Matchmaker

Acting on Love Series

Sonia Stanizzo

To dreams. They do come true.

CHAPTER ONE

The club was hopping. Pumping. Beautiful people from all walks of life gyrated on the dance floor. The air smelled of sex, sweat, and overpriced perfume. Alto definitely was living up to its reputation as the hottest nightclub in Manhattan.

Chloe Doyle raised her champagne flute in the air and clinked glasses with her three friends. "Cheers!" Taking a sip, the sweet bubbles tickled her mouth.

"Happy birthday, Chloe," Hazel Rabin said, raising her voice over the throbbing retro music while dancing in her chair. "Here's to turning thirty."

"Stop reminding me." Chloe threw her friend a dirty look. Was she really *thirty*? When had that happened? She still felt like she was in her twenties, but her body sometimes ached and little laugh lines had started to appear around her eyes, much to her chagrin. She wasn't ready to be thirty. Heck, she was barely ready to be twenty-nine.

Hazel pointed her glass in Chloe's direction as beams of pink, red, and yellow light flashed across her face. "Hey, you're still younger than me."

"And me," Blair O'Connell said before finishing her champagne. "Not that it matters because I'm still fabulous."

"That you are," Daniela Maruyama chimed in with a grin. "We're all fabulous, fierce females who only get better with age." She raised her glass and downed it in a gulp. "Face it, Chloe, you're always going to be the baby." She picked up the bottle and refilled everyone's glasses.

"Only by one year." The flippant comment stung more than it should have done. Yes, Chloe was the baby of her family. And yes, she had accomplished a lot—college and a successful career—but it didn't feel like enough. Her friends had so much more going for them than Chloe did. Daniela was happily single, devoting her energy to producing several hit series while somehow managing to find the time to parent a toddler. Meanwhile, her coworkers, Blair and Hazel, were both married to amazing partners with beautiful children. Chloe dreamed of being as fulfilled with her life as her friends were. It had taken her thirty years to figure out what she truly wanted, and now that she had, things were going to change. Time for a new life. She hadn't flown all the way from Sydney, Australia for nothing.

"So," Blair said, twisting the stem of her flute between her fingers, her eyes glassy from a little too much champagne, "you're now in your dirty thirties and still gloriously single, when are you going to unleash yourself on our American men and compare them to your Aussie blokes? I need numbers. Statistics. Who's better in bed? I want a detailed comparison."

Hazel rolled her eyes. "Good God, Blair, you make her sound like a slut."

"Not that there's anything wrong with that," Daniela interjected.

"Not that there's anything wrong with that," Hazel repeated dutifully. "Still, that's one helluva question to ask." Hazel shook her head and nudged Chloe's shoulder. "You don't have to answer her. Blair is just being a perv."

Blair slammed back the rest of her drink. "Yes, she does! Who else am I going to ask, though? You've been with Joyce for twenty-some-odd years, and Daniela's ace. You're not going to give me the data I need," she whined. "Besides, I'm married and have a three-year-old and a six-month-old. The most excitement I get in my bed nowadays is when Carter has a nightmare and crawls between Mitch and me. Look around"—she gestured broadly at the crowd almost smacking Daniela in the face—"this place is packed with hotties, and I look like sex on heels in this dress. But can I sample any of them? Noooooo. So, if I can encourage my friend to make the most of her single life and live vicariously through her... I will!" Blair slapped a hand on the table.

Hazel paused her glass at her lips, then laughed. "Fair enough."

Chloe hid a grimace. If only her friends knew that Chloe had nothing to compare American men to. She'd been so focused on becoming as successful as her two brothers that she'd completely neglected the social side of her life. The only friends she had were family, clients, or coworkers. And as for dating, the word nonexistent leapt to mind. The only guy she'd ever been remotely interested in had been a friend of her brothers. And even if she'd managed to break the bro code, he'd long since moved away to God knows where. That had been when she was eighteen, and there hadn't been anyone else since. It was something she wanted to change. Desperately.

Flipping her grimace to a grin, Chloe said, "Yes, you are hot in that dress, and you could hook up with any guy in this club. Or girl. Or person," she added in deference to Hazel.

Blair pulled her shoulders back, fluffed out her blonde pixie cut with her fingers, and smirked. "You bet I could." She scanned the packed club of dancers and drinkers with a gleam in her eye. "If I were single, there are plenty of hot guys here I'd like to get to know a *little better*. See any one-night stands you want to partake in?"

Maybe if she was ten years younger, with the excitement of living in a new city, maybe she would have been up for what Blair was suggesting, but she didn't want a one-night stand. She wanted the long haul. "I'm sorry, I will not *unleash* myself on all the men in New York. I'm only looking for one. The faster, the better."

"What do you mean?" Daniela frowned, leaning closer to Chloe.

Chloe ran her finger around the edge of her glass, not quite able to meet her friend's inquisitive gaze. Each of her friends had their life together, and Chloe still felt like something was missing. No, she *knew* that something was missing. "It means that I'm thirty now, and if I wait any longer, my eggs will have shriveled up and died. I moved here to give myself a better chance of finding love, getting married, and starting a family before it's too late."

Daniela made a face but didn't say anything.

Blair had no such compunctions. She pointed a finger at Chloe. "Firstly, your eggs will not shrivel up because you're not that old."

"If you're really that worried about it you can have your eggs harvested," Hazel interjected. "That's what Joyce did."

"That's right," Blair said with a sharp nod. "Secondly, don't they have men in Australia? I've seen some Aussie movies, and my God, the men down under are hot. If they all looked like Chris Hemsworth, I'd never leave the country."

"Yes, there're men in Australia, and no, they don't all look like a Hemsworth." Chloe rolled her eyes. "Dating was never on the menu. Between work and family and more work, I never had the time. And it didn't matter, until suddenly it did."

"What happened?" Daniela asked, her eyes filled with sympathy.

A lance of pain speared Chloe's chest, and she stared into her glass. "Six months ago, I watched a close friend pass away before she got the chance to turn thirty. She had no partner and no kids. Isla thought she had all the time in the world to find her true love and start a family. All she wanted to do was focus on work. Just like me." She swirled the champagne, watching the bubbles pop one by one. "Then she got sick, and her time... her time ran out. She told me that she regretted waiting. I don't want to have those same regrets. Moving here is an opportunity I plan to take advantage of. I want to find love and have everything that goes with it."

Hazel slid her palm along the table and placed it on top of Chloe's hand. "I'm sorry about your friend. Are you okay?"

"Do you want to go? Is this"—Daniela motioned to the club—"too much, too soon?"

Shaking her head, Chloe gave her a small smile. "I'm fine. I just miss her, you know, but I know she wouldn't want me to be miserable."

"I'm sorry about your friend too," Blair echoed. "But wouldn't she want you to have fun with the sexy people of New York? You can't expect to find the love of your life with the first person you meet. You're going to have to try out a few before you find your match. Kick the tires, so to speak."

"I know the chance of finding love with the first man I meet is low, so I was thinking I could try a dating site and narrow down the choices. That way, I can find someone who I'm compatible with and won't have to meet too many guys." The thought of having to meet a lot of men sent shivers up her spine. Men either wanted to use her for her Hollywood connections or were intimidated by her success. There didn't seem to be any middle ground.

Blair screwed up her nose. "Look around you. You're in a New York nightclub full of eligible men. A lot of *hot* ones too." She scanned the room, her gaze pausing at a man standing at the black marble bar. She gave him a flirty smile and wiggled her fingers. "You don't need to go on a dating site. Alto is a walking, gyrating dating app."

Chloe hissed, "Oh my God, why did you do that? Now he's coming over. You're married, you shouldn't be flirting across the room with strange men." Chloe wanted to slide under the table and hide. She hated being put on the spot like this.

"I'm married. Not blind. Besides, I did it for you. You never know, he could be Mr. Right." She pointed a finger at Chloe. "Quick. Smooth your hair and adjust your boobs. Oh, and would it kill you to smile? You want to make a good impression, you know."

Chloe frowned instead. "I don't care about first impressions. I don't want to meet men at a club. They're only looking for one thing. Sex."

"Exactly." Blair's eyes twinkled with mischief. "What a perfect way to celebrate your birthday!"

Chloe couldn't help but giggle. Blair was too much. Sometimes Chloe wished she was brave enough to step out of her comfort zone and have a little excitement in her life. But a one-night stand with a tall, handsome stranger she met at a nightclub was way, way, *way* outside of her comfort zone.

The man from the bar sauntered through the crowd of people to stand at their table. "Ladies. Can I join you?" He grinned, showing bright-white teeth that glowed under the club's black light.

Before Chloe could object, Blair said, "Sure." She pointed to the seat next to Chloe, and he sat next to her. With Daniela on her other side, she was blocked in.

Chloe glared at Blair, who hid a smirk behind her hand. After she got her giggling under control, she smiled at Mr. Dental Commercial and handled the introductions.

Mr. Dental Commercial slid his arm on the back of the booth behind Chloe, scooching way too close for comfort. She shifted closer to Daniela.

Giving Chloe a long, lingering look that made Chloe's skin crawl, he asked, "What's that accent?"

"Australian."

He blinked. "Huh. I was thinking you sounded Swedish. Australia… Sweden." He leered closer. "Women from both countries are sexy."

Chloe turned to her friends and mouthed, *Swedish? What the fuck?* If this was the type of man you picked up at nightclubs, then she definitely wasn't going to find her ideal life partner here. Did he think his charm—or lack of charm—worked on women?

Blair mouthed back, *He's cute, though.*

Cute? Who cared about cute? He could be the sexiest man alive, or even the last man alive, and Chloe still wouldn't touch him.

"Who'd like to dance?" Mr. Dental Commercial glanced at each woman like they'd all pounce at the invitation.

"No," Daniela said, not bothering with an explanation.

His gaze landed on her before moving on to Hazel and Blair. Chloe felt like she was a piece of meat in a butcher's display. No way she was going to dance with this creep. Not in a million years!

"I'm sorry, but Hazel and I are married." Blair dropped her bottom lip and held up her left hand, showing the rock on her wedding finger. "But Chloe is single," she said, apparently missing the memo that this guy was a dud.

Mr. Dental Commercial turned his attention back to her and dropped the arm on the back of the booth onto her shoulder. "Let's dance."

What the hell were her friends doing to her? She'd told them she wanted to find love. She didn't want some random guy who only wanted to screw the first woman he could get his hands on.

"Ummm, well," Chloe glared at her friends hoping they'd help her get out of this situation, but Blair just smirked behind her champagne flute while Hazel mouthed, *hideous disease* and Daniela whispered, "tell him to fuck off." Neither were good options, but at least Hazel's had the best chance of getting this sleazebag to go away without anyone getting hurt. "Awww, gosh, thanks. I'd love to, but I've just discovered I have this rash." Chloe scratched a spot on her inner thigh. "I probably shouldn't dance in case it's contagious, but if you're okay with it, I am too." She plastered an over-the-top smile on her face and shuffled closer to him to the sound of Daniela's muffled giggles.

His eyes popped out of his head, and he propelled himself from the booth like his ass was on fire. "I... ahh... sorry, gotta go. Maybe another time!"

Chloe and her friends burst out laughing as they watched him swerve through the crowd like a motorcycle in crosstown traffic. Served him right for being such a creep!

When he was well and truly gone, Chloe glared at Blair. "Why did you put me through that? God, I feel like I need a shower to wash him off of me."

"He was cute, though, and he only wanted to dance. You didn't have to scare him off like that." Blair giggled.

"Besides, you got rid of him well enough," Hazel said as she dabbed the corners of her eyes with a cocktail napkin. "But I have to agree with Chloe, that guy was horrible. We'll need to do better next time."

"Oh, no—no—no. Please don't try to do better. That was enough to scare me off random guys from clubs for life." She flung her arm in the direction of where Mr. Dental Commercial had disappeared into the crowd.

"Okay, fine. Lighten up and have fun." Blair raised her arms above her head and swayed in time with the music. "It's your birthday. Live a little. You've got plenty of time to tie yourself down."

A flash of anger flowed through her. Blair wasn't getting it. "Have I? You've been married for years, and I've never even had a boyfriend. Time's running out for me. At the rate I'm going, I'll never have kids."

Daniela opened her mouth.

But Chloe shut her up with a glare. "And don't you dare say that I don't need a man to have kids. I know you didn't need or want one. But that's not me, okay?" She thought about the struggles that her mother and sister-in-law Mya had had being single mothers and shuddered. "I don't have it in me to raise a kid on my own like you."

Closing her mouth, Daniela sank back into her seat.

Hazel rubbed her hand on Chloe's shoulder. "Hey, time's not running out. You're still young enough to get everything you want from life."

"Agreed. Stop telling us you're too old. I have a friend who had her first baby at forty-two. Stop overthinking it. Go out, have fun, and when you least expect it, someone will come into your life," Blair agreed.

With a nod, Hazel continued. "You'll only make it harder for yourself if you put so much pressure on finding the right guy straight away. You need to have fun. Flirt with cute guys. Go on dates. When you loosen up, that's when you'll find love."

Maybe they were right. Maybe she was putting too much pressure on herself to find the right guy on the first go. If she didn't have the number thirty hanging over her head, she'd be more optimistic. But that didn't mean she was going to waste her time on men like Mr. Dental Commercial. There had to be better options out there, right?

Blair's eyes narrowed as she stared at Chloe. "When you said that you've never had a boyfriend, you were exaggerating, right?"

Chloe shuffled on her seat and averted her gaze to watch beams of colored lights bounce off the mirrored walls above the bar. "No, I've never had a boyfriend."

"What about in high school?" Blair asked.

"No." She pulled the hem of her skirt down.

"College?"

Chloe huffed. "Blair, what part of '*I've never had a boyfriend*' do you not understand?" She flicked her head back and drained the champagne from her glass.

"How is that possible?" Blair's eyes widened with shock.

"Ethan scared the crap out of any guy who came within five meters of me," she snapped, still annoyed at her oldest brother's protectiveness. "In university, I buried my nose in my books and was too busy studying to go to parties or out clubbing. When I started working as an agent, my hours didn't give me much time for a social life." Blair and Hazel nodded in understanding; they empathized with the demands on her time from needy clients. And when she did manage to get out to meet people, no man had managed to grab her attention. Or woman, either. Was something wrong with her?

"That's just crazy." Blair shook her head with disbelief. "What do you do about sex? From the way you reacted to our—"

"Your," Daniela interjected.

"—My suggestion," Blair amended, "of picking up a guy tonight, you're not a one-night stand kind of girl. Are you?"

"Knock it off, Blair. What Chloe does is none of your business. Stop being so nosy," Hazel said, putting on her managerial voice.

Ignoring Hazel, Blair said, "We're grown-up women; we can talk about sex. I miss the days when I could hook up with a guy and have mind-blowing sex with a stranger. Not that I'd change my life. I love Mitch and the kids. Oh, but to be free for a day! To have no-strings-attached sex again. Not having to schedule it for when the kids are asleep would be amazing." Blair sighed and sagged into her seat. "Please, remind me how great it is, Chloe."

"I'm not sure what to say?" She didn't know what to say because she had nothing to tell them. She didn't do one-night stands. She didn't do *sex*.

"Who was the last guy you hooked up with?" Blair asked.

"Hooked up?" She'd kissed a guy while drunk at a function she'd attended about six months ago. But Chloe knew Blair meant the last person she'd had sex with. "I...umm..."

"You don't have to answer," Daniela said, annoyed.

"Jeez, Chloe, I never knew you were so shy talking about sex," Blair giggled.

"It's not that. I just haven't... had sex." Heat traveled up her neck and flared over her face.

"It's been a while, then," Hazel said, misunderstanding what she meant. "I remember when I was single. I went through a drought that lasted nearly a year. Those were the worst few months of my life. My vibrator got a massive workout."

"No," Chloe fiddled with the strap of her dress on her shoulder, "I haven't had sex at *all*." Finally, her biggest and most embarrassing secret was out; she waited for her friends' shocked reactions.

"You're kidding, right?" Blair asked with a giggle.

Chloe shook her head and rubbed her sweaty palms on her thighs.

"You've never had sex?" Hazel asked in a high-pitched tone.

"Shhh." Even though they were in a nightclub with music blaring, Chloe swung her head over her shoulders to make sure no one overheard. She leaned forward and said loud enough for only her friends to hear, "No, I've never had sex."

"And there is nothing wrong with that, right?" Daniela glared at the other two pointedly.

"Of course not," Hazel said quickly under Daniela's gimlet gaze.

"So the real question is: 'Why haven't you?'" Blair said.

"I told you how things got in the way of having a boyfriend or even a brief relationship." She sighed in frustration. "It's one of the reasons why I moved here. I'm ready to punch that V-card. I'm here to find the right guy."

"The right guy?" Blair asked. "Whose first time has ever been with the *right guy*? Or the right person," she amended, glancing at Hazel and Daniela. "You've seriously waited this long for him to have sex? Not that there's anything wrong with waiting for someone special. In fact, I think that's kinda sweet. It's just not something you hear very often from someone your age.".

Chloe twisted the ring on her finger. "I know it's weird, but it's not like I've gone out of my way to avoid having sex." Except if she was honest with herself, only one person had made her crave that level of intimacy. But that had to be a fluke, right? Happenstance.

"It is a little strange," Hazel said. "Especially since you aren't a super-duper conservative."

"The question is, do you want to have sex?" Daniela fiddled with her napkin. "It's okay if you don't."

"Believe me, I want to have sex." God, she really, really did.

"This is a problem that can easily be fixed." Blair crooked her finger at someone near the bar.

"If you call that guy back, I swear I won't talk to you again," Chloe growled.

Blair waved a hand. "Forget about him. You can do so much better."

A woman walked toward them, a small smile on her lips.

"Um, I don't bat for the same team," Chloe said in case her friend wanted her to experiment.

Hazel winked. "You might like it."

As the woman joined them at their table, Chloe noticed a notepad in her hand. Her shoulders sagged as she breathed out a long sigh of relief. She wasn't a hookup, but instead was a waitress.

"What can I get you?" the waitress asked.

"We'll have two shots of screaming orgasms each, please. Actually, make that three each," Blair said. The waitress nodded and left to get their order. "Hopefully, it won't be the alcohol that gives you one tonight." She wiggled her eyebrows at Chloe. "But just in case..."

"Three! What are you trying to do to me?" Chloe slapped a hand on the table. They might need to carry her out of the club.

"I'm trying to loosen you up. It's your birthday. You need to have fun. Dance with hot guys. Then maybe you'll pick a nice one to end your thirty-year drought with," Blair said as if they were talking about having chocolate cake after a long diet.

"Blair, I'm not having sex with some guy I meet at a club."

"Why not? You said yourself you wanted to have sex—"

Chloe cut her off. "Yes, with someone it means something with."

"And you will," Blair soothed. "In the meantime, you need to discover how your vagina works. What you like and what you don't like. You don't want to meet the man of your dreams and then screw it all up because you don't know where to have him put his dick."

Chloe choked on a laugh while Daniela and Hazel snickered. "I'm hoping he'll know where to put it. And besides, if a man had feelings for me, he wouldn't care how inexperienced I am."

"Yes, true, but how much more fun will you have if you find the man of your dreams and know what you're doing? There won't be any of that awkward stage. It takes time and practice to have an amazing orgasm. And you don't strike me as the kind of person to self-satisfy."

Chloe stared at Blair.

"She means masturbate," Hazel supplied.

Chloe continued to stare.

"Do you masturbate?" Daniela wanted to know.

"I am not answering that!" Her friends didn't need to know that she had a bedside table drawer full of sexual aids. That was between her and her supplier.

"Fine," Blair said with a wave of her hand. "But believe you me, you can't rely on a man to know how to press your buttons. You'll have to guide him. Unless he's extremely skilled, but that's hard to find."

Chloe hated to admit it, but Blair had a point.

The waitress arrived with their drinks and placed them on the table stopping any more talk of orgasms. The tray of shots came in glasses that glowed in bright blue and yellow. They each picked one up and raised them in the air.

Daniela lifted her glass. "To being thirty."

"To being thirty and finally having sex," Blair toasted.

"To being thirty and learning to have *great* sex," Hazel said with a grin.

Chloe stared at her friends and couldn't help the smirk that spread across her face. Pointing a finger at Blair, she said, "If I toast to that, it doesn't mean I'm picking up some random guy tonight."

"We'll see how the night goes." Blair smirked and shot back her drink, pulling a face and shimmying her shoulders as she banged the glass on the table.

"To trying new things." Hazel downed her shot too and copied Blair's facial expressions and shimmy.

"To having fun." Daniela didn't do the shimmy, but she was definitely smirking just as broadly as the other two.

Sighing, Chloe picked up her glass and lifted it in the air. "To losing my virginity."

CHAPTER TWO

Theodore Campbell sat at a table overlooking the crowded dance floor of his nightclub with his brother Blake and best friend Logan. All throughout the club people seemed to be celebrating: engagements, weddings, birth dates. Theo and his friends were celebrating a milestone too: his finalized divorce. Although Theo's friends acted jovial, a tightness pressed into his chest. Not because he still loved his ex-wife, Layla, but because he'd failed her in their marriage. Failure was a bitter pill to swallow.

Blake poured bourbon into the glasses and passed them to Theo and Logan. "To being officially single again." He tilted his tumbler in Theo's direction before knocking it back in one swallow.

Theo grunted.

Logan frowned at his friend. "To getting laid whenever you damn well want without any consequences." He too guzzled his drink down.

Theo stifled the urge to roll his eyes. "That's what you want. I've been getting laid without consequence since Layla and I separated." At first, a few hours a night fucking nameless women had helped him forget about his failed marriage. But all too soon, Theo had grown tired of multiple hookups. They didn't change anything. Once the euphoria of the moment was over, he still felt like shit.

"Well, it's going to be a long time before I commit to one woman. Man, that shit's exhausting," Logan said while pouring more bourbon in his glass.

"So you're swearing off women?" Blake asked, shooting a wink at Theo.

"I didn't say that." Logan grinned. "I said, no more *relationships*. I'll take all the women I can get. In fact, I've spotted a few tonight I'd be happy to take home."

Theo and Blake chuckled. That was Logan, always looking for the next bit of ass.

"Speaking of women. What's your plan now that you're free? Are you ready for another commitment?" Blake asked Theo.

"Same as it's been since I split from Layla." Theo inwardly shuddered at the thought of remarrying; he'd never put another woman through the pain he'd put Layla through. It had been too much. Too painful. Better to be like Logan, a committed bachelor.

His brother's eyes narrowed. "That's not what I wanted to hear. Since your split, you've thrown yourself into work. If we hadn't dragged you out tonight to celebrate your divorce, you'd still be in the office." Blake glanced at his watch. "And it's midnight on a Saturday night. That's fucked up."

Theo shrugged. Work was the only thing that had kept him sane these last few months. "You should be thanking me. This club and the five others around the country—not to mention our property portfolio—are making us a shitload of money."

Blake lifted his glass in a salute. "Not complaining, man. Just looking out for my big brother. All work and no play makes you an ass-hole."

Logan chuckled, "I don't think that's how the saying goes."

"Maybe if you weren't playing around so much and helped me out more, I wouldn't be in the office so late," Theo grumbled, annoyed and maybe a smidge defensive. He knew that even if Blake did work the same hours as Theo that he'd still choose to spend most of his time in the office. Work had value. Work kept him sane. He didn't need anything else in his life.

Blake shook his head. "I do more than my share. Normal people have a life. You should try it; maybe Layla wouldn't have left you if you'd focused on her as much as you do this club." His brother cringed as soon as the words left his mouth. "Shit, I didn't mean that."

But Blake was right. When the cracks had formed in his marriage, he'd thrown himself into work to distract himself from the problems they were facing. Maybe if he'd stuck around more, tried a little harder, things might have been different.

A shimmer of light coming from the dance floor caught Theo's eye. Theo sipped his bourbon and watched a woman in a sequined, bloodred dress sway in time with the music. She held her arms up over her head, tilting her face to the ceiling. Her wavy dark-brown hair swung down her back almost reaching her pert ass. Transfixed, Theo watched as she gathered her locks in her hands and pushed them to the side over one shoulder, exposing her creamy skin in a backless dress.

He couldn't take his eyes off her.

Her outfit glittered under the lights of the club, shooting colors in all directions like a rainbow goddess. When she dropped her hands to her legs and ran them up her thighs, he almost groaned out loud. This rainbow goddess was driving him wild. She was teasing him, tormenting him. God, he could watch her all night. He wondered if she was wearing panties under the dress she was inching ever higher. But before he got his answer, she raised her arms over her head again.

A groan escaped him, and he scrubbed a hand over his face. He felt like a damned teenager trying to score a look up a girl's dress. That wasn't him. He wasn't like all of those pervs down below, getting their rocks off on ogling women having a good time.

Feeling a tightening behind the fly of his trousers, he said, "I need to stretch my legs." He rose from his seat, heading for the bar.

"Wait—" Blake called after him, but Theo didn't look back.

When he approached the bar, the bartender poured him a whiskey and slid it over the shiny black counter. "Massive crowd tonight. The DJ's awesome. He knows how to make everyone party," he said over the music.

Theo nodded. "Thanks for the update, Ruben." He took a sip of the smooth amber liquid. "And the drink."

"Anytime," Ruben said and moved on to his next customer.

Theo perched on a stool, not yet ready to go back and sit with Blake and Logan. He needed some time alone. He needed peace. Well, as much peace as he could get with hundreds of people gyrating around him.

Before he could take a sip of his drink, two blonde women sidled up to him. "Hey, mind if we join you?" Blonde Number One said, twirling a lock of brittle-looking hair around her finger. "You look like you could use some company."

Blonde Number Two flicked her hair off her shoulder and leaned forward to give him an eyeful down her low-cut dress at impressive-looking tits. "We're *great* company."

He knew exactly what kind of "great company" they'd be. He could spend a few hours with these women temporarily forgetting his mistakes and memories. But as he looked at their tight bodies and big breasts in their figure-hugging dresses, his dick didn't stir. Not even a twitch. "Sorry, ladies, I'm afraid I won't be much fun tonight."

Blonde Number One, rubbing her breasts against his arm, purred in his ear, "I know lots of ways to help you have fun."

"I'm sure you do. Maybe another time," he said to placate her, trying to keep the annoyance out of his tone. *Not going to happen. Not tonight or ever.*

Blonde Number Two pouted. "What can we do to change your mind?"

Instead of answering, he met Ruben's gaze and held his hand up, indicating that he wanted the man to come over. When the bartender arrived, he said, "Give these beautiful ladies whatever they want to drink for the rest of the night. No charge."

The women's eyes brightened.

Ruben shot him a look filled with concern but only said, "Yes, sir."

Eager to escape, he said, "Enjoy your night, ladies." And with that, he left them at the bar.

As he made his way back to Blake and Logan, a flash of red sequins from the dance floor caught his eye. He stopped at the edge away from the crush of people. The same woman from earlier still shimmed and swayed among the crowd. Theo's gaze followed the swing of her hips as she danced to the beat of the music.

It mesmerized him.

Watching her got the blood pumping in his veins, unfortunately heading straight to his dick. When the crowd swallowed her up, he stood on the balls of his feet to search over people's heads to find her. A beat later, the lights shone on her, and she glittered like a red star.

He couldn't take his eyes off her.

Caught in some magic spell she unwittingly placed over him, he wanted to take her to his apartment, peel the red scrap of material from her body, and feel her move against him like she moved on the dance floor. For the first time in a long time, something hot and fierce stirred inside him. He wanted her.

And when Theo Campbell wanted something, he fucking got it.

CHAPTER THREE

On the dance floor, Hazel sashayed over to Chloe and yelled in her ear, "Don't look now, but there's a guy on your left who's staring at you."

"What? Who?" Chloe swiveled her head from left to right, but all she saw was a swarm of people around her.

Putting a hand on her forehead, Hazel said, "I'm so glad I said, 'don't look.'"

"Wow, he's gorgeous." Blair fanned her face. "He's seriously checking you out. I'd bet he'd help you with your *little problem*." Blair threw her arms in the air and twirled in a circle. "Chloe's getting laid tonight!"

Daniela took one look at Blair and just rolled her eyes.

"I'm *not* sleeping with some guy checking me out," she said with a laugh. "Besides, the dance floor's crowded; he's probably looking at someone else." Anyway, she was having fun dancing with her friends. It had been ages since she'd gone out and let her hair down, metaphorically. Hopefully the new change in her life would bring on other new changes—like a life partner.

Hazel grabbed Chloe by the arms, twisting her around slightly. "Look over my shoulder—*don't* make it obvious," she said when Chloe tilted her head. "See the guy at the edge of the dance floor with a glass in his hand, wearing the black pants and shirt?"

Chloe nodded. "The one with the biceps and gray tie?" God, he *was* gorgeous!

"Yep, that's the guy," she said, sounding pleased with herself. "Is he still looking this way?"

"Yes, and he looks familiar..." Chloe squinted to focus through the flickering light; there was something about him... She sucked in a quick breath. "I know him! That's Theodore Campbell."

"Who's Theodore Campbell?" Hazel asked.

"My brother Ethan's best friend," she explained. "Theo left Australia twelve years ago, and I haven't seen him since." A bubble of happiness exploded in her chest at seeing an old friend. She paused, frowning. "What's he doing here?"

"Checking you out and wanting to jump your bones, that's what," Blair said, dancing around Chloe with a playful grin on her face.

Chloe laughed. "Not hardly. He always saw me as Ethan's little sister and never looked twice at me." She grimaced as a memory of glow sticks and dances leapt to mind. "God, I tried so hard to grab his attention." How many times had she followed her brother and his friends around just to get a glimpse of Theo, get a minute of his attention? Too many times, that's what.

"You had a crush on your big brother's best friend? That's so adorable," Daniela teased.

"It was pathetic, and you know it." Chloe rolled her eyes. Mooning over a boy who barely knew she existed, it was something she didn't like remembering. But that didn't mean that she needed to avoid Theo altogether. "I'm going to go say hi to him. I'll be right back."

"Take your time. He could be your birthday surprise!" Blair called out.

Chloe shook her head and chuckled, zigzagging through the crowd, taking care not to get caught up with any dancers as she made her way over to Theo. When she finally stood in front of him, she threw her arms open wide and gave him a quick hug. "Oh my God! It's been an age. How are you?"

He stared at her for a beat with a slight crease between his eyebrows before he answered, "I'm good. How are you?"

That was not the response she'd hoped for, but she soldiered on, "I'm great. It's wonderful seeing you again after so long. What have you been up to?"

"You know, this and that. Work takes up most of my time." He took a sip of his drink and kept staring at her.

She took the time to catalog all of the changes in him. The Australian accent was gone, and he sounded like a true New Yorker. But that wasn't the only change. The face of the young man she remembered was replaced by something harder, stronger. The easy smile she loved so much looked forced, like it was something he didn't do often. He wore his light-brown hair longer on top than she remembered. And from the way he filled out his shirt and pants, he'd bulked up. This wasn't the lanky university student she'd pined over for years; he was fully mature, a man's man.

Theo's piercing blue gaze flicked over her. Starting from her face to skim down her body in a way he'd never done when they were teenagers. Actually, back then, he'd hardly looked at her at all. If he had, it had been because he was teasing her for being an annoying little kid.

So why was he looking at her now like he wanted to strip her naked? Then, it hit her. *Theo doesn't remember me!*

She didn't know whether to be offended or not. She'd only tagged after him like a puppy wanting attention for years. How could he forget her? She hadn't changed that much, had she? Her hair was still the same chestnut brown, her face was still the same face she'd had at eighteen. Was he pulling a prank on her, or had he truly forgotten her? She needed to know for sure, so she set up a trap. "It was so good meeting up with you at The Rainbow Room last year. I had so much fun."

"It was. We should do it again sometime," he said, his face remaining impassive. He knocked back the rest of his drink and put the glass on the tray of a passing waiter. He stepped closer. Their chests almost touching. "I have a place upstairs where we can get away from the crowd and noise so we can catch up."

Oh my God. He really doesn't remember me!

If he did, he'd never want to go somewhere "quieter" to catch up. Especially with Ethan's younger sister. *The closeness of their bodies made Chloe's heart race.*

Chloe tilted her face up and was about to tell him who she was, then she slammed her lips shut. This was the guy she'd crushed over for years. The guy she'd dreamed of kissing one day. The one guy who'd filled her dreams. The only guy she'd ever felt anything for. She'd lost her chance when he'd left Australia. Well, if she was honest with herself, she'd never really had a chance. There's no way Theo would have gotten close enough to her to tie her shoelaces with her big brothers around. But it hadn't stopped her from dreaming about what it would feel like to kiss Theo.

What if this was her chance to put those teenage dreams into action? If he didn't know who she was, there was nothing stopping him from taking things further. Instead of an eighteen-year-old pining for a kiss, Chloe wanted more. A lot more. She was damn sick of being a thirty-year-old virgin. She wanted sex, and from Theo's heated gaze, he wanted her and wasn't taking her somewhere quieter just to *talk*.

Could she go to bed with Theo? She'd told her friends she wouldn't hook up with a random guy in a club, but Theo wasn't a stranger. He might not know who she was, but she knew him. Surely that would be okay? Besides, he wanted to sleep with her as much as she wanted to sleep with him. Not to mention, he was so much hotter than the boy who'd left all those years ago. This was her one chance. She should take it.

She put a hand on his arm and leaned forward, her lips a hairbreadth from his ear. "I like your idea of going somewhere quieter."

He trailed his fingers across her lower back and nuzzled his lips just under her ear, causing goose bumps to explode up and down her spine. "Let's go."

This was really happening. Oh God, this was really happening! For a second, her bravado slipped. She wanted to do this, but could she go through with it knowing she wasn't being up front with him? She stared into his eyes, and the desire shooting from them pulled her into their blue depths. *Mind made up; no going back now.* "I'll tell my friends I'm leaving."

"You looked like you were getting well acquainted with your childhood crush," Blair said with a grin when she slipped back to their table.

"He doesn't remember me," Chloe raised her voice loud enough for them to hear her over the music. "And I didn't tell him who I am. I don't have time to explain now because we're going somewhere *quieter*."

Daniela's eyes narrowed while Hazel and Blair's lit up with excitement.

"Why are you standing around talking to us? Go over there and have sex." Blair put her hands on Chloe's chest and pushed her away.

Chloe pressed her heels into the floor and didn't budge. Putting her palms on her warm cheeks, she said, "Oh God, can I do this?"

"Do you want to?" Daniela asked pointedly.

"Yes." The answer came quickly. She desperately wanted him to be her first lover. "What if I totally suck at it and make a fool of myself?" How mortifying would it be if she was a dud in bed!

"You'll be fine. Just follow his lead. He looks like the kind of guy who knows his way around the bedroom," Hazel said.

"And a man who knows where to put his dick." Blair grinned, referring to their earlier conversation.

Chloe pulled back her shoulders and blew out a long breath. "Okay, I can do this. Wish me luck."

"Good luck!" Blair and Hazel called out with joy.

"And be careful!" Daniela echoed.

Chloe waved to her friends with a giggle and made her way back to Theo, mentally checking what underwear she'd worn and when she'd last waxed. Luckily the dress didn't allow for much underneath, and her downstairs area had had a tidy up two days ago. So everything was good to go.

Theo stood where she'd left him, watching her with the same intense stare. Flutters of excitement took off in her stomach. Thank God she wasn't nervous. If she were, that could be disastrous. Nervousness led to sneezes, and sneezes were never sexy.

"Ready?" he asked.

She nodded, not trusting her voice wouldn't come out in a decidedly unsexy squeak. Instead, she plastered on what she hoped was a sultry smile.

It must have worked because he said, "Follow me." He held out his hand for her to take. When she clasped it, their fingers linked together. The simple touch caused her heart rate to escalate. They threaded their way through the tables and booths to a dark corridor away from the main part of the club where a security guard stood at the entrance.

"Good evening, Mr. Campbell," the man said.

"Hey, Carl. Any problems tonight?"

The guard grinned. "Nothing I couldn't handle, sir."

Theo tapped the man's shoulder. "Great, I'll see you later."

"Yes, sir." The guard pressed a button on the wall.

Why had the security guard been so formal? Did Theo work here? She didn't have more time to wonder about it because behind the guard, a hidden panel slid open to reveal a door leading into a darkened hallway. They hurried through it to a lobby resplendent in marble and oak with Theo waving to an imposing doorman. Two black glass doors slid open as they approached; it was quite possibly the fanciest elevator Chloe had ever seen. Stepping inside, Theo pressed a button for the top level. She'd expected them to leave the club entirely, not go to a higher level in the same building. Where were they going? Crossing her arms over her chest, she worried she'd read the situation wrong and he really did want to "catch up."

Theo stepped behind her and pressed up against her back. Reaching around her chest, he held on to her hands. The warmth of his chest, even through his shirt, spread over her bare back. He placed a kiss below her ear and trailed his lips along the curve of her neck.

No, Chloe hadn't read the situation wrong. *Thank God!* She dropped her head back onto his shoulder, biting her lip to stop from moaning when he placed wet kisses on her racing pulse. Her body pressed against his.

Theo released her hands, splaying his palms against her stomach to pull her closer. The intimate contact enhanced the impressive erection throbbing against her arse. Reaching her arms over her head, she linked her hands behind his neck and watched in the reflection of the dark glass doors as Theo's fingers trailed along her ribs. He paused for a second at the curve of her breast, his eyes meeting hers. At her nod, his finger brushed at the crease before floating over a peaked nipple.

A jolt of pure pleasure raced through her at the light touch. She sucked in a breath and arched into his hand. Her skin flushed hot; her panties grew damp. She didn't recognize the wanton woman she saw reflected in the elevator's doors. If one touch could do this to her, just imagine what having sex would feel like. There was no way that a strange guy she'd just met in a club could make her feel like this: wanton, uninhibited, unhinged. But this was Theo, she trusted him, and holy hell, he made her body burn.

Arriving at its destination, the elevator dinged, breaking the connection. Oh God, she'd lost herself in the moment. If Theo'd pressed the emergency stop button, she would have been happy to have her first time in the sleek elevator. If being with Theo was this good already, she couldn't wait for what was to come.

The doors opened into an ornate foyer with a single door visible. Theo reached into his pocket, and the door opened with a slight pop. She stepped inside, her eyes drawn to the wall of windows and the flickering lights beyond. Her heels clicked on the dark timber floors as he led her to the living room. Museum-quality artwork in blue and white tones decorated the walls, complementing the expensive furniture. When they hadn't left the building, she had assumed he was taking her to some kind of VIP room. She hadn't expected to be taken to a luxury penthouse overlooking New York City.

"You live here?" Who lived in an apartment over a nightclub?

"I do." He pulled two glasses from a cabinet behind a bar set up in the corner of the room and opened a fridge stocked with wine and champagne bottles. Selecting a bottle, he poured champagne into the crystal flutes, passing one to Chloe.

"You like the nightlife so much you need to be this close?" She took a sip of Dom Pérignon—a lot fancier than the bubbles she'd had with her friends.

Theo chuckled. "I own the club."

"Huh."

"I have offices on a lower floor," he continued, his eyes intent on her face. "I work long hours, so it makes sense to live as close to work as possible. That way I don't have to wait to play." His voice was husky and filled with need.

Drawn to him, she placed a hand on his arm. "You grew up to be a nightclub owner. That's wonderful. I thought you wanted to be—"

He raised an eyebrow.

Shit! She'd almost let the cat out of the bag. If she wanted to lose her virginity tonight, she couldn't talk to him like she'd once known him. Because once he learned she was Ethan's sister, he'd put a stop to it for sure. "I mean, usually kids dream about growing up to be doctors, lawyers, or police officers," she said, trying to cover her earlier gaffe. "Becoming a club owner is unusual." She averted her gaze and took a long sip of champagne. She knew there was some kind of bro code about touching your best friend's sister. She hoped now that they were older, it didn't matter anymore.

Theo downed the rest of his drink and put it on the white marble counter of the bar, gazing at her through hooded eyes. The time for talking about childhood dreams was over. It was time for her to live hers.

Theo plucked the glass from her hand and put it next to his. He placed a kiss on her shoulder, like he had in the elevator, before trailing his lips to the sensitive spot under her ear. She sucked in a sharp breath when he nipped her earlobe. How could that be an erogenous zone? Unaware of her confusion, he dropped his hands on her hips and pulled her against him. The warmth of his hard body spread over her. Confusion gone, she wrapped her hands around his waist. This was it. This was what she wanted. She could analyze how she felt later; now she was going to live in the moment.

His lips floated from her neck to her jaw before hovering above her lips. Chloe's chest heaved in and out with anticipation. She'd pictured this moment so many times, but she'd never believed it could happen. Yet, here she was, standing in Theo's arms, awaiting his kiss. She swallowed hard when he cupped her face with his hand. Eyes never leaving hers, he rubbed a thumb over her bottom lip and lowered his head, claiming her mouth. Her eyes slipped shut as he parted her lips with his tongue and swept it inside. He tasted of sweet champagne and something more that she couldn't identify. The kiss started slow and sweet, gentle even. But it wasn't enough. She wanted more. She needed more. As if sensing her impatience, the tempo picked up, turning more erotic. The feel of his firm lips, the taste of his tongue flooded her senses, making her become wanton. His kiss awakened something inside her, something she'd doubted she'd even had, and she couldn't wait to discover all the ways he'd put his tongue to good use.

Skimming his palms up her waist and around to her bare back, his fingers ghosted over her heated skin. This moment was already so much better than she'd imagined as a kid. Her teenage brain hadn't been mature enough to really fantasize about being touched like this by Theo. The teenager inside of her wanted to giggle like a schoolgirl and do a happy dance.

Theodore Campbell kissed me! Theodore Campbell is still kissing me.

The kiss deepened, his tongue twirling with hers, and when she thought he'd sucked the oxygen from her lungs, he ripped away from her lips. "Let's take this to the bedroom."

Oh yes, let's take this to the bedroom, the eager part of her thought. But another part of her cautioned that having sex with Theo without him knowing who she was would be wrong. She should stop what they were doing and tell him who he was taking to bed. Even though she wanted Theo, deceiving him didn't sit right. Maybe he was too old to follow any bro code, and if he knew the truth, he'd still have sex with her. Could she take the risk and tell him, or should she keep it to herself?

Don't be an idiot, if you tell him you'll never see him again. What's the harm in keeping a little secret? The little voice in her head butted in while her body yelled at her conscience to shut the fuck up and take what she'd always dreamed about. Indecision warred within her. But when he held out his hand once again, she found herself grasping it and letting him lead her to the unknown.

Chandeliers lit the way through the penthouse to the bedroom, which was just as impressive as the living room but with more windows framing the city in different directions. A bedside lamp cast the room in dim golden light. Standing at the edge of the bed, Theo kicked off his shoes and reached for the buttons on his shirt.

"Wait." Chloe held out her hand to stop him, and his fingers paused at the buttons. As much as she'd love to watch him strip naked, she wanted to get as much as she could from her one night with him. She wanted to undress him herself. She would never have the opportunity again. She stepped closer and even in her six-inch heels, he still towered over her. "Let me do it."

He dropped his arms by his side, a slow smile drifting across his lips. "Go ahead, I like a woman who takes charge."

Up to a point, she knew what to do and could be assertive. When it was time for the main event, she'd have to hand over the reins to Theo. The thought excited her.

Her fingers trembled as she worked on the buttons. One button. Two. After what felt like forever, Chloe finally had all the buttons undone and pulled the shirt open. Tugging it from the waistband of his trousers, she pushed it off his broad shoulders. It floated onto the floor with a swish to reveal his magnificent shoulders and chest. She wanted to touch him, so she did. His muscles bunched as she skimmed her hands from his chest and down over his hard six-pack. She flicked open the buttons of his pants, unzipped them, and tugged at them so they fell to his feet where he stepped out of them.

Her insides heated up as she trailed her gaze over him. God, Theo doesn't look like the boy she used to spy on at the beach. Gone was the slender teenager. Now, a man stood in his place, built strong and hard with a sprinkle of dark chest hair that trailed down and disappeared behind his black boxer briefs where a bulge strained behind the fabric. She wanted to reach out and wrap her hand around his thick cock, feel every inch of him.

Before she could make a move, his arms wrapped around her waist, and he jerked her to him. Their lips smashed together, their tongues tangled. He kissed her long and deep, knocking the breath from her. She couldn't think of a better way to die.

His hand slid down her body to cup her arse. Not able to wait a moment longer to touch him, she slid her hand between their bodies and took hold of the firmness pressing against her stomach.

He threw his head back and hissed, "Fuck me!" as she pumped him with long, slow strokes.

She grinned. That was the plan. Standing on tiptoe, she ran her tongue along his neck and breathed in his masculine scent. *I can't believe this is happening!* She might have waited thirty years to lose her virginity, but the way Theo kissed and touched her, Chloe had no doubt it was going to be worth it.

Leaning down, Theo skimmed kisses along her collarbone and the tops of her breasts. A hand glided to her inner thigh, bunching up her dress, slipping it higher and higher. With featherlight strokes, he brushed a finger over her wet panties. "You're ready for me," he said while sucking on the side of her neck.

Oh boy, she was more than ready!

"You're wearing too many clothes," he continued. He pulled his hand out from under her dress as the other pushed one spaghetti strap off her shoulder. Slowly, way too slowly, he flicked the other strap off, causing the sequined fabric to fall to her waist. Pulling away, he stared at her heaving chest. "Beautiful," he said in a rough whisper.

The dress didn't allow for a bra, so she stood almost naked in front of him. Time to go the rest of the way. Giving her hips a wiggle, the dress slithered to the floor, leaving her in just her heels and panties.

As she started to step out of her shoes, he stopped her. "Leave them on. I want you wearing them as I fuck you," he growled in her ear.

Her breath caught. Holy cow! His sexy voice alone could make her orgasm on the spot. This come-to-life fantasy was everything she wanted and more.

Theo sat on the edge of the bed and lifted Chloe by the hips to straddle him. Keeping hold of her hips, he moved her in a rocking motion against him. Heat pooled between her legs at their close contact.

Skimming his hands up the sides of her torso to her breasts, he massaged them and plucked at her nipples, sending little jolts of pleasure straight to her core. He replaced his hands with open-mouthed kisses, sucking a rosy peak into his mouth, and the jolts intensified, becoming lightning bolts. "Oh, God... yes," she moaned. Her breath quickened. She rocked faster against him, needing more. She needed him inside her. "I want... now..."

"Soon, baby, soon." Theo must have sensed how close she was to exploding, but he didn't give her what she so desperately wanted: his cock inside her.

When she rocked faster against him and whimpered unintelligible words, he flipped her onto her back on the mattress. Rising to stand at the edge of the bed, he stared at her from her head to her stiletto heels. Even though he wasn't touching her, she felt his gaze like a burning caress.

Theo clasped her ankle and lifted it to his mouth, leisurely kissing and stroking his tongue along her calf and up to her inner thigh. He hovered over her lacy black panties. Chloe felt his hot breath on her already feverish skin. When he didn't go any further, she looked down at his dark head. Confused, she lifted her hips, encouraging him to continue. Instead of putting his hot mouth on her throbbing sex, he traced a thumb over the light-brown birthmark in the shape of a jagged heart next to her bikini line.

"I've seen something like this before," he said.

A dart of fear ran through her. "Birthmarks are common," she tried to explain. Had he stopped because birthmarks turned him off? She'd never worried about it before. No one saw it unless she was wearing a swimsuit.

His eyes flicked up to her, and the heat that had blazed from them moments ago fizzled out. Her chest tightened with disappointment, and she tilted her face up to the ceiling. She'd never thought he could be so shallow. The boy she used to know never would have cared about a silly little birthmark, but this new and hunky Theo apparently did. Time to gather what was left of her pride and scurry home. Chloe shifted on the bed, trying to sit up, but Theo didn't move and he had the bottom half of her body pinned down.

He traced the birthmark with one finger. "I've only ever seen a mark like this, and in the same spot, on one person. It was on"—his eyes widened—"Oh fuck!" He sprang from the bed. One hand landed on his hip with the other threaded through his hair. "Glowy Chloe! What the fuck?"

Oh no! Her heart dropped to her feet. He'd given her that nickname after an embarrassing incident at their high school disco. Her cover had been blown.

Jumping from the bed, Chloe grabbed her dress and shimmied back into it. *Shit!* What should she do now? Glancing to the bedroom door, she calculated how fast she could make it out of the room, through the apartment, and to the elevator before he caught up to her and demanded an explanation. With the heels she was wearing, she didn't like her chances at a fast getaway.

"Glowy, don't even *think* about running out."

Dammit, he'd read her mind.

"Why didn't you tell me who you were?" He snatched his trousers off the floor and shoved his legs inside them, not bothering to button them up.

"I... you didn't..." Then something occurred to her. "How did you know about my birthmark?" No point pretending she didn't recognize him. He'd see straight through her bullshit.

He scrubbed a hand at the back of his neck. "You told me."

She shook her head. "No, I didn't."

"Then Ethan must have mentioned it. Fuck! Ethan." He racked his fingers through his hair. "If Ethan finds out about this, he'll shoot me where I stand."

Chloe ignored his remark about Ethan. She was more interested to know how he knew about the birthmark. "Why would my brother tell you about a birthmark near my underwear? It's not like he'd be looking there."

Theo shot her a look. "Glowy, I don't remember how I know; I just do. Now why the hell didn't you tell me who you were? I nearly fucked you!" He paced in front of her.

A lance of pain hit her right in the heart, but she shoved it to the side to deal with later. She had bigger problems right now, like how did she explain and get herself out of this mess? She didn't think that telling him, "*Hey, I wanted to live out my childhood fantasies of you but in a more X-rated way. And you not recognizing me was the only way to do it,*" would work.

Yeah, that'd go over like a lead balloon.

So she said, "I came over to you to say hi, and then you acted as if you knew me. When you said you wanted to "catch up." I had no idea you wanted sex." She cringed inwardly at the pathetic lie, but it was the best she could come up with.

Tipping his head to the side, he pointed a finger at her. "You knew damn well I didn't recognize you. The last time I saw you, you were going through a peroxide blonde with pink streaks phase with a body a lot scrawnier. If you knew who I was, why did you let me bring you up here?" He dug his thumb and finger into his eye sockets like he wanted to wipe the vision of what they'd been doing from his mind.

The lancet morphed into a dagger.

Blinking back tears, she said, "I wanted to have a little fun, okay? I'm in a new country and don't know many people. I'm drunk, and it's my birthday." She winced internally as soon as the words left her mouth, but she soldiered on, "Can't a girl celebrate without being interrogated?" She crossed her arms over her chest with a huff. All she wanted was one night with Theo. One damn night! Was it too much to ask? Now he looked at her like he wanted to throw up. *Just the reaction every woman wants to see*, she thought morosely.

"Chloe, I'm not the man you should celebrate with. I'm your brother's best friend. Out of all the guys in the club, you could have had anyone; you didn't need to pick me."

Maybe she could have gone home with one of the men who'd tried grinding themselves against her like they were dirty dancing on the dance floor. But none of them had interested her. Not a single one.

"I wanted you." She walked to him and placed a palm on his chest, trailing it south, hoping for a response.

She got one, but not the one she wanted. Theo grasped her wrist in a tight hold. "Don't." His jaw clenched, but he didn't move away.

But the alcohol from earlier overrode her sense of right and wrong. Stepping closer, Chloe's heaving chest touched his. She slid her free hand between their bodies and repeated the move from earlier. Again, Theo stopped her from reaching her destination. With their bodies still pressed together, she tilted her head to look up into his face, getting caught in his dark, hooded eyes. His gaze flicked to her mouth and stayed there. Was he going to kiss her? She wanted that. She wanted that so very much. Her body was burning up. Willing Theo to forget about obligations to her brother and take what he wanted, she stretched up toward him, trying to close the distance between them.

But all too soon, her hands were free and cold air wafted between them as he shoved her away. "We're not doing this, Glowy."

Anger and frustration coursed through her. "Don't pretend you don't want me"—she held her chin high—"because what we were doing tells me otherwise."

Theo scrubbed his hands over his face. "I didn't recognize you."

"So? Why should that change anything?"

"It changes *everything*."

"Because of Ethan? Damn it, we're adults; we can do what the hell we want."

"Look, Chloe. I'm sorry I brought you here. Go home and sober up. In the morning, you'll see what a mistake this was." He turned his back and pulled a phone from his pocket. After a beat, he started instructing someone on the other end to hail a taxi for her downstairs.

She'd been summarily dismissed. The reality of what she'd almost done and how she'd thrown herself at him hit... hard. A flush of heat spread up her neck and bloomed on her face. Oh God, how pathetic! Not wanting to face him, she didn't wait for him to get off the phone and dashed from the bedroom to the elevator.

Theo didn't stop her. Why would he? To tell her he'd changed his mind? No, he'd made it clear he wouldn't have sex with her, that he could only see her as Ethan's sister. But for a moment, she could have sworn interest sparked from his eyes when he looked at her even after he learned the truth. If she hadn't been Ethan's sister, she'd be in his bed right now. Instead, she was going home... alone... still a virgin at thirty years old.

Happy freaking birthday to me.

Chapter Four

The shrill ring of a phone jerked Chloe awake. She pried open her eyes just a crack; light from her bedroom window blinded her. Groaning, she covered her face with her arm. "Why didn't I put my phone on silent?"

She rolled over onto her stomach, fumbling for the phone on her nightstand. Squinting at the screen, she answered, "Ethan, why are you calling me at the arse crack of dawn?"

Her brother chuckled. "It's ten thirty. I thought you'd be awake."

Chloe sat up and swung her legs off the bed. Before her feet hit the floor, her stomach rolled, and she took a deep breath to stop herself from spilling her guts on the carpet. "I had a big night." And she was paying for it with a splitting headache.

"I'm sorry I missed your birthday. I tried getting away from filming, but I had a scene I had to finish before we move to our next location." Her brother sounded contrite... and also way too loud.

She rubbed her pounding temples. "That's okay, we'll catch up another time. I spoke to Holly yesterday. She said the movie is going well and she's meeting you when you're done filming in Boston."

Chloe's whole family was in the entertainment industry. Her brother Ethan was an actor, and her sister-in-law Holly was a makeup artist and often did the makeup for her husband's films. Her other brother, Aiden, was also an actor but now was producing a popular TV series, and her mother, Nancy, was a makeup artist who worked for major productions. Even her newest sister-in-law, Mya, couldn't escape the entertainment industry bug.

"Holly'll be here tomorrow. I have a day off before I'm needed on set again, so I decided to take the train in to take my little sister out to lunch to celebrate her birthday like the good big brother I am," he said pseudo magnanimously.

Chloe ignored the last bit and focused on the most important bit of information. "You're here in New York?!"

"Yeah, and I've booked a table at Lucciola's for twelve o'clock, so don't be late."

Normally, Chloe would be excited to spend time with her brother, but her stomach lurched at the thought of food. "I wish you'd called first. I would have loved to meet you, but I'm not feeling up to it."

"Are you sick?"

"Kind of," she answered. She managed to get to her feet and staggered to the bathroom. Clutching the side of the sink, she glanced with horror in the mirror. Staring back at her was a pale face with dark circles under her eyes. A tangled bird's nest sat on top of her head. She looked like death and didn't feel much better.

"Wait... when you said you had a big night, does that mean you got drunk?" Ethan asked with a disapproving tone.

"Umm, I had a few drinks."

More than a few drinks, she amended internally as memories of last night came flooding back. She slumped onto the edge of the bathtub and dropped her head in her hand. Nausea rose up her throat, but not because of the alcohol. This time, it was caused by something much *much* worse. She dragged air through her nose; it did nothing to settle her rolling stomach. Oh my God, she'd almost had sex with Theo! Theo Campbell! Ethan's childhood best friend. The best friend who he still kept in contact with.

The same Theo... who'd rejected her. She cringed. Had last night really happened? From the roiling in her stomach and the existential dread creeping up her spine, the answer was yes.

After getting home, she'd crawled into bed and fallen into a deep, dreamless sleep, forgetting about the most embarrassing night of her life for a few blissful hours. God, why had she thought pretending not to know Theo was a good idea? And when he'd recognized her and put a stop to things, she'd thrown herself at him, trying to change his mind. Apparently Drunk-Chloe had the decision-making ability of a rabbit. She slapped a palm to her forehead, which caused even more pain to slice through her brain.

Okay, she could salvage this. New York was a big city. What were the chances of running into him again? She'd keep clear of his club, and then she'd never have to see him again even though every cell in her body wanted to do just that. She doubted she'd ever forget the way he'd made her feel. How her body buzzed with ecstasy when he touched her. How her heart raced when he looked at her like she was the sexiest woman he'd ever seen. And then how the fear shot from his eyes when he learned her identity.

She must have made some kind of groaning noise because Ethan asked, "Are you hungover?"

"A little." She pushed off the bath to stand at the vanity to rinse her dry mouth with water and picked up her toothbrush.

"You're in a city in a new country. You need to be careful about doing shit like that." Disapproval and anger filled Ethan's voice. "You don't know what kind of trouble you can get yourself into. There are some fucked-up people around here, and with no one looking out for you, you need to be alert to what's going on around you."

"Calm down, Ethan, it was my birthday. My friends took me out to celebrate. Nothing was going to happen to me. I'm thirty years old. I can look out for myself." She might be a grown woman, but sometimes her brothers, especially Ethan, still saw her as a little girl. If she knew her brother, he would try to get her mother or Aiden to come stay with her for her own good.

As she predicted, Ethan said, "I'm going to call Aiden and see if he has time off. He can stay with you while you get settled."

"Ethan, no," she said, rolling her eyes. "Aiden has his own family to worry about. You can't expect him to fly from Australia because I got drunk one night."

"Then I'll get Mum to come."

"Dammit, Ethan, stop treating me like a kid!" She slapped her toothbrush on the sink and forgot she wanted to vomit.

"But you're going out and getting drunk."

"So? It's my life. Keep out of my business."

"Oh, keep out of *your* business," he chuckled. "How many times have you stuck your nose in mine? And Aiden's, for that matter."

"This is different," she huffed. Except she knew it wasn't. She'd even stuck her nose into Aiden's drinking, and Ethan knew it.

"Payback's a bitch," he said in a smug tone.

"Whatever." She knew she sounded like the kid Ethan made her feel like, but she was too hungover to care. "I'm going to pass on lunch. If you have time, come by my apartment before you head out."

"I'm leaving straight after lunch. Take some aspirin, and I'll see you at twelve." With that, he hung up.

Damn Ethan and his bossy boots!

CHAPTER FIVE

Two aspirin, a quick shower, one subway ride, and a brisk walk later she arrived at Lucciola's. She gave the maître d' Ethan's name and was led to a table at the back of the room. Her steps faltered as she approached her brother's table. Unaware of the icy wave washing over her, Ethan stood and wrapped her in a warm hug. Kissing her on the cheek, he said, "Happy birthday."

Over his shoulder, her eyes clashed and held Theo's cool gaze. *What the hell is he doing here?*

"I hope you don't mind that I invited some friends," Ethan said, pulling away. "You remember Theo and Blake Campbell? And this is our friend Logan Carr."

Smiling appreciatively, Logan rose and held out his hand. "Nice to meet you."

Beside him, Blake pushed out of his chair and pulled her into a hug. "It's so good to see you. How long has it been?"

"Umm..." She couldn't remember. With Theo in her peripheral vision, her thoughts were a jumbled mess.

"Twelve years," Theo answered for her. "How are you?" he asked as he too rose to greet Chloe. He embraced her with stiff arms—like they were strangers meeting for the first time and not two people who only hours ago had been naked with their hands all over each other's bodies.

Chloe's cheeks grew warm. She hoped they weren't as red as they felt. She tried to salvage the situation, even as her urge to sneeze grew. "I'm great, thanks. How are you?" She fiddled with the strap on her bag.

"Good." He smiled, though it didn't reach his eyes. Thankfully, he made no mention of last night. She assumed he'd want to keep it to himself as much as she did.

Ethan pulled out the chair next to him, which also happened to be right next to Theo. Talk about awkward. As she shuffled her chair toward the table, their thighs brushed together. The innocent touch spread a tingling sensation over her leg, conjuring not-so-innocent thoughts. She squirmed in her seat. She didn't dare look at Theo in case the way he affected her was written on her face. She scooted a little closer to Ethan. "You didn't mention you were inviting the whole gang," she said, trying to keep her tone light and not annoyed.

"This was the only time I had to meet everyone before I go back to Boston. And thought it'd be a great opportunity for us all to catch up." Ethan smiled at Chloe like he'd just invented sliced bread.

Scratching her nose, she smiled back with stiff lips. "A wonderful idea." She wanted to run from the room. Not only had she experienced one of the most embarrassing moments of her life last night and never wanted to see Theo again, but now she had to sit next to him while smiling and pretending it was great to see him. Where was the nearest rock? She wanted to crawl under it.

"So, Chloe," Logan said, "how long have you been in New York?"

"Only three weeks."

"You're not here on vacation, then?"

"No, I've made the move." She was thankful, yet again, that one of her clients had a pied-à-terre apartment in Hell's Kitchen that they were willing to let her stay in indefinitely. "I found working here is easier for me to do than back home. The time difference was getting too difficult."

"If you need help settling in, I'd be more than happy to help you out," Logan said, his gaze dropping to her chest for a beat.

Okay... Logan was someone to steer clear of.

Ethan spoke up before she could answer, "My little sister has everything under control." He said "little sister" like he was branding it on her forehead, warning Logan to stay away. There he went again, being a big brother and stepping in front of any boys who might be interested.

She knew how to handle men like Logan. How many times had she needed to deal with sleazy clients who thought their fame was the green light to do and say whatever they wanted to her? She wanted to kick Ethan under the table for the way he was treating her and for not trusting that she could defend herself. She wasn't a kid anymore, and she didn't need him to keep away boys—men.

Just to annoy Ethan, she said, "I may be settled into my apartment, but I feel like such a tourist. I've made several trips here over the years for business, but I've been too busy working to enjoy the city. I've always wanted to see the view from the Empire State Building."

Logan chuckled, and a cute dimple cut through his left cheek. But he was anything but *cute*. With his square jawline, strong features, and styled hair, he was gorgeous, and he knew it. Was he husband material, though? Probably not, but she'd bet her Jimmy Choos women fell for his charm.

"I'd love to show you." The words dripped seductively from his lips telling her he'd like to show her more than just the view of New York. Oh hell no, he was definitely not husband material. He was a have-fun-for-a-night-or-two guy, and then he would move on to the next woman as quick as you could pull up your panties. No, thank you. She knew better than to waste her time on Logan.

Before she could say anything, Theo placed his elbows on the table and leaned forward in his chair. "Aren't you too busy at your law firm to play tour guide?"

Incredulous, Chloe swung her head to face Theo. Now she had two men trying to control her life? What the actual hell?

"I'm never too busy to help an old friend of yours out," Logan said, ignoring the death stares Ethan and Theo aimed his way. In fact, he looked like he was enjoying pissing them off, which was another red flag.

"Why don't you take her, Theo?" Ethan turned to stare at Theo, brushing off Logan's offer with a protective glint in his eye. "You know a lot about the city, you'd be the perfect person to show my sister around."

Wait, what?

Both Chloe and Theo stared at Ethan.

Chloe recovered first. "Umm... hello?" She waved a hand in front of her brother's face. "I'm pretty sure I can take myself wherever I want to go."

"Why do it alone when you could have company?" Ethan said, clearly pleased with his suggestion.

Oh no. No way was she going to let Ethan control her like this. "I'm sure Theo has better things to do with his time." She stared hard at Theo, mentally trying to convey a message. *Please tell Ethan you have plans for the next twenty years.*

"What are you doing tonight?" Ethan asked Theo.

"I'm working." Yes! He'd gotten her message.

Theo's finger traced the condensation trickling down his glass, re-minding Chloe about what those fingers had been doing to her last night. She mentally shook herself. *Get a grip!*

"On a Sunday?" Ethan said, snapping Chloe back to their conversation.

Theo shrugged like it was something everyone did with their Sunday evenings. "Yes." He didn't bother to elaborate.

"You work too much. It would be good for you to have a break." Ethan picked up the wine list.

"What if *I* have plans?" Chloe huffed.

Ethan raised an eyebrow. "Do you?"

She flicked her fingernails. "No."

"Okay. Have fun," he said cheerfully as he scanned the wine list.

Turning to face Theo, she said, "You don't have to do this." Then she swiveled in her chair and glared at her brother. "What is wrong with you?"

Ethan's eyes widened faux innocently at her question. "Nothing. You said you wanted to see the sights; I'm helping you out. You don't mind, do you, Theo? If tonight doesn't suit, arrange another time."

Theo's gaze flicked between Chloe and Ethan. If she could read his mind, she'd bet that taking her sightseeing was the last thing he wanted to do.

After a beat, Theo adjusted his tie and said, "I don't mind at all. I'll pick you up at eight thirty and make the reservations. The lights are beautiful at that time."

If she made a scene and protested too much, Ethan might wonder why she was objecting so fiercely and start asking questions. Questions she did *not* want to answer. She plastered a fake smile on her face. "That would be great. Give me your number, and I'll text you my address."

They exchanged details, and then she took a long sip of water. She'd text him later and cancel. It was hard enough sitting next to him. Hours ago, she'd stood naked in front of him. Touched him... done things... No, there's no chance she'd spend another minute alone with him. Not that she thought he'd make the moves on her. It was because she could barely look him in the eye.

"Oh look, here comes the waiter," Blake said, breaking through the tense silence. After giving the waiter their orders, Blake turned to Chloe. "I don't know if you were aware, but when I was younger, I had the biggest crush on you."

Chloe choked on her water as a new and more awkward, tense silence descended. After clearing her throat, she chuckled. "You did?"

"Yeah, but I was too young and you never noticed me. You were busy following Theo around," Blake said.

This time it was Theo's turn to choke on his drink.

"No... I wasn't..." She didn't dare look at Theo in case he saw the truth in her eyes. *God, kill me now.*

"It wasn't just Theo." Ethan nudged her shoulder. "Chloe followed all of us around, Aiden included, because she wanted to run back and tell Mum what we were doing. She was such a snitch."

"I was not snitching." She nudged Ethan back.

"Oh really? Then why *were* you following us around?" Ethan looked between her and Theo, a twinkle in his eye. "*Did* you have a crush on Theo?"

She snorted derisively. "Of course not, he was like a brother to me." *Liar!*

Ethan just raised an eyebrow.

"Okay, fine, you were right, I was spying." That wasn't a complete lie. She had been spying on Theo for her own enjoyment, not to run to their mother and tell her what they were up to. That had just been a bonus.

Ethan shook his head and pretended to look disgusted while Blake and Logan laughed. Chloe risked glancing at Theo. His eyes narrowed at her like he was trying to figure out the truth. Even the arrival of their food didn't save her from Theo's inquisitive gaze. Knowing that she needed to change the subject, she asked Blake about his favorite football team and then sat back to enjoy the chaos she'd caused.

Unfortunately, not everyone was distracted by her ploy. Theo leaned over and whispered in her ear, "You had a crush on me?"

His warm breath washed over her neck, and she shivered with repressed need. "No."

"Liar." He pulled back.

Glancing at the others at the table to check that they were still debating who was the best team, she leaned toward Theo. "I did not have a crush on you. You were too old."

He seemed offended. "I'm only four years older than you."

"For a teenager, that's ancient."

Before he could quiz her more about it, Ethan turned to her and pointed his fork at her plate. "You're not eating."

She looked down at her untouched pasta. Was her lack of appetite the aftereffect of her hangover or because she was sitting so close to Theo? She'd guess the latter. "I'm not hungry."

Ethan frowned. "It's because you're hungover," he said, then turned to his friends. "My sister went out last night and got drunk. Now she's paying the price today."

Chloe's mouth dropped open. *Did he have to announce it to everyone? She glared at her brother.* To her annoyance, Blake and Logan chuckled, but Theo never made a sound.

"Where did you go?" Logan asked.

Chloe tapped her fingers against her glass and pursed her lips. "Oh... ummm. I can't remember the name of the club." She didn't dare glance at Theo. Would he go along with the lie or tell everyone she'd been at his nightclub? He wasn't speaking up, so she took that as a good sign.

"Next time you should check out Theo and Blake's club, Alto," Logan said, winking. "It's one of the best nightclubs in the city."

What should she do? Tell them that was the club she'd been to or pretend she'd never heard of the place? The more she lied, the bigger the chance she'd stuff up and get caught. "That's it! That's the one my friends and I went to." She smiled, hoping it didn't look as stiff as it felt.

Logan's eyes raked over her. "Really? I'm surprised I didn't see you. You're the kind of woman who'd stand out from the crowd." Logan turned to Theo. "Did you see her at the club?"

Theo adjusted the cutlery on the table. "I left early."

"That's right, Carl mentioned you took a woman up to your penthouse." Logan smirked. "Spending the night with a woman should put you in a damn better mood. What happened? Did you pull out your spreadsheets instead of your coc—"

Chloe sprang from her seat, knocking into the table. Glasses and cutlery shook at the force. All eyes swung in her direction. "Oh, arrhh, gosh. Is that the time?" She flicked out her wrist to look at her watch. "I need to go."

"So soon?" Ethan asked, shooting a glare at Logan.

"I just remembered I have a meeting with an actress in half an hour. She'll be pissed if I'm late," she lied. She put a hand on Ethan's shoulder. "Make sure you come for a visit before you go home to Sydney. I want to see you, Holly, and Lily," she said, referring to her infant niece.

Ethan stood and gave Chloe a hug. "I will. Are you sure you don't want me to ask Mum to stay with you for a while? Just until you get settled."

"I'm fine. I have friends to help, so I'm not alone. Stop worrying."

"I'll always worry about my kid sister." He kissed her on the cheek.

She frowned. "I'm not a kid anymore."

He gave her shoulders a light squeeze. "You'll always be my kid sister, no matter how old you are."

She rolled her eyes.

"I'm available to help her out if she needs anyone." Logan put his hand up.

Chloe heard the double entendre but said, "See? I have a lot of people I can turn to." Although, Logan wouldn't be her first choice no matter how good-looking he was.

Ethan didn't seem convinced.

"I'm fine," she reassured him. "I'll call you every day if it makes you feel better. Probably at inconvenient times, but I'll call you."

"Okay, okay, don't get too carried away." Ethan held up his hands in defeat.

Chloe said her goodbyes to Blake and Logan with quick hugs, but when it came to Theo, she lingered just a beat longer, her palms splayed over his strong back. This would be the last time she held him in her arms, so she wanted to make the most of it. It was only an innocent embrace, but what wasn't so innocent was the way her body wanted to grind against his. Breaking away with a jolt, she turned on her heel and got the hell out of there. No way could she see him again. With the way she'd reacted to a mere touch, she'd probably only embarrass herself again.

CHAPTER SIX

Theo breathed out a relieved sigh when Chloe left. Sitting so close had been torture. The sweet floral smell of her perfume, her light musical laughter, and the way she tucked her long dark-brown hair behind her ear exposing her neck had bewitched him, and it took a huge effort for him not to reach out and trail a finger along her smooth skin. Thank God that Ethan was there. With Ethan sitting at the table, it was a reminder for Theo to keep his hands to himself.

Shortly after Chloe left the restaurant, Blake and Logan said their goodbyes. Theo hung around until Ethan had to leave to catch his train.

Once everyone had left, Ethan leaned back in his chair and said, "I have a favor to ask you."

"Shoot, what is it?" Theo said and sipped his coffee.

"I need you to watch out for Chloe," Ethan said, his eyes intent. "Spend some time with her until she's settled in New York."

Theo choked on his coffee and spluttered, "What? You can't be serious!"

"Deadly. You saw how she was today. Jumpy, evasive, hungover." Ethan stressed the last word. "I'm worried about Chloe in New York on her own. With our family scattered around the world at the moment, she has no one she can rely on if she needs anything."

"What could she need?" Theo said putting down his cup.

"For starters, she needs to stay away from men like Logan. He's a great guy, but I saw the way he eyeballed her. If he had a minute alone with her, he'd make a move."

"What's wrong with that?" Everything was wrong with that. Logan went through women on a regular basis. A man like that wasn't good enough for Chloe, he thought somewhat hypocritically considering his recent sexual streak. Although, who was he to decide if Logan was good enough for her or not? It was none of his business who she wanted to screw around with. Maybe his concern was due to her being Ethan's little sister and he was protective of her the same way. *Yeah, right.* He immediately dismissed the thought. At lunch he wasn't being brotherly when he kept remembering how sexy she'd looked sprawled on his bed wearing nothing but a lacy black G-string. How he'd almost fucked her, and how disappointed he'd felt when he had to stop.

"You can't be serious? He's a fuck-em-and-leave-em kind of guy. And I don't want my sister included in his conquests. She deserves someone better than that," Ethan said, uncannily echoing Theo's own thoughts.

"I can tell Logan to stay away."

"But what about the next guy?"

"She's thirty—like she said, she can look after herself. Plus, like she said, she has friends here."

Ethan thrummed his fingers on the table. "Her friends have their own lives. They won't have the time to watch out for her."

What about my life? But he knew that Ethan wouldn't listen to that kind of logic. Plus he hated to admit it, but his friend had a point. If her friends were the same women Chloe had been dancing with last night, then they sucked at looking after Chloe. Visions of her in her red sequined dress sparkling under the club's lights as she swayed in time with the music filled his mind. He'd wanted her from the moment he saw her. Would have had her if she hadn't been Ethan's sister. And dammit, he still wanted her. But he couldn't go there. You don't touch your best friend's little sister, not when you couldn't offer her anything more than a fling. And especially not when you wanted to do all the things that your best friend had asked you to protect her from. Dammit, he was as bad as Logan!

It had been hard enough staying away from her when they'd been younger. When she blossomed in her late teens, he couldn't help but notice the changes in her. The way she'd matured from gangly to gorgeous had sent his blood pumping. He'd noticed her long legs in the short skirts and shorts she liked to wear. Noticed the damn birthmark on her hip that had driven him crazy when she'd worn a bikini—all he'd wanted to do was lick his tongue over it. He'd had to keep his feelings to himself and ignore her when she'd hung out with them. If Ethan or Aiden had gotten a whiff that he was interested, they would have kicked his ass across Sydney.

Pulling himself out of old memories, he said, "She'll be fine. Don't worry so much."

"I called her this morning, and she was hungover," Ethan said, repeating himself from earlier. "What if some guy had taken advantage of her while she was drunk? Who knows where she could have ended up?"

She'd ended up in his bed, and he'd been the guy who had been about to take advantage of her. And damn, if that didn't sting. Luckily, he'd recognized her before he'd fucked her and had gotten her home safely. "I'm taking her out tonight; I'm not sure what more you want me to do?"

That seemed to be the opening Ethan was looking for because his eyes brightened. "Keep hanging out with her. Take her out places. There are a lot of sights around the city you could show her. Just make sure she's not out every night getting drunk and ending up in strange dudes' beds. That kind of thing." When Theo opened his mouth to protest, Ethan put up his hand. "I know it's a lot to ask, but you're my best friend. I trust you. There's no one here I trust more. Please say you'll do it."

Theo tried another tactic. "If Chloe finds out about this, won't she be pissed?"

"Don't say anything to her, and she'll never know," Ethan said with a shrug and a wink.

Theo scrubbed a hand at the back of his neck. What excuse could he give Ethan to not do it? The truth? Tell him that he'd almost fucked Chloe? That he still wanted to see her naked in his bed? That wouldn't work. Not to mention that Ethan would probably beat the snot out of him if he found out the truth. There was nothing he could do. They were friends, he couldn't turn him down.

Scrubbing a hand through his hair, he relented, "Okay, but once I think she's fine and there's nothing for you to worry about, I'm done."

Ethan frowned for a beat then stuck out his hand. "Deal."

Theo hesitated for a second before he took it to shake. God, he hoped this didn't blow up in his face.

CHAPTER SEVEN

Stepping out of the shower, Theo heard his cell buzz in his bedroom. Wrapping a towel around his waist, he padded into his room, picked the phone up from the bedside table, and read the message.

Chloe: You don't have to do this. We can cancel the sightseeing trip and Ethan will never have to know.

She was giving him an out. He should take it. Instead, he typed:

Theo: I'm not canceling.

Chloe: Why? I know you don't want to go with me.

Why? Because he'd promised his best friend he'd watch out for his grown-ass sister. That's why. And it was her ass he couldn't stop thinking about.

Theo: Who said I didn't want to take you?

He did want to "take" her but not sightseeing.

Propping his phone between his ear and shoulder, he grabbed his jeans from the bed and slid his legs inside.

Chloe: Oh, please. The message was followed by an eye roll emoji. *You looked like you'd rather have your hair braided.*

Theo laughed. She was right. There were dozens of things he'd rather do than go to an overly expensive tourist trap. But it wasn't because he didn't want to see Chloe, it was because he didn't know if he could keep his hands to himself. Still, he wasn't canceling. He'd made a promise, and he'd see it through.

Theo: I'll be at your apartment in 15 minutes. Be ready!

He stared at the phone waiting for her to argue more, but it remained silent. When he was sure she wouldn't reply, he finished dressing and called for a driver to meet him in the garage. He usually liked driving himself, but even he found the Empire State Building too much of a hassle.

Fifteen minutes later, Theo was waiting out in front of Chloe's building. What the hell was he doing? He should have canceled like Chloe had suggested. Best to get this over with; he sent her a text.

Theo: *I'm here.*

A message pinged back a few seconds later.

Chloe: You still haven't changed your mind?

Theo: No.

Chloe: Fine. I'll be down in a minute.

Theo didn't have to wait long for Chloe to arrive. When she spotted him, she gave him a small, shy smile that made his chest squeeze tight. Dressed in jeans, a loose-fitting gray V-neck sweater, and a long black coat, she walked toward him like a model on a runway, not a woman on a busy New York sidewalk.

Oh God! He'd never been so scared to take someone out in his life.

A gust of wind blew a lock of her long dark wavy hair in front of her face, and she gathered it in her hands and twisted it so it sat over her shoulder like she'd done in the club. And like what *he'd* done in the club, he zeroed in on her creamy smooth neck. The same neck he'd kissed, running his tongue over her racing pulse. He needed to stop thinking about that night, or he'd never be able to get through the next couple of hours.

As she stood in front of him, he pushed away from the car and swung the back passenger door open. "Let's go." The words came out harsher than intended.

Chloe's eyebrows rose at his tone. "Are you sure you want to do this?"

"I'm here, aren't I?" Again, his tone was sharp.

"Okay... I think I'll go back inside." She turned to leave.

Theo grabbed hold of her wrist before she walked away, turning her around. "I'm sorry." His voice softened. "I've had a lot on my mind... with work." More like with the gorgeous woman standing in front of him making him hard just looking at her.

She glanced at his hand on her arm. "We really can cancel."

"No, I want to take you." And he did. They'd once been friends. Sure, he'd mostly hung out with Ethan, but there'd been times when they'd all hung out together. She was fun, and they'd always gotten along. Why couldn't this be two friends catching up after so many years apart? There was just one thing making this situation not your normal "catch up," and he needed to say something so they could move on.

He dropped her wrist and slid his hands in his pockets. "About the night at—"

She held her hand up. "Please, can we forget about it? Nothing happened."

"Something *did* happen. I should never have asked you to my place."

"Is that something you do often? Ask random women to your apartment."

He didn't—couldn't—answer.

"I'll take that as a yes." She frowned and gazed at something in the distance. "It was a mistake. I've never been so embarrassed in my life. I want to pretend it never happened. Got it?"

"Got it. But there's nothing to be embarrassed about. Like you said, you were drunk and were celebrating your birthday." He offered her a small smile. "I've done dumber things when under the influence."

She gave him a shy smile in return. "So, we agree to forget it ever happened?"

Forget? No fucking way. How could he forget one of the best sexual experiences of his life, well... until it all went to shit. "Sure, already forgotten."

She bowed her head and looked at something on the ground. "And we will never talk about it again?"

"Talk about what?"

Her shoulders sagged in relief. "Thanks."

"Let's go see the Empire State Building." He swung his arm and gestured for her to sit in the back seat.

"I have to say, even though it's such a touristy thing to do, I'm excited," she said before getting in the car.

He sat next to her, making sure he put enough distance between them. To distract himself from Chloe's sweet, floral scent and their close proximity, Theo pointed out sights like the MOMA, St. Patrick's Cathedral, and Rockefeller Center as they drove through the busy streets.

When they arrived and entered the elevator, Theo was thankful the building was packed with tourists and there was no way of there being a repeat performance of the last time they'd been in one. It didn't stop him from picturing what had happened, though. He flicked a glance at Chloe; her eyes were fixed on the ascending numbers, and he'd bet his left nut she was thinking about it too.

Thankfully, the ride up was quick. After a quick scan of the exhibit, they stepped out onto the observation deck. A brisk breeze hit them, and Chloe buttoned up her coat. His instinct was to pull her close to him to keep her warm, but he stopped himself just in time. What the hell was wrong with him? Ever since he'd gotten his hands on her, thoughts of touching her and getting her naked again plagued him. Damn Ethan for putting him through this torture!

Turning toward him, she asked, "Where do we start?"

"Wherever you like."

Chloe scanned the busy deck, saw a gap in the crowd, and made her way through to the railing. Theo followed her.

With her hands holding the crisscrossed bars she gasped, "Oh, wow. This is so beautiful."

"Yeah, it is." Theo wasn't talking about the view. He watched Chloe's face light up with excitement. More beautiful than any city landscape. The wind picked up her hair, and she did that twisty thing with the locks again. The gesture drove him wild. He tore his eyes away and glanced out at the lights stretching over New York.

She pointed and bounced on her feet. "I think I can see the Statue of Liberty."

Theo chuckled at her enthusiasm. He doubted it.

Moving around the deck, she kept stopping and staring out into the distance with a huge smile on her face. "Do you ever come up here?"

"Once. It was right after I moved here; I'd forgotten how great the view is." He'd never bothered coming back, it was such a touristy thing to do, and after twelve years living in the city, he was a New Yorker through and through. Besides, he got a pretty spectacular view of the city from his penthouse.

Chloe stared at him like he had two heads. "I think I'd make this a regular trip. I don't think I could get tired of looking at those lights."

They made their way around a little more, stopping every few seconds to take in the view. They'd be here all night if they kept up this slow pace. But the sheer joy on her face was contagious. He started looking at the scenery like it was his first time too.

"I'm not sure what I'm looking at or where all the landmarks are," she admitted after a while.

Theo shuffled closer—careful not to touch—and pointed. "That's the Chrysler Building." They moved around the platform, and he pointed out the Brooklyn Bridge and the Flatiron Building.

"Where's your nightclub?" she asked.

"It's gonna be tough to spot, all the buildings blend together. Do you see Central Park?" He pointed to the north.

She nodded.

"Move your gaze to the bottom left and over a touch."

She squinted her eyes and leaned forward.

"Do you want to use the binoculars?" There was a pair next to them.

She screwed up her nose. "No thanks. Who knows what's on those things? Point it out for me."

He moved in closer to get her vision in line with his pointed finger. "There are a few buildings in front of it but mine's a bit taller. If you squint really hard, you can see a blue-and-white round symbol on the top of it. Do you see it now?"

She shook her head. "Nope."

He raised his hands and hesitated for a beat before putting them on her shoulders. He turned her a touch to the left and pointed again. His body pressed against her side, and he felt her go still.

Lowering his head closer to her face to get a better sense of what she could see, he said, "Can you see it now?" He drew in a deep breath to suppress the growing desire.

"There are too many buildings. I'm not sure," her voice came out in a husky whisper.

She turned her head to the side, their lips just inches apart. Her gaze dropped to his mouth, and her tongue darted out slightly to lick her bottom lip. He groaned inwardly. All he needed to do was lean in a fraction and kiss her.

One millimeter...

Two millimeters...

Someone jostled them from behind, and the connection broke. Theo cleared his voice and stepped away while Chloe busied herself with wrapping her coat more firmly around her.

"Let's go around again," Theo said, deciding not to point anything else out to her. There was no way he was standing so close to her again. When he did, his brain switched off, and his dick shot to attention. Being near her made him forget about his failed marriage and vow to never marry again. Chloe was a dangerous temptation, one he couldn't seem to avoid.

He groaned, aloud this time.

Chloe touched his arm, snapping his attention to her. "Theo, is something wrong?" She scanned his face.

He shifted uncomfortably. "I'm fine. It's getting cold, we should leave."

Chloe's face dropped slightly. He felt like a jerk for cutting their night short and disappointing her.

The ride on the way down was just as quiet as the one on the way up.

When they stepped out of the building, they rushed into the double-parked car.

After a few minutes of uncomfortable silence, Chloe turned in her seat. "Are you sure you're okay? It looked like something upset you."

"Heights make me a little squeamish sometimes." Another lie. They kept dripping from his mouth. He changed the subject. "How did you like the Empire State Building? Did it meet your expectations?"

She sank back into the seat. "Oh my God. It was beautiful. You were right about going at night. The lights were spectacular."

"Any more tourist destinations you want to see?"

"Are you offering to take me?" she asked coyly. He must have pulled a face because she laughed. "Don't worry, I won't make you go." The car pulled up in front of her building. "Thank you for a great evening."

"It was fun." That wasn't a lie. Up until he remembered his disastrous marriage, he'd been having a great time.

"Good night." She got out of the car, and he watched her make her way inside.

He breathed out a heavy sigh and tilted his head on the back of the seat. Thank fuck the night was over. And it wasn't because he didn't enjoy her company; it was because he liked her company a little too much.

CHAPTER EIGHT

A couple of days after her shortened visit to the Empire State Building, Chloe met up with her friends—Daniela had asked for a rain check due to a minor crisis on her hit procedural—for a catch up and some truly excellent diner fare. After putting in their orders for pancakes, waffles, and meatloaf, Chloe brought Hazel and Blair up to date. She covered all of the basics: needy clients, overprotective older brothers, and frustrating almost first times. Her friends listened sympathetically until she reached the last bit.

"Wait…" Hazel said, incredulous, "you almost did the deed and he stopped, just like that?"

"Just like that."

Blair shook her head. "That sucks dirty diaper dumps."

"It does."

"And there's no hope of convincing Theo to change his mind?" Blair pressed.

"Not while he's following the bro code," Chloe answered.

"So there's absolutely, positively, nothing going on between you?" Blair asked with a little glint in her eye.

"Nope. Nothing. I'm not seeing him again." Disappointment pressed heavy on her chest.

"Well, that's his loss and Tyler's gain," Blair said with an excited grin.

Chloe pushed her pancakes aside and asked, "Who's Tyler?"

"He works with Mitch," she answered. "You'll like him, I promise. He's cute. Has a great job. And he's single. He'd be perfect for you."

"Thank God he's single. Wouldn't want you setting her up with a married man," Hazel said with sarcasm, dabbing at the corners of her mouth with a napkin.

Blair rolled her eyes. "Anyway, I was talking to Mitch about how you're looking to settle down, and he agreed that Tyler is good husband material." She fiddled with her glass, and her gaze flickered away for a beat before she said, "And we set up a date for the two of you tomorrow night."

"What!" Chloe nearly propelled herself from her chair. "Why would you do that?"

"Well, after you left with Theo, the three of us got to talking. Daniela suggested that you put out more than one fishing line."

"So you're saying this is Daniela's fault," Chloe said flatly.

"It was her idea," Hazel chimed in.

"That's right. And it's a good one!" Blair insisted, pushing her meatloaf aside to rest her elbows on the table. "How else are you going to find any prospects if we don't help you? You're new to New York. We're your only friends. It's our God-given duty to act as match-makers for you." Blair's eyes grew sly, and she added, "Unless you want to try your luck with some creepy dating site and meet up with who-knows-what kind of psychopath."

Blair had a point. Chloe'd browsed those sites, and they'd made her cringe. The men on there couldn't think women believed all the bullshit they wrote about themselves, could they? After all, how many six-foot linebackers who liked long walks on the beach and volunteered with sick kids could there be?

Wanting another opinion on the matter, she asked Hazel, "What do you think about this blind date? Should I go?"

Her friend shrugged. "It's up to you, but Blair's right. Going on a blind date with someone she knows is better than meeting up with a stranger no one knows."

Chloe crossed her arms over her chest. "Fine, I'll go. Send me the time and place to meet him."

"Yes." Blair's fist pumped the air, and she whipped her phone off the table and typed on it with a huge grin on her face. "And done. You are going to have the best night of your life. I can feel it."

Chloe wished she felt a smidgen of her friend's enthusiasm.

CHAPTER NINE

B lair was wrong.

It was nowhere near the best night of her life. She'd even say it rated near the bottom. She hadn't had much experience in dating, so her expectations weren't even high. But this date was a joke from the start.

She barely had a chance to introduce herself before Tyler stood, flicked out his wrist, looked at his watch, and announced, "You're late."

Chloe closed her mouth with a click. Yeah, she'd been a teensy bit late, but that was because the subway she'd been on had started running local rather than express—a common New York problem. She'd have been later if she'd taken a taxi—the cabbies got one whiff of her accent and started adding in unnecessary turns. Taken aback by his abrupt tone, Chloe thought he was going to leave since he seemed so annoyed.

He trailed his gaze from her head to her toe. "You're tall."

And he was short. Probably even shorter than Tom Cruise. In her enthusiastic description of Tyler, Blair had forgotten to mention that fact. If she had, Chloe would have worn flats rather than her favorite Jimmy Choos. And while she didn't have an issue with his height herself, from the way he screwed up his nose, she'd bet he did.

He pulled out her chair and gestured for her to sit. At least he had some manners; that was something! So while the date hadn't started well, it could only go up from here.

Hopefully...

It nose-dived. Fast!

He ignored all of her efforts at making conversation during their appetizers. When he did take the time to speak to her, he asked her what she did for a living, only to mock her career. By the time their entrées arrived, he'd had five shots of whiskey and two glasses of wine and was slouched back on the chair, clearly legless.

Staring at her, he grinned for the first time. "How far away do you live?"

She felt like a piece of meat in a lion cage. "Not far," she lied. There was no way she was going to give this guy her address.

His grin became a leer. "Great, I feel like a nightcap. Let's go to your place." He clicked his fingers, signaling for the bill.

"My place for what?" There was no way she'd be inviting him over for coffee let alone more alcohol.

"I haven't taken you to dinner just to eat." The sleazy way he ogled her chest told her exactly what he wanted, and it wasn't another drink.

Her skin crawled. Something within her snapped, and she realized that there was absolutely nothing keeping her here. She'd tried to be polite. She'd tried to be nice. But Tyler was beyond hope, and quite frankly, not worth her time. Grabbing her purse, she leapt to her feet, nearly barreling into the waiter with the check. She handed the waiter a few bills to cover her half of the meal and the tip—no point in stiffing him even if she'd had a miserable time. "I'd like to say this date was enjoyable, but I can't lie. You won't be seeing me again."

He sprang from his chair, wobbled on his feet, and clutched her arm. "Where are you going?"

Flicking his clammy hand off her arm, she said between gritted teeth, "Home. *Alone.*" With that she stormed from the restaurant, ignoring his slurred insults thrown at her back.

As she made it outside, she drew in a deep breath. *What was Blair thinking, setting me up with such a jerk?* Pulling her phone from her bag, she dialed her friend's number.

Blair answered, "Hey, Chloe, is your date finished already?"

"I'm going to kill you." She clutched the mobile in her hand.

"Why? What happened?"

"Everything!" Chloe waved down a taxi and got in, giving the cabbie her address. "I should have ended it the moment I stepped into that restaurant."

"It was that bad?"

"Worse. First, he accused me of being late. Then, he sized me up like a cow at the market and told me I was too tall. By the way, thank you for telling me he was the size of a small child."

"Sorry about that," Blair apologized around a chuckle. "I thought you wouldn't care."

"*I* didn't," she said, stressing the I. "But I think *he* did. He must have little-man syndrome, because he barely spoke to me."

"He's quite chatty when I see him," Blair said.

"That's because he's probably drunk. Once he had a few shots in his system, he wasn't shy about wanting to go to my place because he hadn't taken me to dinner just to *eat*."

Blair gasped, "He did not say that."

"Oh yes, he very much did."

"I'm so sorry, Chloe. He was always so nice. Even Mitch thought he was a good guy. I promise I'll do better next time."

Chloe sighed and stared out of the cab window. "I think I'm done with blind dates."

"You can't give up yet. You just started. I know the perfect guy I can set you up with."

Chloe rested her head against the glass. "You said Tyler was the perfect guy, and look how that turned out."

"This time it will be better. I promise."

Chloe wasn't so sure, but she reluctantly agreed. What other choices did she have? Internet guys? No, she wasn't ready to go down that road. Maybe Blair's next choice wouldn't be such a disaster.

Chapter Ten

"Mr. Campbell, Mr. Vandersluis has arrived for your meeting," Annabelle, Theo's assistant, announced.

"Thank you." Theo shrugged into his suit jacket and made his way to the boardroom.

"Andrew," Theo greeted as he entered the room and extended his arm, "good to see you."

Andrew shook his proffered hand. "It's been a long time." Andrew glanced around the elaborate room with floor-to-ceiling windows overlooking Central Park. His face screwed up with distaste as he took in the mahogany table, black leather chairs, and Marc Chagall painting on the far wall. "I see business is doing well for you."

"I can't complain," Theo said, taking a seat. He gestured to Andrew to do the same.

It wasn't a secret Andrew Vandersluis held a grudge against the Campbell brothers. Their business had skyrocketed, making them millions, while Andrew's was nose-diving fast.

Blake joined them in small talk as Annabelle poured coffee. When she left the room, Andrew leaned back in his chair. "I don't think you've called me all this way for a chat. What is it I can do for you?"

"I've heard you want to sell your building near the Javits," Theo said, cutting to the chase.

Andrew lifted an eyebrow. "Who told you that?"

Giving a shrug, he said, "Word gets around." He had people scouting locations and gathering information on properties in New York. There wasn't much Theo didn't know about Manhattan.

Andrew's face hardened. "I'm gathering you've called me here because you're interested in buying."

Theo placed his elbows on the armrests of his chair and steepled his fingers. "Only if the price is right."

He nodded to Blake, and his brother slid a folder to Andrew. "You'll find our offer in there," Blake said.

Andrew paused with his hand on the folder, staring at Blake and then Theo before opening it and flicking through the pages inside. Andrew's face grew red. "Is this some kind of joke?"

"It's a fair price. Because I know what state the building's in. I know there's a lot of work to be done to bring it up to scratch and up to code. And I know you've paid for *reports* that smudge over the truth about what it's really like."

A vein ticced at the side of Andrew's neck. "If you think there's something wrong with it—"

"I *know* there is." Theo gave him a hard stare. "And I know you do too."

Andrew shifted in his seat. "Why are you interested if you know it's in such poor condition?"

"It's a good location. We can do a lot with it," he said with a shrug. It was the truth as far as he was willing to admit. There was no way he was going to tell Andrew that his building near the Javits was sitting atop prime bedrock. "Are you going to sell to us or not?"

Andrew opened the folder back up, pulled out the piece of paper with their offer written on it, and scoffed. "You couldn't buy the ground floor with this amount."

"Our offer is more than generous." Theo hooked an ankle on top of his knee, awaiting Andrew's inevitable temper tantrum.

"If you accept our terms, we can have our lawyers settle the sale within two months." Blake added. "Plenty of time to pay those sharks circling you after that Atlantic City deal went bust."

Red mottled up Andrew's cheeks. "I'm not accepting this." He flung the folder, sailing it across the desk. "You might have fooled my father into selling this place to you for next to nothing, but you're not dealing with an old man. I don't intend to sell to you."

Theo had expected this and had prepared for this eventuality. Spearing Andrew with a steely gaze, he said, "You won't get a better offer, I promise you that. But I'll give you time to think it over." He paused. "But don't even attempt to try to pull one over on me. It won't work. You won't like the result." Theo pressed a button on the intercom. "It's been a pleasure doing business with you. I'll have Annabelle show you out."

"I can find my own way." Andrew pushed himself out of the chair and stomped from the room.

"That went well." Blake blew out a breath and kicked his feet on top of the shiny table. "He's a fool if he rejects our offer. Selling that property is the only way he's going to avoid losing everything."

"I'm sure he knows that, otherwise he wouldn't be hiding the fact the building needs a total overhaul. Honestly, if we weren't planning on knocking it down and starting fresh, I wouldn't bother with it. He needs to sell it—and for top dollar. But no one is going to pay what he's asking even if they know about the actual geologic survey. He wants way too much," Theo said, drumming his fingers on the table.

"Agreed." Blake picked up the folder. "Are you sure that he won't go to one of our competitors?"

"He'll try, but most don't have the capital... or the vision. Most see that area north of the Javits as a has-been... especially since that stop on the 7 train hasn't gone in." Blake hummed in agreement. Theo continued, "But that building is in a prime position. I'm not letting him sell it to anyone else. He's already got a reputation for selling substandard property, no one trusts him. That location is ours." Theo always got what he wanted—images of Chloe came to mind—well, most of the time.

In his pocket, Theo's phone vibrated with a text. He pulled it out. *Shit.* Ethan. He scrubbed a hand over his face.

"Bad news?" Blake asked.

"No, it's Ethan." Probably wanting updates on Chloe. Who fucking kept tabs on their sister like that? One overprotective brother, that's who.

"Is everything okay? You're frowning at your cell like you want to smash it."

His brother wasn't far off. "Yeah, I'd like to punch Ethan in the head and knock him on his ass for putting me in an awkward situation."

"What situation?" Blake twirled a pen between his fingers.

Blowing out a long breath, Theo said, "He wants me to keep an eye on Chloe while she settles into life in New York."

Blake stopped twirling the pen and clasped it in his hand. "Why?"

Theo rose from his seat, marched to the windows, and stared out at Central Park. "He's worried men will take advantage of her because she's alone in the city with no family to watch out for her."

"What is this? The Dark Ages? Can't she take care of herself?"

"I tried telling him that, but he wouldn't see reason."

"That doesn't sound like Ethan." Blake's chair squeaked. "But I guess I wouldn't know. Chloe's not my sister. So just tell Ethan no, you won't do it."

"It's not that simple." Not to mention, he'd tried and Ethan had guilt-tripped him into agreeing, but Blake didn't need to know that.

But his brother knew he was hiding something. "What's the real problem? What aren't you telling me?"

"The problem is, I'm one of those men she needs to stay away from." Oh shit. He'd said too much. Blake was already like a dog with a bone gnawing to get every little bit of information; now there was no way that he was going to let the subject drop.

Theo heard Blake's feet hit the floor. "What are you talking about?"

Turning around, Theo dug his hands into the pockets of his trousers. "Things got a little awkward between us." That was putting it mildly.

Blake's eyebrow rose. "When you went sightseeing?"

"No. Last Saturday night when we were at the club." He really didn't want to go into it.

But Blake wouldn't let it go. "The night we were celebrating your divorce?" Blake frowned.

There were two things Theo wanted to remove from his brain from that night. His failed marriage becoming official and almost fucking his best friend's sister. His divorce was easy to push to the back of his mind. Chloe... not so easy. The sounds she'd made, the sweet taste of her smooth skin on his tongue. Even the innocent time they'd spent on the observation deck didn't feel so innocent when he'd pressed against her side and wanted to kiss her mouth. He needed to wipe the memories of Chloe away because if he didn't, there was no way he could move on with his life.

"Yes. I bumped into Chloe."

"Really? You never mentioned that when we met her and Ethan for lunch. You acted like you hadn't seen each other in years—oh hell, *she's* the woman you left the club with." Blake slapped his leg and laughed. "Ethan doesn't know, and now he wants you to watch out for his sister. He's handing her to you on a silver platter!"

"Laugh it up. You think I don't know how ironic it is?" Theo tugged his tie from side to side to loosen it around his neck. "It gets worse. When I brought her to my penthouse, I didn't know who she was."

Blake stopped laughing. "You didn't recognize her?"

"No." How had he not recognized her? It didn't matter that the last time he'd seen her, she'd been blonde with her hair cut above her shoulders wearing denim shorts and oversized T-shirts. Her fine facial features and warm smile hadn't changed. He should have remembered her regardless. His only excuse was that night at the club, he'd been too blinded by lust to see clearly.

"And I take it she didn't tell you who she was?" Blake frowned.

He shook his head.

"Did she recognize you?"

"She did."

"Then why didn't she say anything?"

"I asked her that when I realized who she was, and she said she was drunk and wanted to have fun on her birthday with some-one she trusted. Who knows what she meant by that? She probably knew I wouldn't touch her because she's Ethan's sister. Thank God I stopped before it went too far." He wouldn't mention it had been the heart-shaped birthmark that had given her away. Blake would wonder why he knew about it. "After that night, I didn't think I'd see her again. She'd left without giving me her number, and you know how big New York is."

"But then Ethan arranged lunch with us all and convinced you to take her out. Oh, man... this is hilarious." Blake wiped tears from his eyes. At Theo's harsh look, his laughter died down. "What are you going to do?"

"What can I do? If I tell Ethan no, he'll wonder why. How am I supposed to explain that the reason why I can't keep an eye out for Chloe is because I want her naked in my bed?" Shit, he never meant to say that.

"Even after you found out who she was, you still want to have sex with her?" At Blake's question, Theo clenched his jaw and nodded. His brother let out a low, slow whistle. "Man, that's going to be fucking hard, pun absolutely intended. Good luck with that."

"Yeah, Thanks." Theo rolled his eyes.

"And how are you going to hang around her without her getting suspicious?" Blake asked.

"I'll think of something."

"Honestly, Ethan should be okay with you dating Chloe if that's what she wants. He'd be a hypocrite otherwise. She's not a sixteen-year-old girl anymore, and this isn't the sixteen hundreds. You both get to decide who and how you date."

"Ethan won't be happy if I screwed Chloe for the fun of it. You don't love and leave your best friend's sister. Especially if you want a best friend afterward."

"You've got a point." Blake rose, slapped Theo on the back, and chuckled. "Well, good luck. I'm glad it's you, not me."

Too bad it was him. And he had no idea what in the fresh hell he was going to do. Maybe staple his cock to his leg to prevent it from making his life hell. It might hurt, but the alternatives were worse.

CHAPTER ELEVEN

Chloe gave herself one final look over in her full-length mirror. For date number two, she'd opted for black skinny jeans and a white high-neck satin blouse.

Blair had promised this time her date, Henry, wouldn't be such a dud. Instead of meeting for dinner and having to sit through another potential disaster meal, Chloe agreed to drinks. Something quick if the date was bad, and if it wasn't, they could linger longer.

The buzzer to her apartment rang. "Who could that be?" Hazel, Daniela, and Blair were the only friends she had in New York, and they hadn't sent her a text saying they were stopping over. She rushed to the living area and pressed the intercom. "Hello?"

"Hi." There was a pause then, "It's Theo."

At the sound of his voice, her heart fluttered. He didn't need to say his name, she knew who belonged to the deep, gravelly voice the moment he said hi.

"Oh, hey," she said. Why was he at her apartment?

"Can I come up?"

"Umm, sure. I'll buzz you in."

Waiting for him to arrive, she paced the small living area of her apartment, tidying magazines on the coffee table and fluffing pillows on the sofa. When he knocked on the door, she nearly jumped from her skin. She knew he was on his way, but jitters bounced around in her stomach at seeing him again. She opened the door, and her heart skidded to a stop. Dressed in a white shirt tucked into gray trousers, the thin fabric enhanced his broad shoulders and narrow waist. His light-brown hair was neatly brushed off his face. God, he was sexy as hell. She'd tried convincing herself she'd exaggerated his good looks in her mind, but with him standing in front of her looking like a gift from God—or more like the devil tempting her with sin—she'd been delusional. He was so much hotter.

"Can I come in?" He smiled, and creases fanned out from the corners of his clear blue eyes.

"Oh, sure." She gestured for him to enter. "Can I get you anything? Coffee, a drink?" *A bed we can have sex on? Stop it! Stop thinking about Theo in that way.* When he looked good enough to eat, it was hard to keep her thoughts pure.

"No, I'm good. Thanks." He slipped his hands in his pockets and glanced around the room. "Nice place."

And it was. She'd sublet an apartment from a client, and thankfully the actor had good taste—or at least a good interior decorator. It had dark timber floors, a brick feature wall, and a two-seater gray leather sofa. The whole place was smaller than she was used to, but she still loved it. "My apartment could fit into the linen cupboard in your penthouse."

He swung his head toward her, pinning her with his stare.

She slammed her lips closed. Why did she have to mention his penthouse? She wanted to forget about that night, and from his actions, he did too.

Quickly changing the subject, she said, "What are you doing here?" She had a date in thirty minutes. Luckily, she'd gotten ready early and had plenty of time before she needed to meet Henry.

"I wanted to talk to you about the night at the club." He propped a hip on the side of the sofa arm.

She glanced at the floor. "You promised we were going to pretend it never happened."

"I know I did. But I wanted to make sure you were really okay." Was it her imagination, or did his eyes soften as he said those words?

"Of course I am. Nothing happened," she said. They've been through this. Why was he dragging it back up?

He tilted his head to the side and examined her face. "So, we're good?"

"Yep. Uh-huh." She nodded. "I was drunk and feeling a little sorry for myself. That's an instant scratch from my memory bank."

Theo frowned. "Why were you feeling sorry for yourself?"

Never in a million years could she tell Theo that she was still a virgin at her age. Would he think she was some kind of freak? She couldn't bear that pain.

"I turned thirty. That's a huge number. I wasn't dealing with it very well." That wasn't a complete lie. She *was* feeling sorry for herself for turning thirty, but it wasn't because of her age. It was all the things she hadn't done before she'd reached it that depressed her. Finding love and the man of her dreams, having sex, getting married, and starting a family. Time was ticking, and she had a lot of work to do to get those things checked off her list before it was too late.

Speaking of late, she had a date she needed to get to. She looked at the clock on the wall. Dammit, she needed to get to the bar fast; that meant she had to leave now.

Theo regarded her, confusion crossing his face. "Thirty is when your life really begins. It's when you know who you are, what you want, and have the maturity to go for it."

And that's what she was doing. Starting now... by going on a blind date. "I'm sorry, I have to cut this visit short. I'm actually on my way out." And having him in her apartment—in her tiny living room—was sucking the air out of the space, causing her heart to race. Maybe she should cancel her date and stay home with Theo instead. She'd gladly skip her date for another kiss—another touch.

"Where are you going?" he asked, snapping her mind out of her fantasy.

"Oh... umm... I have a date, and if I don't get going ASAP, I'll be late." She picked up her purse and keys from the coffee table.

"I'll drive you." He pushed away from the sofa.

"No, that's not necess—"

"I insist." His mouth tightened. "You don't want to keep your date waiting." Why did it sound like he gritted those words out?

"Okay, thanks." She reached for the door.

"Wait," he called, and she turned around. "You missed a button."

The top she wore had two small buttons at the side of her neck. She always had trouble threading them through the tiny holes. Before she could reach up to fix it, Theo's hands were on her shoulder. His fingers brushing against the exposed skin on her neck. A wave of heat flushed over her, and she held her breath. It seemed to take him forever to button it, so she turned her head to glance at his face. Clear blue eyes stared down at her and settled on her lips. Just like he had at the Empire State Building. Again, she wondered if he was going to kiss her. *Prayed* he'd kiss her! She bit her lower lip in anticipation.

He squeezed his eyes shut for a beat, took a deep breath, and then stepped away. "Done. Let's go." He rushed past her and out of the apartment.

With a heavy sigh, Chloe's shoulders slumped, and she grabbed her coat and followed him out. What had she expected? A repeat performance of the night at the club? No, he'd never step over the friendship boundaries.

Even if they both wanted to.

CHAPTER TWELVE

What the fuck was wrong with him? He couldn't be in a room with Chloe without wanting to strip off her clothes and throw her on a bed. Hell, any piece of furniture would do. His cock had stood at attention all because he'd touched her goddamn shoulder. Her *shoulder!* His body didn't normally react this way. He couldn't run out of her apartment fast enough.

As she slid onto the leather passenger seat, his gaze dropped to her legs. Even though she wore black jeans that hid her skin, they didn't hide their toned shape. He pictured himself removing them slowly, trailing his tongue along the way, and draping them over his shoulders as he rammed into her. God, he needed to get himself under control—fast.

He peeled his gaze away and concentrated on the road. After she gave him the name and location of the bar she was going to, he turned up the music on the radio and navigated his car through the streets. If he couldn't hear her voice, then maybe he could keep his mind focused on the road and not on the porno playing in his mind. Ethan needed to watch Chloe himself or get someone else to do it. Theo was out.

After I drop her off, I'll call Ethan. And tell him what? That he was lusting after his sister? Wanted to get his hands on her body until she screamed his name? He couldn't tell Ethan any of that, and Theo also couldn't back out of his promise. A promise to a friend was as strong as titanium. All he needed to do was get laid—with some *other* woman—and all would be right again. He'd have his itch scratched, and then he'd go back to seeing Chloe as Ethan's little sister—all interest in her forgotten.

Yeah, right.

By the time they reached the bar, his fingers ached from gripping the steering wheel. He needed a stiff drink or two to ease the tension.

"Thanks for the ride," she said in that distracting voice of hers.

"No problem."

She smiled and hesitated with her hand on the door.

Since he was still on the case, he'd better do his pseudo–big brother duty. "Who's the guy? Have you been on many dates with him?"

She shook her head. "His name is Henry. I'll be meeting him for the first time. My friend set me up on a blind date."

His spine stiffened. "You don't know the guy at all? You're meeting a stranger?"

"Blair said he's nice." Her brows creased. "I'm hoping he's better than the last guy she set me up with."

He swiveled in his seat to face her. "This isn't the first blind date you've been on?"

She shook her head.

Shit. Maybe Ethan's concern for her was justified. Who knew what weirdos she'd been set up with? "What was wrong with the last guy?"

She shuddered. "Too many things to explain."

"Blair is setting you up with creeps? What kind of friend would do that?" He needed to drive her back to her apartment, not hand her to some asshole.

"It wasn't her fault. He'd given her and her husband the impression he was a nice guy."

"And you trust her with her next choice? What if he's not what they think he is either?" The urge to turn the car around grew stronger.

She shrugged one shoulder and sighed. "I have to try. I don't know anyone in New York, so I need all the help I can get." Opening the door, she swung her legs from the car. "Thanks again for the ride."

He drew her to a stop, tugging on her wrist. With her skin so soft and delicate under his fingers, he wanted to trail his hand up her arm to her neck and pull her to him, not let her walk into that bar to meet a stranger. But he let go, cleared his throat, and said, "If you get into any trouble, call me."

She smiled over her shoulder and nodded. He rubbed his chin and watched her walk into the bar to meet a guy who could be some psychopath.

God, he was starting to sound like Ethan.

Although, his friend did have a point. If she was meeting with random strangers, it wouldn't hurt if someone watched out for her. Handing his car off to a nearby valet, he walked to a bar opposite the one Chloe sat in waiting for her date. The window he was seated at gave him a clear view of her.

He told himself this wasn't creepy at all. This was what Ethan had asked him to do—keep an eye on Chloe—and that justified what he was doing because she was meeting a random guy. But if she knew he was spying on her, he had no doubt that she'd knock his lights out. As a kid, he'd seen her throw a punch or two at her brothers, knocking them on their asses.

While she sat and waited for her date, she ordered a glass of wine, flicked through her phone, and twirled the ends of her hair around her finger. She wiggled in the seat and adjusted the neckline of her top; she drummed her fingers on the table and drank the wine.

As time went on and her date hadn't yet showed up, the routine repeated until she was on her fourth glass. It had been almost an hour since he'd dropped her off, and the guy still hadn't made an appearance. Her date had stood her up. What a stupid fucker! Did he know what kind of woman waited for him? Obviously not, because there was no way a man in his right mind would ghost a woman like Chloe.

Chloe flicked through her phone again and must have made up her mind not to wait any longer because she called the waiter over and paid her bill. Rising from her chair, she swayed slightly. She clutched the table until her legs were steady then walked out of the bar. She'd had a lot to drink, and on an empty stomach, alcohol became more potent. He needed to get her home safe.

Leaving money on his table, he rushed outside, dodging cars as he crossed the street to get to her. "Chloe!"

She kept staggering along the sidewalk. Tripping over her feet, she steadied herself by clutching a lamppost.

Shit!

He picked up the pace. People around him gave him curious looks as he pushed past them. "Chloe!" he yelled. Again, no response. "Glowy!" She spun around and wobbled. He caught her just in time, holding on to her shoulders to steady her.

"Hey, are you okay?" He stared into her glassy eyes.

"Oh, hey, hi, Theo. I'm fine... good... great... never better. I've had the best night of my life." She shook her shoulders from his grasp and flung her arms out wide. "Dating in New York is s-super."

"I'm taking you home." He once again put his hands on her shoulders and made to turn her around to lead her to his car. But she put her hands on his chest and pushed him away.

"I'm not ready to go home. I have not been on one decent d-date yet." She stamped her foot like a child. "I didn't move from Aus-straya to go on shitty dates. I'm going to find one myself." She swung around and took a few steps.

He grabbed her wrist and led her from the middle of the sidewalk to the shadows of a building away from pedestrians. "Where are you going?"

"To a nightclub to find a date." She rolled her eyes at him. "Hey," she pointed her finger at him. "You own a club. Let's go to yours." She grabbed his hand and tried pulling him.

Theo didn't budge. "It's not open tonight." A truth. Alto was never open on Tuesdays.

Her lip dropped. Then she smiled, and her eyes lit up. "You're the owner, right? You can open up for us."

Ah… the logic of inebriation. "The club's empty. How will you find a date?"

She slapped a hand to her forehead. "This night keeps getting worse and worse."

"It can't be that bad. You seem to have a nice buzz going on," he chuckled.

She giggled. "A bottle of wine will do that."

"Come on. Let me take you home."

She blew a strand of hair from her eyes. "I don't want to go home."

"What do you want to do?" he asked.

"Dance."

"Dance?" he repeated.

"Yep, the night might have started off like hairy donkey balls, but that doesn't mean it has to end like crap. Dancing makes me happy." She did a wonky twirl, and he caught her around the waist before she toppled over.

Their bodies bumped together, and her hands landed on his chest. Their eyes locked. Then she lowered her head and played with the top button of his shirt. He held his breath when her fingers brushed the skin on his neck. It took all his might to let her go and step back.

She pouted. "I'm not going to find a date tonight in your club, but you can still open up for me."

"What for?"

"To dance." She pulled a face like he was stupid.

God, watching out for Chloe was hard work. The girl didn't have an ounce of logic, particularly when inebriated. All of a sudden, Chloe's charade on her birthday made sense; she was a naive and careless drunk. It was a problem. A problem that wouldn't be as big of an issue if she were still in Australia, but in a city like New York, it would be. Especially with the kind of guys who trolled clubs—he would know, he owned one. Fuck, Ethan owed him big time.

"You want to dance in an empty club?"

"Yes." She blinked up at him through long, thick lashes and glassy green eyes.

He blew out a long breath. "Fine. But before we go, you need to eat." And hopefully that would sober her up enough to change her mind about going to the club and dancing.

"Pizza. I'm craving pizza." She did a little happy dance, drawing his eyes to her hips. Christ, she was killing him. He needed the night to end.

They walked a few feet to a restaurant that sold pizza by the slice and sat at a table outside. The city buzzed with life around them.

Cars honked at each other. Across the road, an elderly Black man with a cane was selling canvases of New York City landmarks. Most pedestrians hurried past him without a glance. Chloe didn't seem to notice any of it, too engrossed in her food.

Watching Chloe across from him, there was something Theo was engrossed in too, and it wasn't pizza.

"This is so good," Chloe moaned around a mouthful of food. "I've never been able to buy pizza by the slice in Sydney. Another great reason to move to New York."

"Why did you leave Australia?" Theo asked, trying to ignore the moans of pleasure and the way her tongue darted out of her mouth to lick her lips.

"Work mostly." She folded her pizza like a true New Yorker before taking another bite.

"Mostly?"

Chloe sucked sauce from her finger, and he almost groaned out loud. "My clients are mainly in the States. A lot of them weren't comfortable doing things solely over the phone and via email and video chat. Flying back and forth to New York and LA was killing my social life," she explained, nibbling on her slice. "Oh my God, this is the best pepperoni pizza I've ever eaten."

There were better places to order pizza. Much, much better. The greasy slice probably tasted good because she still wasn't sober.

"You want a better social life? Is that why you went on a blind date?"

She screwed her nose up with disgust. "What was I thinking? Two dates, and they both sucked. Well, the second didn't even show up, so technically I can't call it a date." Wiping her hands on the napkin, she threw it on the empty paper plate.

"Instead of blind dates, why don't you join some kind of gym or activity where you can meet new friends?"

She laughed, but her eyes didn't match her smile. "You make me sound like a sad and lonely person."

"Are you?"

"What? Sad and lonely?"

He nodded.

Instead of answering the question, she reached over to his plate and picked up his uneaten slice of pizza. "Are you going to eat that?" She bit into it before he could answer.

He chuckled. "Help yourself."

"This is so good," she mumbled.

Was she changing the subject on purpose, or was she really that hungry? He had a feeling there was more to why she'd moved to New York than she was saying. But it wasn't his place to pry. He was here to watch out for her and report back to Ethan that everything was okay.

As she chewed her food, she stared at Theo with narrowed eyes and pointed a finger in his direction. "Why are you here?"

He leaned back in his chair. "I'm feeding you."

"No, you were outside of the bar where I got stood up. Why?"

So she'd noticed his fortuitous arrival, he'd hoped she was too drunk to question it. "I was having a drink at a bar nearby and happened to see you when you stumbled out. I was checking if you were okay."

"I did *not* stumble," she huffed.

He raised an eyebrow.

"These heels are too high." She shrugged a shoulder, then asked, "Who were you at the bar with?"

"No one."

"You were drinking alone?" Her eyes narrowed. "Why?"

"Can't a man have a scotch alone in peace every now and again?"

She pulled her lips to the side for a second as she stared at him. "You came to my apartment, offered me a lift, and conveniently showed up as I was leaving the bar. Were you stalking me?"

He noticed a spot of red sauce next to her mouth, distracting him for a second. He wanted to lick it off and had to pull his attention back to what she was saying. "Don't be ridiculous."

Again, she pursed her lips. "So if you're not stalking me, did you come to my apartment to pick up where we'd left off in your penthouse? Because you made it clear you don't want me."

Don't want her? Christ, if she wasn't Ethan's sister, he would have had her naked before they'd even left her apartment. "No, like I said, I wanted to make sure we were okay about the night at the club. It was a coincidence I was having a drink nearby." He rubbed his hands over his thighs. God, he hated lying.

"I don't believe you." She pointed a finger at him. "You've changed your mind, haven't you? You don't care that I'm Ethan's sister, and now you want to jump my bones. Well, you missed your chance, buddy! I'm not interested." She leaned back in her chair and folded her arms.

Theo choked back a laugh. Once the alcohol wore off, she was going to regret the words spilling from her mouth.

"I haven't changed my mind." Damn, he wished he could.

"Right..." She twirled a finger in front of his face. "I see the sex-me-up eyes you give me. You want me b-a-a-d."

He needed to shut this conversation down. Not only would she regret what she'd said in the morning, he didn't want to accidentally tell her she was right about him wanting her.

"Ethan asked me to watch out for you while you got settled," he blurted out. Secrets were a bitch to keep. It sucked up too much energy. He should know, because he'd been keeping one for years and it weighed around his neck.

Chloe's hand dropped. "Ethan asked you to spy on me? Are you kidding?!" Her voice rose. "I'm gonna kill him." She sprang from the chair. All drunken talk about *sex-me-up eyes* forgotten.

Theo stood too, stepping in front of her. "Shhh... calm down."

"Don't shush me! How dare he think he can do this to me? Do I get spies to chase him around the world to keep an eye on him? No! You know why?" She didn't wait for his response. "He's a freaking grown man, that's why." Pointing a finger at her chest, she added, "I'm thirty. Not three. He needs to start treating me like an adult."

"He's worried about you." He glanced over his shoulder. They were attracting attention. "Let's go somewhere where we can talk in private." He put his hand on the small of her back to guide her.

She sidestepped his touch. "I'm not going anywhere until you explain what the hell Ethan's trying to do." She frowned and stared at him for a beat before her eyes grew wide. "Did you have something to do with Henry not showing up? Did Ethan tell you to sabotage my date?"

"No, God. I would never do that."

She made a scoffing sound as she grabbed her purse off the table and pulled out her phone. "Don't get offended when I tell you I think you're full of shit," she said with a sarcastic tone. "I'm calling Ethan and telling him to stay the hell out of my life."

Why did he have to open his big mouth? Theo placed a hand on her wrist. "Wait!"

"Why should I?" she snarled.

"Just take a minute. Breathe. And think about this. If you tell him you know, he'll be pissed at me for telling you."

"So? You look like a guy who can handle someone being pissed at you." She waved her hand up and down like his appearance explained his personality. "I'm pissed at you, and you're handling it just fine."

She had a point. "True, but it won't do you any good."

"What do you mean?" She tilted her head to the side.

"If Ethan is worried enough about you being in the city on your own to send me out to keep an eye on you, after he finds out you know, he'll just find someone else to take my place. Maybe fly your mother or Aiden here." Why was he stopping her again? If he let her make the call, he'd be free from his obligation to Ethan.

Biting the corner of her lip she said, "They'd come here too, even though Mya is pregnant."

He'd forgotten Aiden was newly married but nodded anyway. "On the next available flight if Ethan asked them to."

Her fists clenched by her side. "I'm still so angry at him."

"Big brothers are painful. Just ask Blake. He bitches about me to Logan all the time."

Her eyes lit up, and a smile spread across her face. "Logan... That's right. Logan. You have friends, right?"

Oh no, no, no. She couldn't be interested in Logan, could she? He was a dog. Couldn't keep his dick in his pants for two seconds. Ethan would skin him alive—assuming he let Logan anywhere near her. "Arrh, yes, I have friends."

She tapped his chest with the palm of her hand. "Then you're just the guy who can help me."

Why did he feel like this was going to be worse than helping Ethan? "I'm not setting you up with Logan if that's what you're thinking." He'd rather have a root canal on all of his teeth without anesthesia first.

"No, I don't want to date Logan." She shook her head loosely. "He's a dog."

Oh thank God, she'd noticed. "So ask your friends for help with whatever you're thinking about." He was done doing favors.

"Clearly, they can't help. I'm done with their suggestions." She paused. "Although, really, they were only Blair's suggestions."

"Then ask someone else." He shuffled back a couple of steps.

"Nope. You're the perfect person, and if you don't want me running to Ethan and telling him your cover was blown in three hours, you're going to do it." She looked at him like she'd pulled one over on him, and he had no other choice.

He chuckled. "You said yourself I wouldn't care if someone was pissed at me."

She dropped her hands on her hips. "Well, if that doesn't scare you, how do you think your relationship with Ethan will be after I tell him we almost slept together?"

He crossed his arms over his chest. "I dare you to tell him." He wasn't falling for her bluff. There was no chance she would tell her brother about that night.

She stared long and hard at him, then jabbed a finger at his chest. "Is there nothing that scares you?"

Fuck, yes. What scared the crap out of him was her standing mere inches away from him with her hand on his chest. He was fucking petrified of pulling her into his arms and kissing the hell out of her. Placing a hand on her arm, he said, "Chloe, you're upset. Let me take you home."

She shrugged off his hand. "Will you help me or not?"

He let out a long breath and dropped his head forward. He asked with dread, "Help you with what?"

"Finding a husband."

CHAPTER THIRTEEN

Theo's face went blank for a second before he laughed. *Laughed* right in her face! Holding her chin high, she glared at him until he stopped.

When he realized she wasn't laughing with him, he sobered up, but his lips still twitched. "You're joking, right?"

"No, I'm not joking. Does it look like I am?"

"With you scowling at me, I guess not." Then his lips curled into a grin. "Glowy wants a husband?"

Pain blossomed through her chest. "If you're going to make fun of me, I'm leaving. I'll walk into the next bar and try my luck with someone in there." Nudging past him, she didn't get two steps away before he wrapped his hand around her wrist, pulling her back.

"You are not going into a bar to find some random guy." His eyes darkened and bored into hers.

Her breath caught at his fierce expression. "Why not?"

"Because you don't know who you'll meet."

"Then help me," she pleaded.

"No."

"Why not?" she said again. "Oh, wait. You'll have to get Ethan's permission first. I hate you both at the moment." She turned away. "You can both go to hell, I'm not answerable to either of you."

"How about I drive you home and, on the way, you can tell me why you want a husband." His tone was gentle, the kind used with frightened animals or small children. She was neither of those.

She whipped her head around to check if he was laughing at her again. His face was emotionless, but mirth still twinkled in his eyes.

Jerk.

"I'm not ready to go home." She'd only be reminded of another failed date and her time line being pushed back further. "You promised we could dance in your club."

He held up a hand. "I said *you* can dance. I don't dance."

"You own a nightclub, and you don't dance?"

"Nope."

"Well, I want to dance," she said with a pout. "It's better than standing here while you make fun of me or going back to my apartment only to be reminded that I'm going to be alone forever."

Theo frowned. "You're not going to be alone forever."

Her eyes narrowed. "If Ethan has his way, I will be."

"Ethan didn't ask me to stop you from seeing anyone. He only wanted to make sure you were safe." She stared at him. She didn't know what to believe. Unwilling to keep discussing this in the middle of the street, he said, "Come on. My car's not far, and I'll take you to my club."

They sat in silence during the drive. Once inside the building, he led her into the club. It was eerie seeing the room empty of people. The space looked ten times bigger. Chairs were stacked on tables, and the faint smell of stale alcohol clung to the air.

Theo led her to the dance floor and said, "Wait here." He disappeared into a room behind the bar. A few seconds later, lights burst through the room, bouncing different colors off the mirrored walls, ceiling, and floor. Next, he walked to the DJ stand. With a flick of a button, a slow song blasted through speakers.

With long ambling strides, Theo made it onto the dance floor; his white shirtsleeves were rolled up to the elbows, showing strong forearms. He'd unbuttoned a couple of buttons, giving her a peek of bronze skin. If she weren't so mad at him, she'd rip open the shirt to get a better look at his rock-hard chest and abs. But she *was* mad, and dammit, she still wanted to tear his clothes off. Not that he'd let her. *Damn Ethan!*

She cleared her throat and the image of his to-die-for body from her mind. "I thought you said you don't dance?"

"I'm here to make sure you don't fall on your ass," he said with a grin. The closer he got to her, the faster her heart rate kicked up.

No doubt he'd catch her with no problem if she fell. He was so much bigger and harder than she remembered. The young man she'd once known had been gangly, still growing into his skin. His arms that had once been long and limber were now thick with muscle, but she knew they could be gentle—she'd been wrapped in them not long ago. A shiver raced over her skin as he approached.

Chloe wasn't a teenager anymore, and Theo wasn't the same boy she'd once known. The hardness she saw from him told her something had changed in his life, or maybe, it was just a boy growing into a man, which made him ten times more exciting. There was no way she could dance with him now. How could she let him take her into his arms—press up against him—and not take things further? He'd only reject her again. And God, she'd had enough rejection the past few days to last her a lifetime. "I've changed my mind. I don't want to dance."

Without asking her why, he pulled a remote from his pocket, pressed a button, and the music cut off. Even the lights dimmed from the multicolored brightness to a pale golden glow.

The ambience of the club changed the instant the music and lights turned off. Shadows lingering in corners chased away the cheerful party vibes. The dark atmosphere matched her mood.

The clicking sound of her heels echoed through the quiet room as she walked to a black leather booth and slid onto the seat. She tipped her head back and stared at the ceiling. Was the move to New York worth it? Coming all this way because she thought she'd find happiness here? So far, it wasn't turning out like she'd hoped.

Theo sat opposite her and placed two glasses on the table. "It's soda water. Can I get you something else?"

The thought of more alcohol made her stomach churn. She took a sip. "This is good. Thanks."

"Tell me why you're looking for a husband," he said, his voice oddly intent. "Has this got anything to do with you thinking you're going to be alone forever? You know that's bullshit, right?"

"Is it? I'm thirty and don't have a husband or children. Everyone around me has started families. I want one too." She thought about Isla again and how her life had ended so quickly. "Before it's too late."

"It's not too late. You're still young enough to have everything you want."

She traced a finger over the condensation on the glass. "Not if I keep going on pathetic dates." She looked up at him, her heart in her eyes. "That's why I need your help."

"I'm not finding a husband for you." She frowned with disappointment. "What makes you think I can?"

"In your line of work, you'd have a lot of contacts. I bet you'd know a bunch of single men—like Logan." She already knew his friend wasn't husband material, but she wanted to test him. Would he lead her to the right kind of man if he gave in and helped her? She needed to know.

"Logan is not who you're looking for." A fierce scowl appeared on his face like he hated the thought of her with someone like Logan. "He's the love-them-and-leave-them kind of guy."

She placed her palms on the smooth tabletop and leaned forward. "See? You know the good from the bad. Help me."

"I'm sorry. I don't know anyone who I could set you up with."

"I don't believe you."

He shrugged. "It's the truth."

"You own nightclubs and must have a ton of men working for you. Not to mention the single friends I'm sure you have," she scoffed. "But you don't know anyone you can set me up with."

"I'm afraid that's true." Theo pulled an apologetic face.

Oh, she'd bet he wasn't sorry at all. She slid across the seat and got to her feet in a huff. "I thought we were friends." She marched across the dance floor toward the exit.

"We *are* friends," he called out to her.

She stopped and turned around. "Friends *help* each other."

"I can't help you with this." He rose from the booth and strode toward her.

"Why? And don't give me that bullshit excuse of not knowing any single men." She crossed her arms over her chest.

With a sound of exasperation, he said, "I don't have time to play matchmaker. I have businesses that require my attention twenty-four seven. I'm not one of your girlfriends who you can sit around and talk about boys with."

The way he said it made her feel like a tween all over again. She shook her head and spun on her heels. His physical features weren't the only thing that had changed these past twelve years. So had his personality. He'd become a grade *A* jerk.

"Where are you going?"

"None of your business," she threw over her shoulder.

"You're not going to another bar, are you?"

She didn't answer.

He caught up to her and stood in front of her, blocking her exit. "Don't go to another bar."

"Or what? You're going to run to Ethan and tell on me?" She gave a mirthless laugh. "See if I care."

"Don't go to another bar." he stepped closer, his voice more urgent—insistent.

Her breathing quickened at the heat building between them. "Don't panic. I'm not going to another bar; I'm going home. I've had enough of men for one night, and that includes you." She stepped around him. "Goodbye, Theo. I better not find you stalking me again."

Chapter Fourteen

The next morning, Theo stared out over the city buildings and streets. The gray skies had opened up, and rain pelted the glass of his office. Blake sat at Theo's desk going through plans of the building they wanted to purchase from Andrew Vandersluis. He still hadn't agreed to sell to them, so Theo quietly let an undoctored assessment of the property circulate through the real estate world. He was a man of his word. It was only a matter of time until Vandersluis gave in, and Theo wanted to be prepared.

"So what do you think?" Blake asked.

"Sounds good. Go ahead," he said, distracted by thoughts of last night. Chloe couldn't be serious about wanting his help finding her a husband. It must have been the alcohol talking.

"Okay, I'll offer Andrew an extra two million dollars for the property just because I'm in a generous mood."

Theo spun around. "What?"

Blake grinned at him. "Mention money, and I finally get your attention."

"I heard everything you said," he lied. His thoughts had been con-sumed by Chloe. They had been for days.

Blake chuckled. "Bullshit. What's bothering you?"

Theo scrubbed a hand through his hair, took a deep breath, and told his brother everything. "Chloe wants me to find her a husband."

Blake stared at him with a blank expression. "A husband?"

"Yep." Saying it out loud sounded ridiculous. She couldn't have been serious, could she?

"She asked you to find her a husband? Why?" Blake looked as confused as he felt.

"Because she just turned thirty and believes time is running out for her to start a family."

Blake made a face. "Too old? Man, I wouldn't be thinking about tying myself down to one woman for the rest of my life and starting a family until I'm at least forty," he said with a wink. "If Chloe is serious about this, why did you say no?"

Because his stomach churned at the thought of setting her up with potential husbands. Probably because she was Ethan's little sister, and it just seemed too weird. But he knew the second the thought came into his mind that he was full of shit. He couldn't delve into the real reason. There was no point. He couldn't do anything about it anyway. "I said no because I can't help her. I'm not a fucking matchmaking service."

"No, but you do know a lot of single men who'd jump at the chance to date Chloe. I can't see what the problem is. Give her number to a couple of guys, and let her take it from there."

Theo dug his hands in his trouser pockets. "If it's that easy, you help her."

Shrugging, Blake tilted his chair back. "I would, except my friends are too immature for Chloe. They're still screwing around. No one's planning on settling down. You could always ask—"

"Don't even think about Logan." Theo glared at his brother.

Blake held up his palms. "Jeez, calm down. He'd be the worst guy to set her up with. I was going to say, what about your buddy, Darius? I heard he broke up with his girl a couple of months ago. He could be looking to start dating again."

"That's a rebound."

"Okay, well... there's Sebastian who you run with some mornings. I know he's single. He was hooking up with some chick in the bar last week."

Theo raised an eyebrow. "Seb hooks up with multiple women on a regular basis. He's not husband material."

"Then how about Owen? He's a decent guy." Blake suggested.

He didn't have a ready-made excuse for that one. Owen was a decent guy. He was an accountant whose firm contracted with theirs and also a friend. He didn't screw around and wasn't an asshole. "He's going bald."

Blake rolled his eyes. "Listen to yourself. 'He's going bald'? I mean, come on! It sounds like you don't want to set her up with anyone because you have a thing for her." Blake laughed, but when Theo didn't join in, he choked and said, "*Do* you have a thing for her?"

"She's Ethan's sister."

"That doesn't answer my question."

"Look, Chloe asking me to find her a husband is fucked up. I mean, who does that?" Theo said to avoid the question.

"A friend who trusts you enough to help her," Blake answered.

"I'm not doing it. I'm too busy with work. I don't have time to play matchmaker." Theo said, rearranging some paperwork on the desk.

"You work too much. This could be a good distraction for you."

"I'm not doing it," Theo repeated.

"Are you still going to be Ethan's watchdog?"

Theo blew out a breath and dropped his elbows on the desk. "When she found out about that, she warned me to stay away. I'm going to have to tell Ethan she knows. He's so worried about her, he'll probably fly his mother to New York, and that would really piss her off."

"*Or* you could kill two birds with one stone. Set Chloe up with a couple of dates, and that way you can keep an eye on her for Ethan."

"No. Now will you drop it?"

Blake stared at Theo through narrowed eyes. "You like her. That's why you won't help her out. You want her for yourself."

"You're being ridiculous," Theo scoffed.

"Am I? Since when do you refuse to help out a friend? That's if that's *all* she is? You're helping Ethan; help her too."

Theo threw his hands in the air in frustration. "Fine. I will try and find her a husband. Happy? Now shut the fuck up about it."

Blake smirked. "Why does the thought of helping her make you look like you've eaten a rotten egg?" He paused. "Look, if you're interested—"

Theo slapped a file on the desk. "I'm not."

"But if you were, Chloe would be a great woman to move on with."

"My divorce was finalized a week and a half ago. I'm not looking for another wife now or ever."

Blake and his family believed his marriage had ended because he and Layla had drifted apart. They didn't know the real reason it had ended was because he couldn't give his ex-wife everything she wanted. A baby.

Annabelle walked into the room, thankfully ending their conversation. "Excuse me, I have a Chloe Doyle in the waiting room asking to see you. She doesn't have an appointment, but she's insisting it's important."

Blake's face split into a huge grin, and he slapped his thigh. "Speak of the devil. I can't wait to see what she wants."

Scrubbing a hand over his face he said, "Send her in. *You*"—he pointed a finger at his laughing brother—"get the fuck out of my office."

Blake pushed himself from the chair and followed Annabelle. Before he reached the door, he turned around. "Two birds. One stone. Or take her for yourself. I know what option I'd choose if I were you." With that, Blake left the office and, a few seconds later, Chloe stood at his door.

Chloe hovered in the doorway unsure if she'd made the right decision coming to see Theo. When Blake passed by her, he gave her the biggest grin, and she wondered if he knew about her embarrassing behavior last night. Her head pounded—a reminder of too much alcohol and too many terrible decisions.

Pulling back her shoulders, she stepped inside the office. Theo waited, one hip propped on the edge of his heavy wood desk with his arms crossed, accenting his broad shoulders and bulging biceps. God, would she ever get used to seeing how buff he'd grown over the years?

"You're looking fresher this morning, Chloe." A playful grin tugged at his lips.

Her stomach churned. She wasn't sure if it was because of the hangover or last night's embarrassing behavior. "I'm not feeling so fresh."

Theo chuckled, and her heart tripped at the sound. The childhood crush she'd thought was over years ago had reared its head once again, this time bigger than ever before. If she was to find herself a husband, she needed to control the urge of wanting to have her way with Theo. Oh, wait. It would never happen. She was Ethan's sister and therefore a no-go zone. What a dumb rule!

"Umm… about last night." She averted her gaze toward the window and the view of Central Park. "I'm sorry I got mad at you for not wanting to help me with… with…"

"Finding a husband?"

She nodded. "I was drunk, and I should never have asked. I was mad at Ethan for sending you to spy on me, and well, I thought you owed me. I'm not going to tell Ethan I figured out his plan to treat me like a two-year-old. He'd only send my mother here." Her eyes met his. "But that doesn't mean I want you following me around either."

"If I hadn't been watching you last night, who knows what could have happened? You weren't in the greatest condition."

"You think I don't know that?" The bottle of wine she'd consumed pounded in her head. "I know I shouldn't have had so much to drink, and I won't do that again no matter how bad the next date or *no-show* date I end up on is. I'll try my luck with a dating site because Blair's men were duds, and I don't trust her choices anymore."

Theo frowned. "You still want to go on dates with strangers? Do you know how dangerous using dating sites can be?"

Chloe crossed her arms over her chest, mirroring his stance. "You're starting to sound like my brother. Do I have to remind you that I'm an adult?"

"No, you don't." His crystal-blue gaze trailed over her body like a warm caress, and her knees trembled. "It's still dangerous meeting random people online."

She threw her arms out in frustration. "Well, how the hell am I supposed to find a husband, then? You refused to help. I don't know anyone else here. I have no other choice."

"Why are you in such a rush to find a husband? I know you said you're thirty. That's not old, you have plenty of time."

Chloe's shoulders slumped. "You don't know that. Anything can happen, and then I've missed out. Do you remember my friend Isla?"

Theo smiled. "The two of you used to follow us around."

"We didn't—" Theo raised an eyebrow. "Okay, sometimes we did. We were bored." She took a calming breath. "Anyway, Isla died three months before her thirtieth birthday."

Theo pushed himself away from the desk and stood in front of her. "I'm sorry to hear that. She was a great girl."

Chloe nodded, her throat clogging with emotion. She missed her best friend. Six months after her passing, and it was still hard to talk about. "She worked and traveled and lived her life like it never was going to end. She said she was too young to settle down. She thought she had plenty of time for all that." Another breath. "Then she got sick. She started having problems breathing and fainting spells—an undetected heart condition. Treatment came too late. Her one regret was not experiencing true love." A tear slid down her cheek, and she brushed it away.

"Doesn't mean the same thing's going to happen to you," Theo said, placing his hands on her shoulders and rubbing his hands up and down her arms.

The soothing gesture made more tears fall. God, she'd thought she'd had no more tears to shed. Guess she was wrong, because they fell as if she'd just lost Isla all over again. Theo pulled her closer, her face nestled in the crook of his neck. She breathed in the faint smell of sandalwood as he wrapped his arms around her.

"Shh, Chloe, it's okay," he whispered, holding her until the tears dried up and her body stopped shaking.

After a few minutes, she cleared her throat and pulled away. She ducked her head and gave a sheepish grin. "I'm sorry about that. I still miss her. I'm okay now."

Theo searched her face as if to verify the truth of her words. "That's understandable. She was your best friend." Theo's hands moved from her shoulder, up along her neck, and cupped her face, brushing over her damp cheeks.

Chloe held her breath as his gaze fell to her mouth. Anticipation vibrated through her. All too quickly, he dropped his hands and stepped away. Chloe exhaled in a rush. Of course, he wasn't going to kiss her. He was only offering her comfort.

"I'll help you," he said.

"What?"

"With setting you up with a couple of dates."

"Really?"

He gave a stiff nod.

Rushing forward, she flung her arms around his neck and hugged him. "Thank you."

His hands landed on her waist, and for a second, he held her tight. Just as quickly, he pushed her away, but not before she got to feel his hard body pressed against hers giving her a thrill.

"I can't promise I'll find you a husband," he said.

A grin spread across her face. "This is going to work out. I can feel it." She just needed to ignore all the tingly sensations whenever she got too close to Theo.

With Theo frowning at her, she didn't think he shared her optimism. "Don't get your hopes up."

"I'll try not to." Although, how could she not? Theo was her brother's best friend. He wouldn't find her just anyone. He'd make sure the man was decent. Ethan would kill him if he didn't.

Butterflies fluttered in her gut. Could she finally have the life she'd been wishing for? She glanced at Theo, and for a second, she pictured him in the role of husband and father. No. He'd made himself clear. She batted the thought away. It was ridiculous to even imagine it. The attraction could be all in her head—just fantasies and wishful thinking of a teenage girl with a huge crush.

She needed to look toward the future. "Do you have anyone in mind?"

He pinched the bridge of his nose. "I've only just agreed to do this. Give me time."

"Oh, sure. Sorry. It's just that the clock's ticking." She tapped the watch on her wrist.

"I don't think a month or two will make much difference."

Chloe's jaw dropped. "A month or two? No, no. That's too long. Try a day or two."

Theo's eyebrows rose. "I can't organize something in such a short time. I know turning thirty—"

"I've turned thirty," she interrupted. "By the time I find the right man, it could take several dates which might then take a few months to determine if he's the one. If things are looking good, maybe a year's gone by. Hopefully he'll propose quickly—although I might have to plant the seed there—and then it takes months to plan a wedding. We'll get married and want to have some time enjoying married life before we decide to have kids. By then, I'm heading toward thirty-five and the magic words of 'advanced maternal age.'" She took a deep breath. "Basically, my eggs aren't getting any younger. So chop-chop!"

Theo stared at her, blinking rapidly. "You haven't thought this through at all," he said in a voice laden with sarcasm.

Chloe ran her fingers up and down the strap of the bag slung over her shoulder. "When you're my age, it's all you think about."

"I don't, and I'm thirty-four."

Chloe scoffed. "That's because you're a guy and have more time. Your swimmers will still be going strong when you're seventy."

Theo made a face, probably at her bluntness, because he said, "Make sure you don't reveal your five-year plan on the first date. The guy will run screaming."

She pulled a face. "Ha ha. Funny." He could be right, though. "If you're setting me up with men who are ready for commitment, it shouldn't be a problem."

"Trust me. Ease them into it."

"So, starting the conversation with, *will you be my husband and father of my children* is too much?"

"Maybe a little." He grinned.

With all seriousness, she said, "Thank you for doing this. I know you think I'm nuts."

"Not nuts... determined," he said, then added. "But also maybe a little nuts."

She nodded and smiled. "Yes, determined. A much better word. I like determined."

He laughed.

Chloe made her way to the door, stopped, and turned to him. "I'll call you tomorrow. I can't wait to see who you pick for me."

As Theo shook his head, she waved goodbye and sailed from the room. For the first time in months, she had hope for her future.

CHAPTER FIFTEEN

Six days later, Chloe hadn't heard a word from Theo. She'd been tempted to call and ask how finding her a date was going but had held off. She'd told him she'd give him a day or two, and to be fair, that was asking too much. So, she'd waited a week, but he still hadn't called with any news. She'd reached out via text, but he hadn't returned her messages.

In her apartment, she poured coffee into a travel mug and put a contract she was taking to a client in her bag. Locking up, she made her way downstairs and onto the street. The buildings around her were a mix of marble and limestone brick, arches and columns. There was a restaurant on every corner, little stores here and there and skyscrapers touched the skyline. She was tempted to lift her face to the sun, close her eyes, and twirl.

Waving down a taxi, she jumped in and gave the driver the name of the restaurant she was meeting her client at for breakfast. Instead of texting Theo again to find out what the holdup was, she decided to call. Pulling out her phone, she dialed his number. It rang a few times and went to his voice mail.

After the tone, she said, "Hi, Theo, it's Chloe. I've been patient and have given you a week to set me up on a date. If I don't hear back from you by four this afternoon, I'm picking someone from the dating site I joined last night. I've already marked a couple of prospects. Nikolai from New Jersey who owns an auto body shop looks promising. His profile pic is of him shirtless and polishing a muscle car. He has a great body and is kinda cute." With a devious smile, she hung up. She'd barely put her phone back in her bag when it rang. "Hello, Theo."

"You are not going on a date with Nikolai from New Jersey," his deep voice warned.

"Oh, so you *are* getting my messages. I had to wonder since you never returned any of my texts."

"I've been busy."

"Busy setting up dates for me, I hope."

There was silence for a beat. "I haven't found anyone for you yet."

Chloe sagged into the car's seat. "Have you even tried?"

More silence.

She propped her elbow on the window and rubbed her forehead. "Nikolai from New Jersey is looking better and better," she said lightly.

"Chloe—"

"You don't want to help, that's fine. I get it," she said, dropping her teasing tone. "I'm sorry I've troubled you. Bye, Theo."

"Wait! I'll have something set up today and send you the details."

She sat up straighter. "Really?"

"I can't let you go out with a guy from Jersey who's polishing his imaginary muscle car."

Chloe laughed; she'd been caught fair and square. "Thanks, Theo. You're the best."

Before he hung up, he mumbled something like, *I'm a fucking idiot*. She pretended she didn't hear it.

After her meeting, Chloe's phone beeped with a text from Theo.

The message read: *You have a date with Darius Perez tonight at Maybell Bar at 7pm.*

What, no information about this guy? What did he look like? How would she know who he was? She didn't want to push her luck calling Theo and asking—he wasn't happy helping her in the first place. Oh well, she'd work it out for herself. With luck, there wouldn't be too many men sitting on their own in the bar. Chloe read the message again, waiting for a hit of excitement at the prospect of going on a date. Nothing stirred. Hopefully, when she met Darius Perez, sparks would fly.

———◄O►———

That night as Chloe stepped out of the apartment building, a black Mercedes she recognized pulled up beside her. Theo! Her stomach did a little flip as he stepped out of the driver's side. He looked like a movie star—like James Bond in his navy suit and white shirt—only a thousand times hotter.

"What are you doing here?" she asked when he walked over to her. She was trying to get over her crush, which was impossible with him standing in front of her.

"Taking you to your date," he said, his eyes raking over her appreciably.

Her outfit wasn't anything sexy. She wore fitted black pants with an oversized red shirt tucked in the front of the waistband. Gold jewelry hung from her wrists and neck, and she wore leopard print flats in case Darius wasn't tall and had little-man syndrome like the last guy.

She'd kept her look casual and elegant, but from the way Theo's eyes smoldered, she could've been dressed in lingerie. Then he blinked, and the heat was snuffed out like a candle.

She stiffened, pulling away. "You gave me the information; I can get there on my own."

"You don't know who he is or what he looks like. What were you going to do, ask every single guy in the bar if he's Darius Perez?"

That's exactly what she was going to do.

"So tell me what he looks like," she said.

"I'm taking you."

She huffed and put her hands on her hips. "Has Ethan put you up to this? Did he ask you to be my chaperone?" God, when would Ethan stop being so overprotective?

"This has nothing to do with Ethan. Excuse me for wanting to help you out." He, too, put his hands on his hips, mirroring her gesture.

They stood in the middle of the sidewalk glaring at each other, not paying attention to pedestrians walking around them and shooting them dirty looks. "Ethan didn't plan this?"

"No, but if you want to find Darius yourself, go for it." He turned to leave.

She hesitated for a moment, then called, "Wait."

He turned to face her, one eyebrow raised.

"I don't want to be late, so I may as well let you take me." It would be better if Theo introduced them. She wouldn't admit it to him, though.

He nodded in the direction of his Mercedes. "Get in."

She slid into the passenger seat, her mind on other things. Once she was on her date enjoying the company of another man she'd forget about Theo, right? She had to believe it, or she'd have no hope in finding a husband.

What the hell was Theo thinking? He didn't need to take Chloe to her date and introduce her to Darius; they didn't call it a "blind date" for nothing. He'd been unable to get any work done all afternoon because he'd kept picturing Chloe on her date with Darius. Before he could change his mind, he was in his car heading toward her apartment.

Pulling up at the valet stand, he led her inside the noisy bar and to where Darius was waiting. At least he hadn't stood her up like the last jerk. When Darius spotted them, he frowned at Theo like he was wondering what he was doing on their date. "Hey, Theo." Then turning toward Chloe, he smiled. "And who is this?"

"Darius, this is Chloe Doyle. Chloe, Darius Perez."

"Great to meet you." Darius held out his hand.

Chloe took it and leaned in to kiss his cheek. Theo's fists clenched by his sides as she greeted the handsome man. "Lovely to meet you."

Darius pulled out a chair and gestured for Chloe to sit. When Theo didn't leave them alone, they both stared up at him. "Arrh, are you joining us, Theo?" Darius asked with a frown. His dark-brown eyes narrowed.

Chloe glared at him, nodding slightly in the direction of the door. Awkward silence descended.

Theo shook himself free. "No, I'm not. Have... fun." The word lodged in his throat, and he walked away.

Just as Theo was about to leave the bar, someone called out his name. He turned to find his friend Rafael Garza. "Hey, Rafael. Good to see you."

"It's been a while." Rafael clasped his hand in a firm grip.

"Too long. How have you been? How's the family?"

"They're here with me—Ariana's checking out colleges. Join us for a drink, and we can catch up more," Rafael said.

Normally, Theo would be happy to. Since Rafael had moved to Seattle with his husband and daughter two years ago, Theo hadn't seen him. But he didn't want to stay at the bar while Chloe was on her date. "I'd love to, but—"

"Come on, Theo. Will and Ariana are at the table over by the window. They'd love to see you too. Ariana especially would love to see her Tito Theo."

He really would like to catch up with his buddies. Theo glanced at the table where Raphael's husband and teenage daughter were seated then at the one where Chloe and Darius were. If she didn't turn around, she wouldn't see him and think he was spying on her. "Okay, just a quick drink."

The quick drink turned into two and then dinner, and even though he was enjoying the company of his friends, his attention kept drifting over to Chloe. When she placed her hand on Darius's arm, Theo's hand squeezed around his glass. When their heads leaned so close they were almost touching, Theo's jaw clenched.

Fingers clicked in front of his face. Theo's head jerked back. Rafael, Ariana, and Will all stared at him with confused smiles on their faces. "Whoever is sitting at the other end of the bar better watch out, because it looks like you're going to put your fist in their face," Will commented dryly.

"Who is it? Anyone we know?" Rafael asked, glancing over his shoulder.

"It's no one." Theo took a long pull of his beer.

Chloe laughed and tossed her head back, exposing her creamy neck. Was that fucker going to kiss it, trail his tongue along the beating pulse—

"There's that murderous look again." Will twisted in his seat. "Who *are* you staring at?"

Some lucky bastard and the woman he wanted with every fiber of his being but wasn't allowed to have. Hopefully, Darius was the one and Theo wouldn't have to help her find any more dates. Then, she'd be out of his life and *mind* and everything would get back to normal.

Theo was trying to listen to a story Will was telling him when Chloe and Darius rose from their seats, getting ready to leave. *Shit!* He should have been gone by now. Dammit, there was no way of getting up to leave without her spotting him. Slumping in his seat, he tried making himself appear smaller, invisible. When she walked past his table, she did a double take and stopped in her tracks. She absently waved goodbye to Darius as he continued to walk out of the bar. Theo let out a relieved breath she wasn't following him.

"Theo? What are you still doing here?" Then her eyebrows slammed together, and she tossed her head back and gave a mirthless laugh. "Unbelievable. You stayed and watched me on my date! Are you crazy? This is so ridiculous. I am so going to kill my brother."

"Chloe, it's not what you think." He glanced uncomfortably at his smiling friends.

"I am so sick of you and Ethan thinking I'm some pathetic girl who can't live her own life. I can't even look at you right now." She stormed away.

Saying a quick goodbye to his friends, he hurried after her. Before she got to the door, he grabbed her wrist and spun her around.

"Let go of me." She glared at her arm.

"Will you stay and listen to me if I do?"

She clenched her jaw and nodded. Before letting her go, he led her to a quiet corner of the bar then dropped his hand.

"I wasn't spying," he said.

She tossed her head back. "Oh please."

"I'm serious. I was on my way out when I saw an old friend and his family. They asked me to stay for a drink. I haven't seen them in two years, and I wanted to catch up," Theo explained.

"How convenient." She rolled her eyes and crossed her arms over her chest.

"Believe what you want. Setting you up on dates is more trouble than it's worth."

She shot him a look that could freeze the Hudson. "Speaking of the date you set me up with, why didn't you tell me Darius just broke up with his girlfriend of six years? Elizabeth was all he could talk about."

Theo shuffled his feet. He knew Darius was a rebound, and yet he'd asked him over Owen. "I was hoping he'd be over her by now."

"Over her. Over her!" Her voice rose. A couple sitting at a nearby table stared at them. "Well, he's not. I've spent the last hour listening to how he met Elizabeth in college, the many countries they traveled to together, the excitement of buying their first apartment together, and how blissful their lives were. That was until the day he proposed. She said no and broke up with him."

"That's rough," Theo said. He had no idea Darius had been in such a serious relationship.

"According to Darius, it was heartbreaking and his life has never been the same since. He can't look at another woman without thinking about Elizabeth and how in love they were."

"Not if she turned down his proposal, they weren't," Theo mumbled under his breath.

"He was almost in tears, the poor guy." That probably explained the touches of the arm, the closeness when they'd talked. She'd been comforting him, not planning on having sex with him.

"He told me he wasn't sure about going on the date, but you convinced him it was a good idea. That it would help him get over the breakup." She jabbed her finger at his chest. "Why would you set me up with him? You knew he was a rebound, and you let me go out with him anyway."

Theo averted his gaze. "He didn't need too much convincing. He could have said no if he was so heartbroken."

Chloe huffed and pushed past him. "Unbelievable. I thought I could rely on you."

Taking a few quick steps, he blocked her from leaving. "I'm not a fucking matchmaker. You asked me to find someone for you, and I did. If he wasn't perfect, it's not my fault."

"Perfect! I'm not asking for someone *perfect*. Someone who's emotionally available would be a good start. I don't need another friend; I need a boyfriend!" They were nose to nose and yelling at each other. Not caring about the curious stares from the patrons aimed at them. "I can see now you're not the person to help me. You failed with your badly chosen date for me. If Darius is the kind of man you're going to set me up with, I'd have a better chance with online dating."

He jerked back like she'd slapped him. A deadly calm washed over him. The word *failed* wasn't one he swallowed easily. The last time he'd failed at something—his marriage—had been out of his control. This time, he'd deliver what Chloe wanted.

Through gritted teeth, he said, "You want me to find the man of your dreams?"

She pulled a face as if to say, *duh!*

"Fine, I'll find you your Mr. Right. I'll find you the best goddamn man you'll ever meet, and you'll be so grateful, you'll be sending me Christmas cards for the rest of your life thanking me for how fucking awesome your life is." He leaned down so their faces were inches apart. "Okay?"

Her chin jutted out, and she said, "Yes."

"Okay," he stepped away. "I'll take you home."

He shoved the timber doors open and left the bar. Now all he needed to do was find the perfect guy. There was no way he was going to fail at *anything* again.

Chapter Sixteen

When Chloe got home, she was still mad at Theo for not taking his matchmaking duties seriously. But more than that, she was mad at herself; she never should have asked him for his help. What was worth doing was worth doing yourself, and all that.

As much as she hated the thought of online dating, several of her university friends had met their spouses online. Pulling out her phone, she opened up her dating profile and scrolled through the options. None of them leaped out at her.

Not a one.

After twenty minutes of searching, she closed the app even more frustrated than before. She couldn't learn anything useful about a prospective mate from a picture and a profile. There needed to be sparks—passion—and that was definitely lacking in an app.

She glanced at the clock. She could still go out, but what good would that do? Anyone out at a bar was likely trolling for a hookup, not the long haul. And the thought of speed dating gave her the heebie-jeebies.

Which brought her back to square one: asking her friends to hook her up with their single male acquaintances. And at the rate she was going, she was going to be single forever. Darius was far and away the best of the bunch, as pathetic as that was.

Darius was a nice guy—objectively handsome, even—with dark-brown skin and twinkling black eyes. Except for they hadn't been twinkling all that much during their date. Less than five minutes in, they'd become tear filled. As much as Chloe appreciated his ability to show his emotions, she hadn't been attracted to him. At all.

Argh, this is hopeless!

Needing a comforting voice, she dialed Daniela. Hazel and Blair were great, but nothing seemed to faze Daniela, and she desperately needed a steady ear right now.

Her friend picked up on the second ring. "You've got ten minutes. Go."

"In the middle of a crisis?"

"Always," she answered over the sound of a clacking keyboard. "But I've got ten minutes for you."

It was as good as she was going to get. "My life sucks," Chloe stated.

"Join the club."

"No, really. I can't find a husband!"

"And that's a problem?" She could hear the amusement in Daniela's voice.

"It is if you want to get married and have babies."

"Technically speaking, you don't need a husband for the latter."

Daniela would know; she'd had her own child via artificial insemination. Chloe knew she didn't have it in her to be a single parent. Plus she really wanted what her two brothers had with their wives, a partner who she could rely on and love through thick and thin. An image of Theo swam into her thoughts, and she just as quickly shoved him under. "But I want a husband!"

"That's fine."

"But I can't find one!"

"Have you been looking?" Daniela asked in a reasonable tone.

But Chloe was in no mood to be reasonable, not after the night she'd had. "Of course I have!" she snapped, and then ranted for a solid five minutes, filling her friend in on everything from Blair's shitty date options to Ethan's overprotectiveness to Theo's spying and sabotage and even their embarrassing almost one-night stand. She finished up with, "And you want to know the worst thing?"

Her voice filled with laughter, Daniela said, "Enlighten me."

"I wasn't attracted to any of them." She paused and amended, "Well, other than Theo."

"So what's so different about Theo?"

It was a question she hadn't considered. What was different about Theo? He was handsome, but Mr. Dental Commercial, Blake, Logan, and even Darius were handsome and she hadn't felt a thing for them. She'd known him forever, but she could say the same about Blake. The thought of dating Blake made her shudder; it'd be like dating Ethan or Aiden. So why did she want to jump Theo's bones so badly? She didn't really have an answer so she said, "He just is. I've known him forever. Even when I was a kid, I had a crush on him. I used to follow him everywhere."

"Uh-huh." Daniela said it like a light had gone on. "Everything suddenly makes sense."

"It does?" Chloe asked, surprised. "Then why can't I find a husband?"

Her friend paused, and then asked, "Do you want the flippant answer or the real one?"

"Real," she answered without hesitation.

"Because you're not interested in finding a husband. You're only interested in Theo."

"Well, I can't have him! The bro code killed that!"

"That sucks."

"Tell me about it. So what do I do now?" Chloe practically wailed.

Daniela sighed and muttered under her breath. "You're not going to like this, but you're going to have to be patient."

"I can't be patient! I'm on a deadline."

"Your brain might be telling you that, but your attraction doesn't work that way. You're going to need to become close friends, and possibly more, first."

That made no sense, and Chloe told her so.

Sighing even louder, Daniela asked, "What do you know about demisexuality?"

"What's that?"

"It's on the asexuality spectrum," Daniela answered, turning on her clinical producer voice. "It's sometimes called single-target sexuality, but that's not really what it is. Demisexuality is when a person is only interested in sex or romance with somebody who they already have an existing connection to. A deep emotional bond, as it were. Which in your case means Theo, and only Theo."

Chloe rebelled at the thought. "But... I'm attracted to guys."

"Are you? Name a celebrity that you'd want to bang."

Chloe drew a blank. "Well that's not a fair question!" she protested, pacing back and forth in her small living room. "I know too many celebrities, and they're all giant pains in the arse."

Daniela laughed. "You're not wrong." She stifled her giggles. "Okay. Other than Theo, tell me someone you've wanted to have sex with. Or even date. They can be fictional, they can be real, I don't care. They can be the bloody Queen of England—"

"She's dead," Chloe interrupted. "And I'm not into women, re-member?"

"So? Prince William, then," Daniela said, exasperated. "People say he's cute, or was, I wouldn't know."

Chloe struggled for a minute, racking her memories to think if there was anyone that she'd been attracted to. Again, she came up blank.

And Daniela knew it. In a smug voice, she said, "Sounds like you've got some research to do, and your ten minutes are almost up. Anything else I can be of assistance with?"

"You've been enough of a pain in the arse; go back to dealing with whatever crisis you're in the middle of."

"Take care of yourself. Let's meet up for drinks next week."

"It's a plan," she said and hung up. Opening the browser on her phone, she typed in the word "demisexual."

Daniela was right. She did have some research to do.

CHAPTER SEVENTEEN

Three days later, Chloe stepped out of the elevator and into the ultramodern reception area of Theo's office. Walking past Annabelle's shiny white marble desk, she said, "Good morning, is Theo in?"

Annabelle rose from the chair. "Yes, he is. Do you have an appointment?"

"No, but he's expecting me." He wasn't really, but she didn't care. Without waiting for permission to enter, she made her way to Theo's office.

"You can't go in there," Annabelle called, rushing around her desk.

Chloe didn't stop at the receptionist's demand. She was still mad about the botched date he'd set her up on, and she still wasn't sure if she believed that he wasn't spying on her. He *had* been sitting with two men and a teenager, so maybe he was telling the truth? God, that man screwed with her mind; she didn't know what to believe anymore. Anyway, he'd promised to help her find her Mr. Right, and she hadn't heard from him in days. Yeah, she knew she was being impatient, but the clock was ticking on her ovaries. Not to mention, now that she suspected that she might possibly be demisexual, she was in even more of a time crunch.

Chloe swung open the glossy black door and stopped in her tracks. Annabelle almost bumped into her. Inside the office, Theo stood at his desk facing the window looking out over the city—shirtless! Chloe swallowed hard at her view. Theo's broad shoulders, tanned skin, and toned back narrowed into the waist of gray trousers. Oh good Lord! The man was spectacular!

At the interruption, Theo turned his head over his shoulder. His eyes widened when he saw Chloe.

"Excuse me, sir, I tried stopping her," the executive assistant said, not seeming at all bothered that her boss was half-naked in his office. Meanwhile, Chloe's tongue was stuck to the roof of her mouth. *Down, girl!*

"That's okay, Annabelle. Please close the door behind you." When Annabelle left, Theo said, "I spilled coffee on my shirt." He walked to a cupboard on the other side of the room, pulled out a black shirt, and shrugged into it. The front view of Theo's body was even better than the back.

Finding her voice, she said, "Have you found another date for me?"

His hands tucked the shirt inside the waistband of his trousers, and this time she couldn't drag her eyes away. What would he do if she walked over to him and replaced his hands with hers? Oh, my God! What was wrong with her? She needed to get over her Theo obsession, and fast! The quicker she found her future husband, the quicker she could attend to matters that were becoming uncomfortable. Her vibrator took the edge off, but at some point soon, she'd like to feel the real thing.

Theo sat on the edge of the desk, placed his palms on the surface, and crossed his legs at the ankles. "I've asked my friend Owen, and he's agreed to meet you."

She walked farther into the room. "Is he another rebound guy?"

"No." Theo's lips thinned.

She narrowed her eyes at him. "What's wrong with him?"

"Nothing. He works for an accounting firm. He's a good guy." Annoyance flicked across his features.

"So why do you look miserable?" She eyed him skeptically.

"Maybe because this whole situation makes me uncomfortable."

"Well, if he's as good as you say he is, then this should be over soon and you'll never have to help me again." She knew she was being a bit of a brat, but she couldn't help it—he and Ethan were treating her like a child—and she fully expected Theo to call her on it. His frown deepened, but he didn't snark back like she expected. Something was off here, but she couldn't put her finger on what.

"He's in our office today. I'll call him up, and you can make arrangements," he said, leaning over to the intercom on the desk. The movement pulled his shirt tighter across his body so the muscles were defined under the fabric.

God, it was getting hot in here. Was the air conditioning on? She wanted to fan her face. Then his words hit. "He's coming here? Now?"

His finger paused over the button. "Don't you want to meet him before your date? You can decide whether he's your type or not before you commit to meeting him."

"Oh, yeah... that's a great idea. See? I need you. You're so helpful." She twisted a ring on her finger. Jittery nerves spread along her spine.

Again, he frowned. He really must hate doing this for her. Normally she'd feel guilty for asking someone to do something they didn't want to do, but this was important. Her future depended on it. Darius might have been a bad fit, but she had to have faith this time would be better.

Theo pressed the intercom button. "Annabelle, can you please call Owen to my office?"

"Thanks for doing this for me. I appreciate it."

Theo pushed away from the desk and stood in front of her. "I hope it works out for you."

The way he looked at her with creases between his eyebrows and an intense stare, she wasn't sure if she believed him. He took another step forward, and her breath caught. If only Theo could forget about the bro code he had with Ethan and make a move. Images of the night in his penthouse flashed in her mind. She'd do anything to have a night with him. Multiple nights.

She took a step back. No point in wishing for things that would never happen. If she wanted a husband and family, she needed to clear Theo from her mind, or no one would ever measure up. "Tell me a little about Owen."

He rubbed his hand on his chin; it made a scratching sound over the light stubble. "He's about thirty-six and manages the accounting team we work with. We've been friends for about five years."

Chloe waited a moment for him to continue, and when he didn't, she asked, "That's it? What about hobbies? Things he likes. Something more personal."

Theo shrugged. "You can learn all that during your date. It'll give you something to talk about."

Yes, he was right. If she knew everything now, they might be sitting at dinner listening to the sound of crickets, but it didn't help settle the herd of horses stomping on her chest. Her nose tickled.

Someone knocked, and a tall man with wavy dark-brown hair with threads of gray on the sides walked into the office. He wore a charcoal-gray suit, filling it out nicely. With kind green eyes and a warm smile, she could totally see husband potential. Hopefully he had the personality to match. Could this be him? Could he be the man she'd marry and spend the rest of her life with? The man she'd start a family with?

Please don't sneeze. Please don't sneeze, she repeated in her mind, nose twitching.

"Aachoo!"

"Bless you," Theo and Owen said at the same time.

Oh, no. Don't start now! Owen ambled closer. When he smiled, a few lines fanned from the corners of his eyes. He had a handsome face.

"Aachoo!" *Crap!* This couldn't happen now. Dammit, nerves, go away! God, it was mortifying, she'd blamed her sneezing on sinuses so her dates wouldn't think she was a freak. It hadn't happened in years, and she'd thought she'd gotten it under control. Obviously not.

Why didn't it happen when she was with Theo? They'd gotten *very* intimate, and she hadn't had so much as a nose tickle. Was it because they'd been friends first and she was comfortable around him? The night at his penthouse, she'd felt a lot of things—excitement, desire, the joy of losing her virginity with a man she trusted. Nerves? No.

"Are you getting a cold?" Theo asked, looking at her with concern.

"No, just allergies," she lied.

"Owen, this is Chloe Doyle. Chloe, my friend Owen Farina."

Owen approached her. Thinking he was offering his hand in greeting, she held out hers to shake, but he'd gone in for a hug. Realizing they were doing different things, he pulled back as Chloe moved forward to hug him. The whole thing turned out to be a jumbled mess of awkward gestures and embarrassed laughter.

"I'm sorry," Owen said, taking a step back. "Let's try this again. It's lovely to meet you, Chloe." He smiled. His eyes sparkled with laughter as he held out his hand.

Holding back a sneeze, she tried to return the smile. It made her grimace instead. Great. Definitely not the first impression she wanted to make. "Lovely to meet you, too." Not able to hold the sneeze in any longer, she turned her head over her shoulder and let it out as quietly as she could.

It wasn't quiet.

"Theo, you gotta get this office cleaned more often. The dust is going to kill her," Owen chuckled.

Theo scowled; clearly he didn't appreciate Owen's joke. If his face was any harder, it would crack. *What's wrong with him?*

"Theo tells me you're an agent. That sounds interesting," Owen said. "Entertainment, right?"

"That's right. It's entertaining dealing with divas and huge egos sometimes."

Owen laughed. "I bet. I'd love to hear more about it over dinner. I can book us a table at Ronaldo's—they make the best Italian food—for Monday if that suits you? If not, we can arrange another day."

Chloe loved Italian food. Ronaldo's got booked out weeks in advance. She'd heard the food was amazing, and it was one of the places on her list to try. Were the stars aligning? Here was a man who looked to be of right mind, handsome, had a good job, didn't seem to take things too seriously, and had the same taste in food. He really could be the one.

"Aachoo! I'm so sorry about this." She waved her hand around her face. "I promise to have it settled before our date." How, she didn't know, she'd have to deal with that problem later. Maybe hypnosis?

CBD oil? Puppies? "Monday sounds great," she said, flashing Owen a bright smile. "Ever since arriving in New York I've wanted to try that restaurant."

"Then we're off to a good start." He grinned. He really was handsome.

"Owen, I need the report for the Bellevue account on my desk in an hour. You'd better get back to it."

Owen's eyes widened for a beat at Theo's harsh tone. "Sure thing. I'll get right on it." He turned to Chloe. "I'm looking forward to Monday. Theo's given me your number; I'll text you the time," he said, holding his arms out wide so she knew he was going in for a hug not a handshake.

She laughed and stepped into his arms. There was solid muscle under the suit. Chloe liked what she felt. This could work.

A slapping noise behind them broke them apart. They spun around to find that Theo was dropping files onto his desk. It was a pointed—and rude—hint.

"I better run. See you soon." Owen gave Theo a puzzled look before he left the office.

"What is wrong with you?" Chloe asked.

Theo's eyebrows rose, looking confused. "Nothing."

She folded her arms across her chest. "It didn't look like nothing. You were glaring daggers at Owen the whole time he was here. Is there something wrong with him? Something you're not telling me? Because if he's married or in a relationship or secretly dresses in baby clothes, then why the hell are you setting me up with him?"

"There's nothing wrong with him. I'm busy and need that report. Don't worry, he's a great guy." It sounded like it pained him to say those last few words.

"Okay, well... that's good. I'll let you get back to work," she said, turning to leave.

"Chloe," Theo called.

She glanced over her shoulder.

Theo slid his hands into the pockets of his trousers. "I hope it works out for you."

"Thanks. I do too." And she did. But she left his office wondering if he really felt the same.

Theo sat in his office, staring out of the window, a plethora of colored lights spilling out in front of him. He left the liquor sales report he was supposed to be working on unopened on his computer; he couldn't concentrate because the scene from this morning kept playing over and over in his mind. The memory of Owen scanning Chloe from head to toe with a gleam of interest in his eyes stuck. The way she'd smiled back at him with hope in her eyes still burned in his chest.

What the fuck was wrong with him?

It shouldn't bother him if they made googly eyes at each other. If things went well, they'd be doing a hell of a lot more. His hands fisted on the arms of his chair. Damn, why did the thought of them together disturb him so much?

He knew the answer. It was because he was attracted to her and trying fucking hard not to be. He could admit it now. At first, he'd blamed it on being overly protective of her because she was Ethan's sister. But it went deeper than that. Even if he went against the no-touching-siblings rule that was never spoken about but was an oath all friends made—which at their age, really shouldn't matter anymore—he couldn't do anything about it. Not when she wanted a husband and children. Two things he couldn't give any woman anymore. With any luck, her date with Owen would go well and she'd be on her way to a happy life, and he'd finally be able to get her out of his mind.

The phone in his pocket rang, breaking him away from his thoughts. Pulling it out, he groaned. The woman he needed out of his life and mind—fast, was calling. What the hell did she want? "Hey, Chloe."

"Theo... hey. How are you? I hope I'm not disturbing you," she said overly brightly.

"Is everything okay? Why are you calling?" He hoped she wasn't calling to ask him another favor. He wasn't sure his resolve could handle it.

As if his thoughts were prophetic, she stammered, "Oh... arhh... well... I need another favor."

Theo tilted his head on the back of his chair and pinched the bridge of his nose. Why did he have to be right? If her request was anything like her husband-finding favor, he'd have to decline. There was only so much a man could take. "What is it?" curiosity had him asking.

"Today in your office when I was sneezing and I told you I had allergies, I-um... lied."

"Why would you lie about that? So, you *do* have a cold?" Why would she call to tell him that? Maybe she wanted to postpone the date. Or even better, cancel. Still, wouldn't she just call Owen to rearrange?

"No, it's nothing like that. It's more like a...problem."

"What kind of problem?"

After a moment of silence, she said, "Well, the sneezing is a reaction I have when I'm nervous."

He rubbed his forehead. "I don't understand." Who sneezed when they got nervous?

"Umm... when a situation comes up that makes me nervous, I sometimes sneeze."

"Is this a joke?"

"I wish it was. My life would be a little less complicated."

"Isn't your job high stress? Doesn't it make you nervous?" This didn't make any sense.

She laughed self-consciously. "You'd think that, and in the beginning it did happen—why do you think I did so much from Sydney when my biggest clients were in New York? Eventually I got over it, so now even the most intense bargaining sessions are just old hand for me. I know it's psychosomatic, but I can't seem to stop it."

Theo rose from his chair, walked to the window, and scrubbed his hand behind his neck. "Owen made you nervous?" His chest tightened. *She's already attracted to him?*

"Yes—no. It's more the situation. It's when something exciting/terrifying is about to happen. Like a first kiss or meeting my idol or going on an important date. Things like that."

While what she said made sense, it brought up even more questions. "We did a hell of a lot more than *kiss*. You didn't sneeze with me." Did that mean she wasn't attracted to him? The muscles in his jaw clenched. If so, she'd been a damn good actress. There was silence on the other end of the phone. He wondered if she was picturing how much more they'd done together, and if it was constantly on her mind like it was his.

Eventually she said, "I think the reason I don't sneeze with you is because I'm comfortable around you. That's why you're the only person who can help me."

"How am I supposed to stop you from sneezing?"

"I hoped we could go on a date before my dinner with Owen."

"What?" Was she out of her mind? He was trying to stay away from her as much as possible. A date? No fucking way.

"If we do a practice run and I can see how I interact with you, then I can make sure I do the same things with Owen, and hopefully I won't sneeze."

"You can't be serious." Theo walked to a cabinet along one wall of his office and pulled out a bottle of bourbon and a glass. Pouring a finger width, he knocked it back in one swallow.

"I know it must sound crazy—"

"Ha! Batshit crazy."

"Excuse me for not being perfect and completely in control of my body. We can't all be so cool and in control like you," she spat.

Okay... he'd pissed her off. As someone possessing a body part that had a mind of its own, he could empathize, and unfortunately, he didn't think placing a pillow over her nose would conceal her problem like it did his. "You think going to dinner with me will help you?"

"Yes, I do."

God, was he going to regret what he was about to say? Probably, but the words spilled out anyway. "Fine. Let's go on a date. But then, I'm done. After this, no more favors."

She squealed, "Thank you so much! You're the best."

He squeezed his eyes shut. "I'll book a restaurant for tomorrow night."

"Excellent. Text me the details, and I'll meet you there."

"No, I'll pick you up at seven and give you a real date experience. That way we've covered everything." Well, not everything. There would definitely be no good-night kiss when he walked her to her door.

"See, I knew you were the perfect man for the job. See you tomorrow." With that, she hung up.

Theo dropped into his chair, tilted his head back, and stared at the ceiling. Why was he torturing himself this way? Why couldn't he say no to Chloe?

Because he'd do anything for her—even help her get ready for her future husband—because that's the kind of screwed-up guy he was.

CHAPTER EIGHTEEN

C hloe dropped a file on top of the desk, stretching her arms over her shoulders to ease the tension. She'd been reading contracts all day and was finally done. She glanced at the time. Six fifteen.

Shit. Theo will be here soon.

After having a quick shower, she stood in front of her closet, deciding on what to wear for her date. Well, the *dress rehearsal date* to prepare for the real thing. Should she choose something casual? It was only Theo, and it wasn't a real date. Or should she wear something dressier? Like the blue dress she'd bought from that cute boutique. Maybe she should save that for Owen? She flicked through her outfits but ultimately decided on the blue dress. She wanted to dress up, and she could always buy another dress for her dinner with Owen.

Slipping on the dress, she hurried into the bathroom and styled her hair into loose waves, securing one side behind her ear with a gold clip. She made quick work of her makeup—just some subtle eyeshadow and tinted lip gloss.

She turned from side to side in front of the mirror, inspecting her work. Looking good! Ready for dinner, her heart beat with excitement. Taking a deep breath, she had to remind herself this wasn't a *real* date. The only reason they were going to dinner was to fix her sneezing problem.

The doorbell rang, and she rushed to the living room and pressed the intercom. "Hello?"

"It's me." She'd know that deep, melt-your-bones voice anywhere.

"I'll be down in a second."

"No, buzz me up. We have to do this right."

She giggled. "Okay." And pressed the button to let him in.

During the few minutes it took for Theo to reach her door, she smoothed out the skirt of her dress, tucked a stray lock of hair behind her ear, and checked she didn't have any lip gloss on her teeth in the mirror hung near the door.

Theo knocked, and her heart pounded. She took a deep breath and opened her door. The breath caught in her lungs. Oh sweet Jesus! She should be used to seeing Theo dressed immaculately and looking sexier than any man had the right to, but this somehow took the cake. Tonight, he'd dressed in a charcoal suit with a black shirt, filling it out to perfection. Her heart shouldn't jackhammer behind her ribs at the sight. How could it not, though? It wasn't every day the masculine ideal stood at her door.

"These are for you." He held out a bunch of pink gerberas, her favorite flowers, as his gaze roamed over her body approvingly.

Warmth washed over her, and a little happy bubble formed in her chest. "Thank you, but you didn't have to buy me flowers."

"I told you we were doing this right. Gotta help you get married off."

And her little happy bubble burst along with the heat in his gaze. Of course, this was all an act. Nothing more. She'd asked for his help, and he was giving it to her. Simple as that. She had to get her head out of the clouds and focus on what she needed to do to move forward—whether it be with Owen or someone else.

"I'll put these in some water, then we can leave." She hurried into the kitchen, found a vase, and filled it. Before going back to Theo, she put her hands on the counter and drew in several deep breaths to settle her racing heart. This was Theo, her childhood crush, looking sexier and hotter than she ever could have imagined him. These giddy emotions whenever she saw him would pass. She needed her pep talk to work— damn, she was screwed if it didn't.

Back in the living room, she picked up her purse from the coffee table and smiled. "Ready?"

"Let's go." He held open the door.

Once in his Mercedes, he said, "I hope you like seafood."

"Yes, I do." Seafood was one of her favorite things to eat. First the flowers, now the cuisine. Had Theo called Ethan and asked him for a list of her favorite things? Surely not, because if he had, he'd have had to explain why he wanted that information. There was no way he'd tell her brother he was taking her on a date even if it was a pretend one. He really was giving her the first-date treatment.

At the restaurant, the valet greeted them and took the keys to Theo's car. Inside they were greeted by the maître d' who rushed to them and proudly showed them to the best table in the restaurant. Who the hell had Theodore Campbell become since leaving Australia? From the clothes he wore, the car he drove, and the club he owned, she'd say someone who'd made it big. Once seated at their table, the waiter gave them a few minutes to look over the menu.

"Are you taking notes?" Theo eyed her over the menu.

She looked up from where she was debating between the grouper and the lobster risotto. "Excuse me?"

"This date was so you could learn why you're not nervous around me so you can apply it to your date with... Owen." Did he just screw his face up when he said Owen's name?

"Oh, right." She'd forgotten the real reason for the dinner, being so caught up in the fantasy of actually dating Theo. "No sneeze yet. So whatever we're doing is working."

He gave her a crooked smile, and it was so damn sexy her thighs clenched. *Stop it! Stop looking at Theo like some sex god. Or dating other men will never work.* Pulling her attention away from his panty-melting smile, she focused on the menu and gave the waiter who'd returned her order of the lobster risotto.

"It looks like you've done well for yourself these past few years. How did you get to own a nightclub? I always thought you wanted to be a race car driver."

He laughed. "I've replaced fast cars with owning clubs, it's become my new passion."

"Clubs?" They paused in their conversation as the waiter arrived with a bottle of wine and poured it into their glasses. "You have more than one? Do you own the buildings they're in too?" Chloe asked once they were left alone.

"We own six clubs all over the East Coast," he answered, taking a sip of chardonnay, "and yes, we own the buildings. It's not usual, but it makes things easier." He didn't elaborate.

Her chest filled with pride. "Wow, that's amazing. You own them with Blake?"

"Yes, and with my father too. Although he's retired and is more like a silent partner now."

"It makes me happy seeing you doing so well."

They had both seen their fair share of struggles growing up. Chloe's father had died in a boating accident when she was eight, and money had been tight. Thankfully, Ethan and his acting career had pulled them out of poverty.

Theo's father had been injured while renovating their house when a beam had fallen on him and broken his back. It had taken months to recover, and in that time his burgeoning real estate business had foundered. Facing bankruptcy and difficulty finding a new job that could accommodate his wheelchair, he'd moved his family to New York where his brother had offered him a job overseeing renovations of all the property his brother had snapped up during the Great Recession. When his brother had died a few years later, Theo's father had inherited the company and its extensive real estate portfolio.

"I'm not the only one who's doing well. You're a bigshot agent to a lot of pretty impressive actors. Good for you." He paused. "You know, Ethan never told me, how did you get your start?"

"Not much to tell, mostly I was in the right place at the right time. My agency was expanding into Sydney, and they were hiring." She shrugged, there was something so mundane about it, but it was the truth. "I was lucky. I have to pinch myself sometimes. A lot of the people I've met have been amazing. I love my job."

Their food arrived, and they spent the next few minutes enjoying their meals.

"So, what else have you been doing these past twelve years?" Chloe asked.

Theo took a sip of wine and shrugged. "Work, mainly."

"Really? What about a social life, travel… the fun stuff?"

"Work *is* 'the fun stuff.'"

Chloe pushed her plate aside, propped an elbow on the table, and dropped her chin in her hand. "You don't always work. I've heard about the many women you were involved with."

An eyebrow rose, and he smirked. "How do you know that?"

"Oh, well... Ethan used to mention it." Heat crept up her neck. Now she sounded like a stalker. "Being rich and handsome in a city full of beautiful women, I'm surprised you're not married."

The smile that played on his lips dropped. "Ethan never told you?"

"No. You were married?" Ethan'd told her about the womanizing, which had hurt. Why hadn't he told her about Theo's marriage? Surely he'd been a groomsman or at the very least invited to the wedding. He should have told her, maybe if he had she wouldn't have kept secretly pining over Theo.

From what she could tell, Theo was having his own internal conflict because despite the growing silence between them he kept staring into his glass. Finally he said, "Yes."

"From your stone-faced expression, I'm guessing it didn't end amicably."

"It ended as well as any divorce can." He drained his glass. "At least there's no hostility."

And yet misery etched his face. Had she been the love of his life and broken his heart? How could she leave someone like Theo? Or had Theo gotten tired of her? She had to know. "What happened?"

He poured another glass of wine. "We grew apart."

"I'm sorry to hear that. Failed marriages aren't easy."

For a second, he screwed up his face. "It was for the best."

What had happened for them to grow apart and for it to be "for the best"? Because from Theo's reaction, it seemed like he was still hurting. "How long were you married?"

"Five years. The divorce was finalized a few weeks ago."

"No wonder you look like you've swallowed razor blades. It's still fresh."

"We've been separated for over a year. Any feelings are long gone." Theo signaled for a waiter. "Time for dessert," he said, putting an end to the conversation. He may say the feelings were gone, but in the depths of his eyes, pain lingered. Did he still love his ex-wife?

He must. Suddenly so much of his odd behavior made sense; like Darius he was still rebounding. She must have unwittingly reopened the wounds of his failed marriage. She promised to be more considerate in the future and hoped that she wouldn't need his help again.

During dessert, they talked about their friends, family, and work, laughing over the funny stories she told him about her clients and his ongoing saga with a certain DJ. She'd never felt so comfortable around a man in her life. This was what she wanted in a relationship. Someone she could talk, laugh, and share her day with. They'd have dinner, a glass of wine or two, and cuddle on the sofa in front of the TV bickering over what movie they wanted to watch. Then they'd go to bed, and Theo would undress her, roaming his hands over her body as he kissed her long and deep.

"Hey, Glowy." Theo clicked his fingers in front of her face. "Am I boring you?"

Oh God, she'd fantasized about what a relationship would look like and cast Theo in the lead role. "Oh, sorry. What were you saying, and I can't believe you still call me by that horrible name?" she deflected.

"Horrible? I thought you liked it?" he chuckled.

Maybe when she was younger. It had made her feel special that he'd had his own nickname for her. Now that she was older, well, she still liked it; she just didn't want to admit it. "I'm surprised you remember it."

"How could I forget? You and Isla thought you were so cool, sneaking into our tenth-grade disco. With the number of glow sticks around your neck and wrists, you were visible from space," Theo laughed.

Embarrassed, Chloe groaned and covered her face with her hands. The things she used to do to grab Theo's attention. "Why did we do that? We thought we'd fit right in, but no one else in the hall wore them."

"That's because sixteen-year-olds want it as dark as possible so we could hook up. You looked like you'd stepped out from a kids' birthday party."

He wasn't far from the mark. "The glow sticks were leftovers from Isla's twelfth birthday party. I'm so embarrassed," she laughed.

"It was cute." He smiled.

Chloe hadn't been trying to be cute, and it had chipped away at her heart a little when he'd laughed at her glowing like a star in their school hall.

That memory led to others, and soon enough, they realized they were the only couple left in the room. It was time to end the date.

"I'll settle the bill," she said before she got sucked further into his blue eyes and sexy smile.

"It's a date. I'll take care of it." His eyes found their waiter.

"No, this was my idea. The least I can do is pay."

He shook his head. "I'm giving you the full treatment."

A picture of what the full treatment included in her mind didn't end with dinner. She busied herself checking her phone for messages to distract herself from how she'd really like the night to end—in bed with Theodore Campbell.

The ride home was quiet. Chloe kept thinking about what a wonderful evening she'd had with Theo. They were so comfortable together. She could have sat with him all night. If only their relationship could...no. She stopped her fantasizing from getting out of hand. No point wondering what a life with him would be like because he wasn't offering it to her. He was healing from his divorce, and he'd made it clear a relationship wasn't possible between them. But she'd be blind if she said she hadn't noticed the subtle glances of desire aimed her way.

Theo pulled up by a hydrant in front of her apartment, and she made to get out of the car. He put a hand on her arm. "I'll walk you to your apartment."

"You don't need to do that."

"It's a date."

She chuckled. "It's over now." Pausing, she licked her lips. "But a first date should end with a good-night kiss."

He stared at her, silent. The silence stretched for one heartbeat. Then two. Until the silence shifted from anticipatory to awkward.

"I'm guessing the answer is no?" She tried laughing it off even as her heart sank at the look of horror in his eyes. "I'm sorry if the thought of kissing me disgusts you." She turned her back to him. Her hands shook as they fumbled with her purse as she searched for the key to her building.

He placed a hand on her shoulder and turned her to face him. "The thought doesn't disgust me. Do you know how much I want to kiss you? How much I want to strip you naked? How hard it is not to touch you whenever you're around?" His gaze dropped to her lips.

She sucked in a shuddery breath and shook her head. "What's stopping you? And please don't say Ethan because that's a weak excuse. We're adults, we can do whatever we want. We don't need his permission."

"We don't," he agreed. "But he's not the only reason."

"Then what is it?" She had a feeling she already knew the answer.

"You want a husband. I'm not that guy. I'm never getting married again."

Her heart clenched. He'd confirmed her suspicions. "Is it too soon after your divorce? Are you still in love with your wife?"

A cascade of emotions flashed over his face so fast she couldn't register them all. "*Ex*-wife, and no, I don't have feelings for Layla anymore."

Layla.

His ex-wife's name was Layla. The woman who had scarred him so much he was scared of marriage. "Maybe if you give it some time, you'll change your mind."

"Time won't change my mind. Marriage isn't for me."

Her dreams of a life with Theo fractured, crumbled, and shattered. Deep inside of her, she'd always held out hope that Theo might be her forever one, now he was destroying that with every word. "What about a family, don't you want to have children someday?"

His face spasmed. "I'm not having kids." His harsh tone made his answer sound final, like it was set in stone and unbreakable.

If that were true, then he really wasn't the one for her as much as she wished he were. She couldn't dwell on impossibilities with the time line she was against; she needed to wipe him from her mind and focus on a man who could give her the things she wanted.

God, this was going to be tough. Would any man ever measure up to Theo? She prayed someone would, otherwise she was screwed.

Theo scrubbed a hand through his hair and waved the other hand between them. "Whatever this thing between us is can't go any further. I need you to understand that, Chloe."

A pang of regret flooded through her. She nodded. She understood—it didn't mean she liked it.

Needing to get away, she said, "Well... thank you for tonight. I'm grateful for your help with my crazy plan. Fingers crossed it worked." She held up her two entwined fingers. Opening the door, she stepped out into the night. "Good night, Theo."

"Good night."

She closed the door behind her and heaved a heavy sigh. From the steps of her building, she watched Theo drive off.

Tonight's pretend date had been successful. She'd had a beautiful dinner with great company. Theo had been the perfect gentleman. He'd made her laugh, and she felt comfortable around him. Most importantly, she hadn't sneezed.

It had been the perfect date.

Just not with the perfect man.

CHAPTER NINETEEN

T heo scrubbed a hand over his face. Not even back-to-back meetings with suppliers could stop him from thinking about two nights ago.

Now he had her date with Owen looming over his head. Images of what they might do together filled his mind. Would she let Owen walk her to her apartment? Let him kiss her, touch her? Not his business. She could do whatever the hell she wanted. At least that's what he tried to tell himself, but it didn't stop his gut clenching.

Theo and Blake sat in his office scanning through the reports, and like he'd conjured him up, Owen walked in. Theo's jaw clenched. This man was taking Chloe out to dinner in a couple of hours, and he wanted to slam his fist on the timber table.

"Hey, Theo, Blake. I've got the report for the Hanson Liquor account you asked for." He waved the file in the air before dropping the folder on the table.

"Thanks, that was quick. I wasn't expecting it for another couple of hours." Blake picked it up and flicked through the pages.

An anticipatory smile flashed across Owen's face. "I'm leaving early so I got it done."

Something about the man's attitude rubbed him the wrong way. "I better not find any mistakes because you've rushed through this." Theo crossed his arms over his chest.

Owen shook his head. "No mistakes. I double-checked everything."

"Maybe you should triple-check it," Theo said, annoyed at the man's flippant tone. "This account is important."

Blake glanced between Theo and Owen. His eyebrows pulled together, then he said, "I'm sure it's fine. You're always thorough, Owen."

"Thanks," Owen said.

"Where're you heading off to?" Blake asked, clearly trying to steer the conversation into calmer waters without much success.

Unaware of the minefield he'd wandered into, Owen answered, "I've got a date." He turned toward Theo. "Thank you for setting me up with Chloe. We've talked a couple of times over the phone, and she seems like a great woman."

In Theo's peripheral vision, he saw Blake's eyebrows shoot up.

"No problem." Theo picked up the folder and flicked through the pages, not seeing a word or number written through the red haze clouding his vision.

"I think this could be something. We have a lot in common," Owen continued blithely.

"Glad I could help," Theo said through stiff lips.

"I'll be in the office for another half hour if you need me." He smiled, rubbed his hands together, and did a little bounce on his heels. "After that, I'll be meeting Chloe."

"Have a great night," Blake said as Owen headed out of the office.

Theo didn't say a word.

Blake swung around in his chair to face Theo. "He looked excited for the date. I see you took my advice and set him up with Chloe. I think they'd be great together."

Theo's fists clenched by his sides. "Yeah, great."

Blake stared at him for a beat. "You're pissed."

"No, I'm not," he lied and picked up plans for Andrew Vandersluis' building they'd been looking at earlier in the day. He rolled them up, imagining that the plans were Owen's neck. Dammit! He needed to get control of himself.

Blake pointed a finger at Theo. "You like Chloe."

"We're friends." But he knew that it wasn't the answer his brother was looking for.

True to form, Blake didn't let it go. "No, you *really* like Chloe in the 'more than just friends' way."

"It doesn't matter." He couldn't do anything about his feelings for her anyway. Theo collected the plans and rose from the chair to leave.

Blake put a hand on his arm, stopping him. "Hey, don't set her up with guys if you want her for yourself. If you like her, go for it."

"I can't." She wanted more than he could ever give her, but he couldn't say that part out loud. Not to his brother. He hoped Blake would drop it, even as he knew he wouldn't.

"If you think Ethan will be pissed you're with his sister, he'll get over it."

Theo sighed. "It's not that."

"You're not serious about not getting into another relationship, are you?" Blake asked, still pushing because, of course, he was. "People divorce all the time, and they often find love again."

"I'm not looking for love."

"Well, from the way you were *looking* at Owen, I'd say you were ready to kill him. You must feel something pretty strong for Chloe if you can't stand the thought of him dating her." His brother's eyes were intent.

Theo slapped the plans back on the table. "Nothing is going to happen between me and Chloe. I'm not right for her."

"Why the hell not? Just because things didn't work out with Layla doesn't mean you're not right for Chloe."

His brother wasn't going to let this go; he had to tell Blake the truth he'd kept hidden for so long. He wasn't looking forward to this. With a sigh, he said, "Chloe wants kids."

Blake shrugged. "So? Most women do."

"I can't give them to her."

Blake shook his head. "Why not?"

Theo paced the room. "Because I'm... I'm... infertile." There, he'd said it. Now to wait for the fallout.

It wasn't long in coming "What?" Blake stood in front of him slack-jawed. "What the hell do you mean 'infertile'?"

"I'm not repeating myself." He'd never said the words out loud, and they tasted like acid on his tongue. Layla had loved throwing the word in his face because it had been his fault she couldn't get pregnant. But if *he* said it, then it became real. Like his failures couldn't be hidden away and forgotten about. Receiving the finalized divorced papers had reopened the wound, reminding him he was the reason their marriage had failed.

Blake stared at him like he'd transformed into a goat. "You can't have kids? Since when?"

Theo clutched the back of a chair. "We'd been trying to conceive for about a year with no results, so we went to a fertility specialist. Layla had tests done, and she was all clear. My results were a different story." God, this was hard.

"Man, I'm sorry." Blake put a hand on Theo's shoulder, but he shrugged it off. The last thing he wanted was his brother's sympathy.

"That's why I'm no good for Chloe." The words tore at his chest.

"If you explain it to her, maybe she won't care."

Theo shook his head. "I'm not putting her in that situation." He wasn't putting himself in that situation. Not again.

"There are other options... IVF, adoption," Blake continued, "Hell, I'd be willing to jack off into a cup for you."

That was Blake for you—always trying to find a solution. But things weren't so simple. "Layla didn't want to consider IVF, said it was too invasive for something that wasn't guaranteed to work. I brought up adoption, but the light died in her eyes the instant I said it. She wanted her own child. Our child."

"Just because Layla didn't want to try other options doesn't mean Chloe won't. Things might be different with her. You need to give her a chance," Blake said in a reasonable tone.

But Theo wasn't in the mood to be reasonable, not about this. "No, other options take time. Since turning thirty, she's already put herself on a strict time line. I'm not making her wait for something that may never happen." He clenched his fists. "I won't be that cruel."

"What if you're making a mistake and she's willing to take the risk? What if she's the one for you?" Blake asked.

That's it. He was done with this conversation. He'd already said too much. "I'm not making a mistake, and that's the end of this little brotherly heart-to-heart." He knew he was being snide, but he didn't care. He. Was. Done. "If we don't get out of here now, we'll be late for our meeting."

Striding from the room, Theo reconsidered his promises to both Chloe and Ethan. If Chloe's date with Owen didn't work out, he was done helping her. He was done spying on her and reporting back to her brother. He couldn't put himself through this anymore. He couldn't deny he had feelings for her. Handing her over to another man was tearing a hole in his chest. If they lived in the perfect world, they'd be together. But the world was far from perfect. And he wasn't the perfect man. He knew that—hated that. He'd do everything in his power to keep her in his life.

The next time he saw her, he'd tell Chloe he was done playing matchmaker.

CHAPTER TWENTY

C hloe hesitated in front of the restaurant. She hadn't sneezed while getting ready which was a good sign. What would happen when she walked inside? Would her nerves get the better of her? What would cause the sneezing to start?

This was ridiculous! At thirty, she shouldn't feel like an inexperienced teenager on her first date. She'd had dates before—including several sans sneezes. This time she was after something serious. There was more on the line. Destiny could be waiting for her inside.

Thinking about maybe having her dreams realized with Owen, her nose twitched. Shit! Shit! Shit! She waited for the sneeze. When nothing happened, she let out a sigh of relief. Maybe her practice date with Theo had worked. Could their dinner cure her of her condition? Images of Theo flooded her mind.

She mentally shook herself. *Stop it! You're going on a date with Owen. A really nice man. You can't keep thinking of Theo.* Taking a deep breath, she stepped inside the dim restaurant. The host led her to the table where Owen waited. When he saw her, his face lit up, and he stood, pulling out a chair for her.

"Hello, Owen," she smiled. Her nose didn't twitch. So far, so good.

"Chloe, you look beautiful. How are you?" He kissed her on the cheek before she sat down.

No sneeze. Excellent.

The rest of the night went smoothly. Even when he reached over the table and placed his hand on hers, her sinuses didn't play up. Buoyed by her good luck, Chloe let herself relax. Owen was wonderful. He made her laugh with outrageous stories about the things he got up to as a kid. He was serious about wanting a relationship, and they shared the same dreams about having a family. He ticked all the right boxes. Flutters took off in her stomach. She allowed herself to hope, to dream. Her nose tickled, but no sneeze. Was she cured? God, she hoped so.

After dinner, Owen insisted on waiting with her while the valet ordered her a taxi, holding her hand with their fingers entwined together. His hand in hers was strong and warm. It felt nice. A few moments later, a cab pulled alongside them. She turned to face him. "Thank you for a lovely evening."

"Can I see you again?" he asked.

"I'd like that." And she meant it. This had the potential of turning into something more. Excitement at maybe finding the right man danced in her belly.

He smiled and lowered his head; he was going to kiss her. Her heart rate kicked up. Her palms grew sweaty. Just when their lips were about to touch, her nose twitched. Oh God, no! She turned her head to the side and sneezed, breaking the connection.

"I'm so sorry." She held her hand over her mouth. What was wrong with her? She'd never find a husband if she kept doing this.

He chuckled, "It's okay. I'll call you tomorrow." He opened the taxi's door.

She searched his face. Would he call? Or had he worked out she was some kind of weirdo with a sneezing problem, and it was an empty promise? "Good night," she said, sliding onto the seat and giving the taxi driver her address.

She rested her arm along the door and tapped her fingers with frustration. She'd ruined a wonderful date. If she kept going this way, she was going to die a lonely old woman with her virginity intact.

This sucked. But what could she do? When she got really nervous, she sneezed. Except, she never sneezed when alone with Theo. There was comfort in their years of friendship—a comfort tinged with desire. Daniela might be right; she really might be demisexual. If that was the case, then what she needed was to replicate the same familiarity with Owen. Be friends before things moved to the next step. But she didn't have time to take things slow.

Everything had been fine until Owen had gone in for the good-night kiss. Well, she'd kissed Theo and there hadn't been any problems.

A light bulb went off.

Leaning forward, she said, "Excuse me. I've changed my mind, can you take me to Alto club, please?"

Thirty minutes, one wrong turn, and a long wait in line later, cold seeped through Chloe's coat. She wrapped it tightly around her body and soldiered on. She could have texted Theo to let her in, but she needed the time to sort out in her mind what she wanted to say to him before she blurted out her request. Would he do what she'd asked after everything he'd done for her already? Probably not. He'd already told her no more favors. She would just have to convince him to change his mind.

Was he even in the club? Or if he was in his penthouse, would the doorman to his building let her up? Should she go around and find him? No, she'd been in line for fifteen minutes already; she didn't want to lose her spot. She shuffled forward a few steps. She tapped her toe on the pavement. Another ten minutes passed. This was a mistake. As she turned to go, someone called her name.

She turned back; Blake jogged toward her. "I thought I saw you. Why are you waiting in line?"

"Umm... isn't that what you're supposed to do?" She didn't know any other way to get into the club without calling Theo to let her in.

Confusion flashed across Blake's features. "Hasn't Theo put your name on the list? You just have to give security your name and show them your ID, and you have VIP access."

"Oh, I don't know if he has." She'd already asked so much of Theo, asking to get onto Alto's VIP list seemed... well... selfish.

"I'll check. Come on, let's get inside. It's fucking freezing out here." He held on to her hand and guided her into the club. "You're here on your own. Didn't your date go well?" he asked as he checked her coat.

"You know about that? Of course, Theo would have told you."

"Yeah, he did." Then frowned like something troubled him. Before she could ask him if everything was okay, he smiled. "Theo's at our table. Want to join us?"

She nodded, and he led the way. They zigzagged through the crowd until they reached the table. "Look who I found waiting outside the club." He paused, realizing that only Logan and two chic women were seated there. "Hey, where's Theo?"

"He went upstairs to his penthouse. Hey, Chloe, join us for a drink." Logan waved for her to sit.

If she joined them and ignored the reason she'd come to the club, what would that achieve? She'd still have her sneezing issue. "I would love to, but I need to talk to Theo. Do you think I could go up and see him?" she asked Blake. Then a thought hit her. "Is he alone?" What if he was with another woman? A chill prickled down her spine.

"With the mood he's in, he's scared everyone away," Logan said with a laugh.

That didn't sound good. Should she turn around and go home?

"Come on, I'll take you to the elevator." Blake placed his palm on the small of her back and guided her away from the table.

Deciding to stick with the plan, she followed him, not able to stop thinking about the last time she'd walked this way. To the night she'd almost slept with Theo. After she told him what she wanted, would he reject her again? Her stomach rolled.

When they reached those shiny black glass doors, Blake gave her a hug and whispered, "I'll see you later, Chloe."

Stepping inside the carriage, she took a deep breath and watched the numbers ascend. She wiped her sweaty palms on her dress, and before she could settle her racing heart, the doors slid open. She stepped out, expecting that she'd have to knock. But the door to his penthouse stood open. Was he anticipating company? That funny chill made a reappearance.

A lamp in the corner bathed the room in a golden glow. Through the glass windows, a hazy moon hung low in the sky, dimmed by the city lights. A dark silhouette stood in front of the windows, his back toward her with a tumbler in his hand by his side.

"I told you, I'm not going back to the club, and tell Logan to stop texting me," he said with an edge to his voice.

"Logan had his hands full with two women," she said around the frog in her throat.

Theo spun around. "What are you doing here? Shouldn't you be on your date?"

"The date's over." Chloe stepped farther into the room.

Gone were the expensive tailored suit and styled hair. He was dressed in gray sweatpants and black T-shirt. It looked like he'd run his fingers through his hair multiple times. His feet were bare, and he looked just as gorgeous in this casual outfit as he did in a suit.

He walked to her, placing his glass on the coffee table. From the looks of his red-rimmed eyes, it wasn't his first drink. What was he upset about?

"The date's over already? Wasn't Owen 'the one'?" he said, screwing up his nose.

"He could be. I like him." But with Theo standing in front of her, Owen paled in comparison.

"What are you doing here? If you like him so much, shouldn't you be with him?" Theo glared at her. Why was he so angry?

"I should leave. I'm sorry I've disturbed you."

He grabbed onto her wrist, pulling her close but not close enough so they touched. "What are you doing here?" he asked again.

Her head tilted back to look at him. She bit her lip, wondering for a second if she should ask him—could ask him. Then his gaze dropped to her mouth, and she decided she'd do anything to have him kiss her.

"I... arhh...I need to ask a favor."

His hand dropped from her wrist; he took a step back and jammed his fingers through his hair. "No."

"You haven't heard what it is."

"I'm done with favors. The answer is still no."

"But—"

"Chloe, you asked me to find you a date with a decent guy, and I have. You like him, he could be 'the one.' Start planning your wedding and pick names for your firstborn." He smacked a hand on his chest. "What more do you want from me?" His voice was ragged, almost pained.

She closed the gap between them. "I want you to kiss me."

Theo stared at Chloe, waiting for her to laugh and yell, "just joking." She didn't even crack a smile. "You're kidding, right?"

She nibbled her bottom lip. "No."

"You want me to kiss you?" he asked, just to be sure he'd heard correctly.

"Yes."

"This is the favor you're asking?"

She rolled her eyes. "Yes, Theo. It's not that hard to understand. I want you to kiss me."

"Like a kiss on the cheek?" He tapped the side of his face.

This time she laughed. "Let me explain for the people not paying attention. I want you to kiss me. On the lips. Passionately."

He took a few steps back. "What the fuck for?"

Her face fell. "Wow, you don't have to look so repulsed. We've kissed before, and I'm pretty sure you enjoyed it."

"I need another drink." He strode to the bar and splashed bourbon into a glass, knocking it back. Yeah, he'd enjoyed it. A little too fucking much. "The thought doesn't repulse me."

Chloe stared at him. "Well, are you going to do it?"

"No." If he kissed her, he was afraid that he wouldn't be able to stop kissing her, but he wasn't about to tell her that.

Disappointment and hurt flashed over her face before settling into a frankly adorable pout. "Why not?"

He should have known she wasn't going to let it go; she was bull-headed like that. It was one of the things he liked—and also disliked—about her. "I've already stepped over a line I should never have crossed."

She folded her arms over her chest. "If this is about Ethan—"

"You don't mess around with your brother's little sister." It was a lame excuse, and he knew it.

"I'm not sure if you've noticed, I'm not little anymore," she said, arching a brow.

She had him there; he most definitely had noticed. She might have been Ethan's little sister, but she was also a grown woman who excited him like no other. A woman who he could talk with, one he could envision a life with. She was the perfect woman: someone who could be both a friend and a lover. A partner. But he wasn't perfect enough for her, and he cared about her too much to subject her to his baggage. He let his eyes drift over her and said, "That's not the only reason."

"Then what is?" Her chin jutted forward.

Part of him wanted to tease her about looking like a kangaroo looking for a fight, but the greater part of him wanted to cross the room and take her in his arms. To stop himself, he rested a hip on the side of the counter. "There's no denying there's an attraction between us, and it's hard for me to hold back."

"Then don't." A spark of hope shot from her eyes.

"That would be cruel—to both of us," he amended quickly when he saw the hope morph into pain. "I can't give you more. I can't give you what you want. You're looking for a husband, and I'm not him." It was the closest he could come to telling her about his infertility.

Her head dropped so she looked at her lap for a beat. "I know. You don't want marriage and kids."

He nodded. He couldn't bring himself to speak. If he did, he might tell her the truth, and he couldn't bear to see the desire and respect in her eyes fade like it had with Layla. As much as he tried to claim otherwise, the divorce had wounded him more than he could express.

Wrapping her arms even tighter around her body, Chloe took a step back. "And your answer is still no?" she clarified.

He nodded again.

"Okay," she said in a voice that was filled with tears. "Okay."

She turned, arms still wrapped around her midsection, and headed for the still-open front door of his penthouse. A door he'd left open because he was expecting his brother for a nightcap. A door that was only accessible through a special express elevator. A door only one person knew would be open.

Dammit, Blake!

His brother was meddling—playing matchmaker. The irony wasn't lost on Theo. Had Blake known what Chloe wanted? What she was going to ask him? Probably not. He suspected if his brother had known that he would have strapped a jetpack to her back and hurled her upward at the speed of sound.

The universe was laughing at him. He could either rage against it, or he could go with the flow and see where it took him.

He made a decision. "Chloe, wait."

She stopped just outside the threshold of his apartment. "Yes?" Her voice was tiny, muffled, like she was holding back tears.

"Come back here."

She moved approximately three feet into the room.

He sighed. "Just to confirm. You only want a kiss. That's it. Nothing else."

"That's it," she echoed. "I expect nothing more from you. Just a kiss."

"Why are you asking me this?"

Keeping her distance, she met his eyes, hope and pain warring within them. "Our dinner date helped me with Owen. It really did. I didn't sneeze at all—not even a nose twitch—until he went to kiss me good night." A slow blush blossomed over her cheeks. "I made a joke to cover it, and I don't think he was turned off, but do you know how embarrassed I was?"

No, but he knew how each word was a stiletto through his chest. Even though he'd been the one to set Chloe up with Owen, the thought of her actually liking him enough to want to kiss him made Theo want to find something to punch. Repeatedly. He couldn't bear the thought of her kissing, caring, and loving someone else. But wasn't that the point of Chloe dating?

How did his life get so complicated?

Clearly unaware of the turmoil her request was causing within him, Chloe continued, "If you kiss me, I'm hoping—like our date—it will help the next time I see Owen. That way when he tries to kiss me, hopefully I won't sneeze."

Her request was so innocently oblivious it was both annoying and adorable. "I've kissed you before, so we've done the practice round already." And that memory haunted him in his dreams.

"That was before I met Owen. I need to see what we do together so I can do the same with him. I wasn't taking notes last time."

Was this a fucking science experiment? Surely, she couldn't be that innocent—or callous. He called her on it. "Do you know how ridiculous that sounds?"

"I know." Her shoulders drooped. "I know. But you're the only person who never gives me the sneezes."

He raised an eyebrow. "I don't make you nervous?"

"Not normally. But sometimes. But not really. I can't explain it. I just know you're the only one I've kissed like it means something. And

I also know that I have to try something," she said in a rush. "I don't want to be single forever."

He sighed. "That won't happen."

"It might if you don't help me." She pulled a hopeful expression, smiled, and stepped closer.

God help him! This woman was going to kill him. "Just one kiss?" he asked once again. He could handle that, right?

She lifted a shoulder and gave a cheeky smile. "And maybe a little making out?"

"Whoa!" Theo waved his hands out in front of him. "You mentioned nothing about wanting more."

"I'm mentioning it to you now." She tried to sound flirtatious, but her tone couldn't hide the intent behind her words.

An intent he wasn't about to let slide. "You're asking me to perform on demand so you can run off to another man." Couldn't she see how outrageous this was? Outrageous, and yet, he was tempted to be her guinea pig. "You can't keep asking this of me. You just can't!"

Chloe twisted her fingers together. "I know I've asked a lot from you, and I appreciate all you've done. If I don't get help with this, the longer it's going to take to find a boyfriend."

And wasn't that a giant fucking splash of cold water. "Yeah, about that. I quit."

Her eyebrows rose. "What do you mean?"

"If things don't work with Owen, I'm not setting you up with anyone else." He held up a hand to prevent her from protesting. "I haven't got the time to play matchmaker and stand-in boyfriend." He would never have agreed in the first place if he'd known how much she'd want from him. How hard it would be to resist her.

"Fair enough. I promise I won't ask for anything else." She linked her fingers and placed them under her chin, giving him a sweet smile. What she was asking for was anything but sweet.

He blew out a long breath. He just hoped after kissing her one last time he could purge her from his system. "We kiss, make out, and you won't ask any more favors to do with dating, right?"

"Right." She grinned cheekily. "Unless you want to do more. I'm letting you know I'm up for it. The ball is in your court."

Suddenly, nerves pinched the back of his neck. The last time he'd been nervous around a woman was when he'd been thirteen—his first kiss. He'd had plenty of experience since then. Kissing was a piece of cake. "When do you want to start?"

She shrugged. "How about now?"

"Are you sure?" He ambled closer.

She swallowed hard and nodded.

Theo took another step toward her. Her chest rose up and down at a rapid pace. The dress she wore tightened against her chest, but he kept his gaze focused on her face, her eyes, her lips. He cupped his hand on the back of her head and brushed a thumb over the beating pulse in her neck. "Is this what you really want?" His lips hovered above hers.

"Yes," she whispered and rose on the balls of her feet so their noses rubbed together. When he kissed her, her lips parted with a soft sigh. It was just an innocent kiss, and yet a shot of pure lust hit him. Hard. Right between his legs. Dear God, just what had he gotten himself into? How could he hope to get her out of his system with just one kiss?

Her hands caressed over his shoulders, up his neck, to tangle in his hair. Planting his hands on her waist, he tugged her closer. There was no way he could hide the hard-on pressed against her stomach. She didn't seem to mind, her body melting against him. The kiss deepened, more urgent now.

She broke away, dragging in a breath. "This is my teenage fantasy come to life. But so much better." She gave a soft chuckle.

Resting his hands on her hips, he said, "Oh, yeah. So, you did have a crush on me?"

Tilting her head to the side, her tongue swept over her bottom glossy red lip. "Maybe? Just a little."

He groaned at the gesture, thinking about all the things he wanted her to do with that mouth. But this was about her, not him. For her, not him. Just a kiss and making out. Nothing more. Although, that didn't mean he couldn't have a little fun too. Maneuvering her until her knees hit the back of the sofa, he eased her down on top of it. She hooked her hand in the waistband of his sweatpants and tugged him to his knees so he knelt in front of her. His hands went behind her ass, and he slid her forward so her legs wrapped around him. He continued to kiss her mouth before trailing his lips to her neck. She smelled like flowers on a spring day—fragrant and sweet. He breathed in her scent. Her head tilted to the side, exposing the delicate skin of her neck. He ran a finger along it to where it met her shoulder. He helped her out of her coat, revealing still more of that beautiful peachy skin. Only Chloe would wear a dress with spaghetti straps to a casual date in the middle of March. He brushed the strap of her dress off her shoulder and paused, waiting. When she didn't object, he did the same to the other side. The dress sat dangerously close to falling around her waist and exposing what he wanted to get his hands and mouth on.

"When you say 'make out,' does it include a little more skin? Maybe some touching and tasting?" *Please say yes!*

"Absolutely," she gushed. "I'm up for anything!"

He chuckled at her enthusiastic answer.

With his index finger, he tugged her dress down revealing her breasts covered in a dusty-pink push-up bra. Fuck him sideways, she was glorious. Before he could ask to see more, she reached around her back to unhook it. As the lace fell down, he covered one pert rosy nipple with his mouth.

"Oh, God!" She clasped her hands behind his head, drawing him closer. Sinking back onto the soft leather sofa, she moaned with every flick of his tongue.

He pulled back, dropping his hands on her legs, caressing them up her thighs so her dress bunched up around her waist. Her panties were lacy and pink, matching the bra. He groaned.

With his hands brushing against the elastic of her panties, he slid a finger under the fabric, causing her to shiver. As his finger skimmed over her wet folds, she arched her body upward to rest her head against his shoulder. Her warm breath tickled his neck. Her breasts pressed against his chest.

"I want you naked," she demanded with a moan as she pressed soft kisses over his collarbone.

He had no objections. He wanted to feel her flushed skin against his. She yanked his T-shirt over his head and tossed it on the floor. Next, her hands moved to the waist of his pants and tugged. He placed a hand over hers, stopping them from slipping under the waistband.

When she looked at him and frowned, he said, "This is about you, not me. Are you sure?"

"Yes, oh please, yes."

That was about as enthusiastic as you could get. He released her hands and let them wander to whatever destination she wanted. Thank fuck, it was south. She clasped her fingers around his erection and slowly stroked him as she kissed the side of his neck. He was ready to burst. Since when was he a two-pump chump?

To take his mind off the torture she was inflicting on him, he said, "Any signs of a sneeze?"

She raised her head and stared at him, her eyes glazed with desire. "Not even a tickle."

He pulled her hand away before he embarrassed himself, turned her in her seat, and pushed her flat onto her back. With her sprawled out before him, he'd never seen anyone so beautiful. Desire shot through his veins, and he crawled over her. Her legs opened for him, and he settled between them. God, he wanted to sink into her then and there. Feel her rock against him until she shattered in his arms. Just because he couldn't have her like he wanted didn't mean he couldn't make her fall apart.

He kissed her long and hard as his hand massaged her breast. She clutched onto his ass and pressed against him like she needed more of him. Well, he could give her more. With hands on her knees, he pushed her legs up until they fell open naturally. He ground himself against her, cursing the clothes stopping him from sinking inside her.

"Theo, please...I want you to..." she cried.

He wanted to do what he knew she was begging for, but he couldn't go there. Not when he had to walk away. Chloe wasn't a love 'em and leave 'em kind of girl; she wanted forever, and that was something he just could not give her.

"Theo..." her voice shook. "I need... Oh, God, I need—" She bit her lip, cutting herself off.

She was so close that he could feel her trembling under him. He slid his hand between their bodies and inside her panties, then plunged two fingers inside her.

"Oh, God. Yes," she gasped and bucked against his hand

He gritted his teeth, and sweat pebbled on his forehead. The restraint from wanting to replace his fingers with his cock was killing him. With each thrust, her head tossed from side to side. His thumb massaged her sensitive clit, and she clenched around his finger. He pumped into her one last time, hooking his fingers against her G-spot.

She cried out as an orgasm ripped through her body; her warm, wet heat clenched around his fingers. He eased her through her climax, drawing it out, making it last.

This would be the only time they'd do this, and he wanted to give her a memory she could treasure.

———— ◆○◆ ————

The sounds of their choppy breathing filled the air, and Chloe lay still, reveling in the sensations arcing through her body. Feelings she'd never had with a man before—only the battery-operated rabbit she had in her nightstand drawer had even come close to replicating what Theo had managed with just two fingers. God, the way he kissed her, touched her, and made her body stir to life was unbelievable. She wanted to stretch with satisfaction and curl up on the sofa with him until they caught their breath, then she wanted to do it all over again. But this time, she wanted to take it further. They'd been so close. There'd been a moment where she'd thought he might lose control, rip the rest of his clothes off, and claim her virginity. But he hadn't, much to her chagrin.

Theo pulled back and stared at her with a shuttered gaze. What was he thinking? Did he regret what just happened? Because she didn't, it had been the best experience in her life.

Like he'd come to his senses, he quickly tugged her dress up so it covered her breasts. Climbing to his feet, he strode to the bar to pour himself a drink. After knocking it back, he said, "I took things too far. I'm sorry."

Disappointment burst her euphoria bubble. That answered her question—he regretted it. Adjusting her clothes—not even bothering with her bra—she walked over to him. "I wanted to make out."

"*Make out*, you sound like we're in fucking high school." He said the words with a sneer, like they were pathetic. He raked a hand through his hair. "I should've stopped it from going so far. If I hadn't found some control, I would have fucked you on that sofa."

Chloe stepped back at his harsh tone. "I wouldn't have minded. If I'd wanted you to stop, I would have said so." And she would have, trusting that Theo would. It was another reason why she wished she could have him. Maybe she'd done something wrong, something she shouldn't. "Was I...was I okay? I didn't do anything wrong, did I?"

"No, you were great." He rubbed a hand at the back of his neck.

"Then why are you so upset?"

"Because... Because... I'm no good for you. I don't want you thinking that this"—he waved a hand between them—"can go any further."

And there it was, the confirmation of what she already knew. Her chest hurt every time she so much as thought of his rejection of her, but she couldn't seem to stop herself from wanting him. And she knew he desired her too, but desire wasn't enough. There needed to be more, something he seemed to be unwilling to give.

Not wanting to drive a wedge between them, she turned away. "I should go. Thank you for helping me with my sneezing problem."

"I'm glad I could be of service." His voice was strained. Pained?

She met his eyes with determination, her hands clenched at her sides. "I'm not sorry about tonight. I enjoyed myself. A lot." Her voice softened. "But I am sorry you regret it. I don't want there to be any negativity between us. I want us to still be friends, to still be in each other's lives."

He shoved his hair from his face. "I don't think that's a good idea," he said, and pain flooded through her replacing the aftereffects of her orgasm. "I'm done. I won't help you again if things don't work with Owen."

"You're acting like we've done something wrong."

"We have. You're Ethan's sister. I'm supposed to be watching over you, not nearly fucking you."

"Screw Ethan! He's not here, and his opinion doesn't matter. We get to decide what kind of relationship we have. We're the only two people who matter."

His expression softened, but his words were harsh, "You're being naive."

"So what? I don't care." She blinked to push back the tears that threatened. "I've had a crush on you since I was thirteen. And tonight? It was like a dream come true. I don't regret what happened between us. I'm just sorry you do!" Grabbing her coat from the floor, she scanned the room for her purse, found it on the coffee table, and tucked it under her arm.

She was almost to the elevator when his voice stopped her. "I don't regret it." The words were soft, almost tender. But when she turned, his expression hardened.

Hurt blossomed in her chest, and she wrapped her arms around herself. "Oh? Because the way you're looking at me doesn't show you 'had a great time.'"

"Chloe..." He reached out toward her for an instant before letting his hand fall. "I—"

She cut him off. "Stop! Just stop... Don't say anything you don't mean."

He didn't say a word.

"Okay..." She gathered the tattered remains of her confidence around her. "Thank you for a lovely and educational evening. I think I've got my sneezing problem under control."

He nodded, his eyes solemn. "I'm pleased I could be of assistance."

"And before you feel the need to remind me, I remember my promise, I won't ask anything of you ever again. Goodbye, Theodore Campbell. If you change your mind about us, you know where to find me. But I won't bother you again." She blew out of the living room and into the elevator, her heart plummeting as fast as the lift.

CHAPTER TWENTY-ONE

A fter a night spent tossing and turning, Theo entered the office in a mood as black as his coffee... and almost as bitter. It was early, most of the office wasn't expected until closer to nine, but Theo couldn't bear to be back in his penthouse, which still smelled faintly of Chloe's perfume.

He flipped open the nearest file and nearly growled. It was the report he'd requested from Owen. Fucking Owen! Why the fuck had he set Chloe up with him? Just the thought of the accountant touching her was enough to make him see red. But he had no right to be jealous, none. They weren't dating. In fact, he'd been the one to insist on that. It was his own damned fault that he'd hooked the two of them up. This was karma for him playing matchmaker; he was sure of it.

Worse, if he tried to forbid Chloe from seeing Owen, he'd be as bad as Ethan.

Ethan. Fucking Ethan. It all came back to him. If Ethan hadn't been his best friend, Theo would have fucked Chloe on her birthday and gotten her out of his system. A small part of his brain tried to tell him it wouldn't be that easy, but he shoved that part into a steel box and sat on it. He couldn't do anything about Chloe and Owen, but at least he could rectify the problem with Ethan.

Picking up the phone, he dialed Ethan's number. He didn't care what time it might be wherever Ethan was, it was time to get his life back on track.

His friend picked up after a few rings, annoyingly bright and cheerful. "Theo! How's it going? I was just thinking about you!" Translation: he was getting ready to call Theo to check up on Chloe, but Theo had beaten him to the punch.

"I'm done," Theo said without any preamble.

All trace of cheerfulness faded. "What?"

Theo leaned back in his chair and stared up at the ceiling. "You heard me; I'm done. Chloe's not some teenager on spring break, getting smashed and partying hard." He tactfully chose not to mention the time she'd drunk a bottle of wine after being stood up for a date. What Ethan didn't know wouldn't hurt him. And by him, Theo meant himself.

"Yeah, I know, but she's my little sister. That doesn't stop just because she moved half a world away. I need to know she's okay and being looked after, and who else would I trust to look after my sister than my best friend?" It sounded oh so reasonable, and if Theo hadn't known just how good of an actor Ethan was, he might have fallen for it. But being in the business world as long as he'd been, Theo knew when he was getting manipulated.

And he was done. He'd told Chloe he wouldn't let her manipulate him into finding her a husband, and now he was telling his best friend he wouldn't be his spy any longer. Apparently it was twenty-four hours filled with bad decisions and boundary-setting conversations.

"Your sister is fine," he said, arranging the pens on his desk into neat lines. "She's practically a native New Yorker."

"So, you *have* been watching out for her." Relief and pleasure filled Ethan's voice. "I knew I could rely on you. I couldn't trust anyone else."

Theo grunted noncommittally. Oh he'd been watching her, all right. He'd watched her orgasm less than twelve hours ago. Theo slumped in his chair. And if Ethan knew what Theo had gotten up to with his sister, his best friend would be madder than a cut snake.

"So, what's the news?" Ethan asked like he was Perez Hilton on the lookout for the next scoop. "Who's she hanging out with? What's she doing?"

Well, he couldn't rightly answer those questions, now could he? She'd been asking him on dates and practically *doing* him. Wouldn't that go over like a cement helicopter? "You need to talk to her, not me."

"Why? I've asked you to keep an eye on her."

Time to bite the bullet. "And I'm not doing it anymore. She's old enough to watch out for herself, and she's fine." Theo paused, debating with himself. Should he tell his best friend that his sister was on to his game, or should he let him discover that for himself? Decisions, decisions. Deciding that he still wanted to be friends with Ethan, he said, "As a sign of our friendship, you should know that she knows what you've asked of me." And wasn't that a confusing statement if ever there was one?

There was a clattering sound from the other end of the line before Ethan came back with, "Shit, you told her?"

"I had to." Theo massaged the back of his neck. "She knew something was up. I couldn't keep a secret that damning from her. It was you or me, mate, and you were volunteered as tribute."

"I'm surprised she didn't call me and blast my arse."

"She wanted to; I calmed her down. It was the least I could do."

Ethan chuckled. "Damn right, considering you threw me under the bus to begin with."

"You're the one who asked me to spy on her."

"And you said yes," Ethan pointed out.

"Well, I'm unsaying it. Count me out. I'm done."

He could practically hear Ethan frowning at the phone. "Well, I'd appreciate it if you'd still watch out for her. For your best friend's sake."

"No, I'm through playing babysitter." Spending time with Chloe had almost killed him, and if Ethan knew he wanted to get Chloe into his bed, he'd destroy their friendship entirely.

But much like his sister, Ethan wouldn't let it go. Once any of the Doyle siblings got an idea into their head, they wouldn't let it go. It was infuriating. "Come on, mate, just for a few more weeks. Take her out on the town. Show her the sights. Help her settle in."

"No, she's settled in just fine. She doesn't need my help. She's got three good friends she hangs out with and is dat—" He slammed his lips shut.

"Were you about to say 'she's dating'?" Oh no, Ethan sounded way too interested in that. If Ethan had worried about Chloe living in New York on her own, Theo didn't think he'd react well to finding out about his sister dating. Especially not from him.

"Look, talk to Chloe. I'm not getting involved anymore. I've gotta go; I've got my seven thirty waiting for me," he lied. No one was waiting. He just wanted to get out of the hole he'd dug for himself. Throwing a bone to politeness, he said, "We'll catch up some other time." He hung up the phone before Ethan could protest.

He knew Chloe would get a call from her brother. But he didn't care, it wasn't Theo's problem anymore. Although...

He tapped out a quick message:

Hey, heads up. I've told Ethan I'm not spying on you anymore. I'm sorry I ever said I'd help him. He should be calling you soon. I accidentally let slip that you had a date. I just thought you should know.

There. He'd done the right thing, and now he could move on with his life. His lonely life without Chloe.

If things were different, then maybe...

No, there was no point imagining the impossible. He'd never put another woman through what Layla had gone through with his infertility. Failing to give her what she wanted—a baby, his baby—had been a bitter pill to swallow.

He wasn't going down that path again.

CHAPTER TWENTY-TWO

The next evening, Chloe was about to walk into the restaurant to meet Owen when her phone rang. Digging it out of her purse, Ethan's name lit up the screen. Well, Theo had warned her this might happen. She wanted to ignore his call, but he'd probably call again later and interrupt her dinner. Thank goodness she'd arrived a little early so she had time to answer the call.

"Hi, Ethan. This is a bad time. I'm about to meet someone for dinner."

"Who are you meeting?" he asked in a singsong tone like he already knew what was up. Which, to be fair, he did.

Chloe stepped away from the restaurant's entrance to let a couple inside. "You don't say hello anymore? I'm going to tell Mum." If he was going to be the meddling, overprotective brother, she could play the bratty little sister.

She heard him sigh. "Hello, Chloe."

"Much better," she said with a grin.

"Who are you meeting?" he asked again.

Chloe shook her head. Was it so hard to engage in a little small talk before he went straight into the interrogation? Apparently, her brother had eschewed all social niceties. "A friend."

"Is it a guy? I've heard you're dating." No points as to who spilled the beans, at least she'd had a little warning—the jerk.

Chloe pinched the bridge of her nose. She almost wished that Theo was still spying on her for her brother, at least then he'd be the one to get the third degree and not her. She kicked a pebble on the sidewalk. "Why bother asking me? Your spy should've filled you in on all the juicy details." She clutched the phone. "Which let me ask you some-thing: how could you do that to me? Don't you trust me?"

"I'm worried about you on your own." He didn't bother denying it or apologize for invading her privacy and treating her like a child.

Well, she wasn't about to take this lying down. "I don't know how many times I need to tell you this, but I can take care of myself." When a couple walking by paused to look at her, she lowered her voice and pulled out her trump card. "Mum doesn't even treat me this way."

Ethan sighed. "Mum's too nice; she always thinks the best of people. But you're in New York, literally half a world away without any sup-port system should something happen. I promised myself I'd always take care of my family after Dad died. What else would you have me do?"

"You could—and I know I'm going out on a limb here—trust me to make good decisions and take care of myself. I was doing just fine in Sydney."

"But you weren't interested in dating then," he countered quickly. Too quickly. "Ever since Isla died, you've been laser focused on getting married and starting a family. I'm worried about you rushing into things without regard for the consequences. I'm worried about you getting hurt. I'm worried about you dating guys you know nothing about. You could date a psychopath for all you know."

"That's a bit dramatic. Going for another BAFTA nom, are you?" she asked, annoyed. "Owen's a nice guy. Theo wouldn't have set me up with him if he wasn't." Oh shit, she probably shouldn't have said that last part.

Her brother pounced on the information. "Theo set you up? What the fuck? Me and Theo are going to have a little chat the next time I see him."

"Do *not* contact him about anything to do with me again." She squeezed the bridge of her nose, feeling a headache coming on. "I want to find someone to spend the rest of my life with, and he's been helping."

"I didn't ask him to do that. He was supposed to take care of you—"

"I can take care of myself, thank you very much," she said, cutting him off. "I'm done with this conversation. I'm meeting a nice man. Someone who could be perfect for me, and you've pissed me off. If the date ends badly, I'm blaming you. Then I'll have to start all over again with another *stranger*." Her voice rose, and this time she didn't care who heard. "Stay out of my business."

"Chloe—" he sounded contrite, but she wouldn't let him finish.

"Goodbye, Ethan." She hung up and flung the phone into her purse. Dropping her head, she stared at the cracked sidewalk. What did she have to do to get Ethan off her back? She didn't have time to worry about that now; she was late meeting Owen.

Chloe hurried inside the restaurant to where Owen was waiting. When he saw her, he smiled, rose, and pulled out a chair for her.

"Sorry I'm late," she said, hanging her purse on the back of her chair.

"No problem. You look beautiful," he said and placed a hand on her back to kiss her on the cheek before she sat down.

"Thank you." She'd hoped to feel something when he kissed her. A spark or warmth where he touched her. Yes, it was chaste and there was nothing sensual about it, but she wanted *something*.

This was all Ethan's fault! Picking up the menu, she stared at the page, still too pissed with her brother to make conversation with Owen. The last thing she wanted to do was bite his head off. Damn her brother for putting her in this mood.

"Something wrong?" Owen stared at her over his menu. "Nothing on there you like?"

Crap, she needed to get Ethan out of her head, and fast! She plastered a smile on her face. "Sorry, I'm distracted by a call I got before I arrived."

"Anything serious?"

"No, my brother is being dramatic over nothing. But I don't want to talk about him." Or what an overprotective brother she had. She glanced at her menu. "Everything looks delicious. I'm having trouble deciding what I want."

After a few minutes, they ordered dinner, and while they waited, Chloe found herself relaxing and enjoying Owen's company once again. He had a great sense of humor, was passionate about his work, and loved his family. They talked about places they could visit together and when their next date should be. His eyes beamed with interest when he looked at her, and she knew he wanted to take their relationship further.

This was good. This was very good. Chloe actually liked him and would like to see where this was leading, but before she committed to spending more time together, she needed to tell him she was still a virgin. Yes, it was still early in their relationship. A conversation like that could wait until they were ready to take the next step, but Chloe had her schedule and needed to fast-track things. It would be a good test of character.

By the time dessert arrived, she didn't want to put it off any longer. Owen was great; surely he wouldn't have a problem with her virginity.

She swirled her spoon in the strawberry sorbet. "There's something I wanted to talk to you about." Chloe put down her spoon and moved her bowl aside.

"Uh-oh, sounds serious. Are you going to tell me you don't want to see me anymore?" His shoulders slumped, and he rested back in his chair.

"No, not at all. I like you. I want to see you again." She smiled reassuringly. Even though her skin didn't break out in goose bumps when he touched her hand, nor did her body heat up when he looked at her. She hoped it was only a matter of time until it did.

He dabbed his mouth with a napkin and placed it on his plate. "Then what is it?"

She fidgeted with the stem of her wineglass. "There's something you should know about me. If what we have is going to move forward, I think it's important."

"Okay." His forehead furrowed.

"Well, umm, I've never... never done it before. If our relationship continues, you'd be my first." There, she'd said it. Now to see how he'd react. She mentally crossed her fingers.

His brows furrowed. "Done what?"

Okay, that wasn't the ideal response, but the restaurant was rather crowded. She cleared her throat, glanced around her to make sure no one was close by, and said in a deliberately quiet tone, "I've never had sex."

Owen sat statue still. The only things moving were his rapidly blinking eyes. After a moment he said, "You've never had *sex*?"

So... that response was worse—a lot worse—but it still wasn't completely terrible. Chloe's gaze flicked around the room. Thank God for good old New York indifference. She met his gaze and said, "No."

"Never?"

She traced a finger along a crease in the tablecloth. "I'm a virgin."

"You're kidding."

"No."

"A virgin."

"Yes."

He put his palms on the table and leaned forward. "You're how old?"

"Thirty."

"This has to be a joke."

Chloe sighed. This wasn't going at all how she'd imagined. In fact, the only way it could get worse was if he started laughing at her. "It's not."

Owen stared at her, then blinked. Then blinked again. His cheeks puffed out, and he broke down into peals upon peals of laughter, drawing every eye in the restaurant to them. "What's wrong with you?" he asked, clutching his stomach.

"Wh-what?" she stuttered, surprised by his question.

"Are you a überreligious nutjob who's waiting for marriage?"

Her heart sank. "No," she said, subdued.

"Is there something physically wrong with you?" He screwed up his nose and scanned her from head to waist like he was trying to spot a defect with her body. "Are you a fucking freak?"

Freak? Had he really just called her a freak? She glanced around the room and saw several amused and pitying faces watching her. Anger burned in her gut. She'd liked him! Confided in him, and he'd thrown her confession back in her face! She snatched the napkin off her lap, slapped it on the table, and gathered her belongings. "I've changed my mind. I *don't* like you, and I *never* want to see you again." She eyed the watching crowd again. "Thank God I didn't waste more of my time on a selfish arsehole like you."

With her head held high, she stormed from the restaurant. It wasn't until she was seated in the back of a taxi that her shoulders slumped and tears pricked at the back of her eyes. Was this what she was going to expect from men she dated? Would they all see her as a freak and think something was wrong with her? Her mother had always told her people should have sex when they were ready and not a moment before. But apparently Owen didn't subscribe to that philosophy.

She wished she could talk to her mother right now, but she knew her mother would drop everything and fly out to be with her. She couldn't bear to have that.

She propped her elbow on the doorframe and dropped her chin in her hand. She stared sightlessly at the passing traffic and blurry New York lights. Would her life be so bad if she didn't have a husband and children? Could she be fulfilled without them? She'd seen her brothers and friends happy, and Isla had said it was her biggest regret before she died. God, she missed Isla. So many times, she'd pick up the phone to call her, only to remember she'd never hear her voice again. Her friends here, while great, weren't the same. She needed to go home and curl up in bed before the night got any more depressing. Hopefully by morning, it would be a brighter day.

The next morning, while Chloe lay in bed, her phone vibrated on her bedside table. Stretching and yawning, she rolled on her side and picked it up, groaning when she saw Ethan's name. What did he want now? Was he checking up on her after her date even though she'd told him to butt out of her life? She wanted to ignore him, but he wouldn't stop calling until he'd talked to her.

"Hello." She fell back on her pillow.

"Are you alone?"

She rolled her eyes. Would he ever learn to speak cordially on the phone? "Good morning to you too."

"Well, are you?" His voice was distant like he had her on speaker.

"Yes. Not that it's any of your business."

"Chloe... I'm...arrhh...sorry about last night."

She pulled the phone away and looked at the caller ID to make sure it really was Ethan. "Did Holly put you up to this?"

"Ummm..." Ethan said. While in the background, she heard her sister-in-law shout out, "Yes!"

"Oooooh, busted!" she teased. "Hi, Holly. Kiss my niece for me!"

She heard her brother shoo his wife away and pick the phone up, presumably taking it off of speaker. "Laugh it up. See if this isn't the last time I apologize to you, you ingrate." His tone shifted. "But really, I've had it made abundantly clear that I was out of line asking Theo to spy on you and owe you a giant apology. I hope I didn't ruin your date."

"You didn't. He managed to do it all on his own." Oh shit, she'd forgotten just who she was talking to; she blamed it on the out-of-character apology.

"What happened?" Ethan's tone deepened, and she knew he was getting into protective mode.

It was too early in the morning for his crap. She needed coffee if she was going to deal with Ethan in full Papa Wolf mode. She swung her legs from the bed, padded into the kitchen, and flicked on the coffee machine. "We're not as compatible as I first thought." No way could she tell Ethan the truth.

"Can I do anything? I'll come down and keep you company for a couple of days. Boston isn't that far away."

"Don't. Please, just don't," she said, pulling her I Love Australia mug out of the dishwasher. "I'm fine, but you can stop treating me like a kid. I'm going to keep dating, and I don't want to be looking over my shoulder for you or someone you've sent to spy on me."

"It's hard to let you go when I practically raised you," Ethan said sadly.

"And I love you for it. It just sometimes gets a little too much." Chloe sighed, slid onto a stool at the breakfast counter, and sipped her coffee. After their father died, Ethan had taken on the role of protector and provider. Even though she and Aiden were now adults with great careers, he still watched over them, making sure everyone was okay.

Ethan was silent for a moment. "I know. I thought I'd worked on pulling back. I guess it wasn't enough. I just worry about you being alone."

"I'm not alone. I have friends who check in on me and clients that keep me busy."

Ethan let out a breath. She could sense his concern through the phone. "Promise me you'll be careful."

"I promise." And she actually meant it. She had no intention of making the same mistake that she had with Owen by trusting someone else to play matchmaker for her. This time she was going to rely on herself.

"Call me anytime if you get into any trouble. I'll be on the next train down."

She laughed. "Stop worrying."

"Promise you'll call me," he insisted.

"Okay, I will." She wouldn't. If she called Ethan, he'd wrap her in cotton batting and ship her all the way back to Australia.

"You can always contact Theo if I can't get to you quick enough."

Yeah, not in a million years. "Ethan, nothing's going to happen. Don't you have a movie you need to shoot?" She needed to end the call before her brother changed his mind and took the train to New York anyway.

"All right, I'm going. Love you."

"Love you, too."

After hanging up, Chloe took her coffee into the living room and curled up on the sofa. She flicked through her phone and opened the apps to the few dating sites Blair had recommended what seemed like eons ago. Twenty-six messages greeted her. Twenty-six men who'd seen her picture and profile and decided to shoot their shot.

Could she go this way in the dating world? She flicked through the first several messages. Hookup. Hookup. Creepy picture. Marriage proposal. Hookup. Was that a penis? Oh, God!

She tossed her phone on the sofa. Why did finding love have to be so hard?

CHAPTER TWENTY-THREE

Theo sat in his office with Blake and Owen, going over a potential acquisition. Instead of listening to his accountant, all he could think about was Owen's date with Chloe. Had it been good? Had they kissed? Or worse, had he taken her home and slept with her? His jaw clenched, and he had to remind himself it was none of his business.

"What do you think?" Owen asked, cutting into his thoughts.

"I don't like it. Tell them we're not interested." He leaned back on his chair, threw a leg over his knee, and rubbed his chin. The casual posture belied the tension pinching down his spine when he stared at Owen.

"What?!" Owen and Blake both said at the same time.

"Are you mad? They're practically giving us the company," Blake protested.

"And they're willing to settle in half the time," Owen added.

"I don't care if they want to settle tomorrow for a dollar. The answer is still no."

"Are you sure?" Blake asked.

Even though Theo hadn't listened to Owen's report, he'd done some research of his own. "The company is selling cheap because their whiskey is inferior—among other problems."

"We could fix that," Blake said.

"We could, but the company's reputation is slipping fast, and I don't want to focus too much of my attention building it back up."

Blake shrugged and said to Owen, "I'm happy with that decision."

"Right, okay, I'll let them know." The accountant rose to leave.

Like Theo's mouth had a mind of its own and he had no control over it, he asked, "How was your date with Chloe?" Why did he have to torture himself?

Owen shook his head and chuckled. "I won't be seeing her again."

Theo stilled at Owen's mocking tone. "Why not?"

"Did you know she was a thirty-year-old *virgin*?" The chuckles morphed into belly laughs. "Who's still a virgin at her age? There must be something seriously wrong with her. Man, I dodged a bullet," he sneered. "What a freak."

Owen's announcement slapped him in the face. Anger curled in his gut, and he slowly unfolded from the chair, taking a few steps toward the accountant, towering over him. "If you call Chloe a freak again, I swear to God I will rip your fucking heart out."

Owen's laughter ceased, all blood draining from his face, and he swallowed hard. "I—she..."

"Get out of my office before I cancel your firm's contract," he said with a low and deadly tone.

Tail figuratively between his legs, Owen scuttled from the room.

Theo watched his retreating back, regretting not putting a fist through his face. Maybe he could still cancel Owen's contract? But he could do that later. He stormed toward the door.

Blake hurried after him, placing a hand on his shoulder. "Where are you going? If you touch him, he could sue our asses off. You got damned close to the line threatening him like that."

"He deserved worse." Theo shrugged his arm off. "I'm going out."

"We have a meeting in ten minutes."

"Go on your own or cancel. I don't give a fuck."

Lost for words for an instant, Blake gaped at him like a fish, his mouth opening and closing in shock. "But...but...you never miss a meeting. Or leave work. What the hell is going on with you?"

Theo didn't give a shit about work. He needed to get to Chloe.

Chloe was finishing up with her client—a young, up-and-coming romantic comedy actress—when her apartment buzzer went off. Before she could get off her sofa to answer, it buzzed again.

Putting her coffee cup down, Chloe said, "Excuse me, Emily, I'll see who that is."

"No worries." Emily smiled and poured herself another glass of champagne.

Racing into the living room, Chloe pressed the intercom button. "Hello?"

"Chloe, let me up." Theo's voice crackled through the speaker.

What was Theo doing here? Was there a sense of urgency in his voice? "Is everything okay?"

"It will be when you let me in."

She glanced over her shoulder toward Emily. "I'm with a client. Can it wait?" She wouldn't have even given him the option if she and Emily were in the middle of a negotiation.

"No. Get rid of them."

It must be serious. Was Blake okay? "Okay, come up." She pressed the button that opened the foyer door.

Back in her living room, she said to Emily, "I'm sorry, something urgent has happened. Let's meet for lunch later this week to celebrate season two—no more having to return to DJing pop-up raves!"

Sounding like she was suppressing a giggle, Emily asked, "Is everything okay?" She set her glass down and flung her bag over her shoulder.

"I'm not sure. I hope so. I'll call you tomorrow."

As she led Emily out, they were met with a loud knock at the door. What the hell was wrong with Theo? As soon as she opened the door, he barreled inside. She said a quick goodbye to Emily and closed the door behind her.

Taking in Theo's disheveled appearance, she asked, "What's wrong? Has something happened?".

He paced in front of her, loosening his tie even more to flick open another button. "Why didn't you tell me Owen was an asshole?"

She didn't know what she was expecting, but it wasn't that. "What?"

"Is what he said true?" He stopped in front of her, his face hard.

"What did he tell you?" From his stone-cold expression, she knew exactly what he was talking about. Owen had told him about her virginity, the louse.

"He told me you're a virgin. Is it true?" Why did Owen have to tell him? *Shit.* Next, he'd probably put it on a billboard in Times Square. The little snake. God, she wanted to run to her room and lock the door. Hide. Would Theo's reaction be as bad as Owen's?

When she didn't respond, he asked again, "Is it true?"

Her heart pounded against her ribs, and her palms grew sweaty. She glanced down at her feet. "Yes, it's true. I'm a thirty-year-old freaking virgin. Pathetic, huh?"

She waited for him to laugh. When he didn't, she lifted her head. His face was devoid of any emotion. Well, that was better than disgust.

"How is that possible?" Disbelief laced his words.

Chloe blew out a long breath and dropped to the sofa. "I'm not waiting for marriage, and there's nothing wrong with me physically like Owen assumed. Maybe I'm just a freak." Because she really felt like one after last night. It didn't matter what her friends said, at the end of the day knowing something and feeling something were two different things. And while she knew that there was nothing wrong with her still being a virgin, Owen's reaction sure made her feel wrong.

Theo dug his hands into the pockets of his trousers, a vein ticcing in his jaw. "You're not a freak. Owen has a lot to answer for."

It was good hearing him say it, even if she still didn't believe him. She gave him a small smile. "Thanks."

"Chloe, you're beautiful. A wonderful woman." He pulled his tie off and tossed it on the coffee table. "I find it hard to believe that you haven't had sex."

While she knew that he didn't mean to hurt her, his words still stung. She wrapped her arms around herself. "It's not that I don't want to have sex. I just haven't had the opportunity. You remember how overprotective my brothers were when I was a teenager?"

Theo nodded.

"Boys were too scared to look at me twice." At the time, there had been only one boy she'd wanted. The one boy she would've been happy to have her first time with. But he'd left, and she'd never got the chance.

"And when you got older?"

"I buried my head in books and was constantly studying. Boys my age partied and slept around with whoever opened their legs. I wasn't into that. When I first started working as an agent with only local Australian talent, no one interested me. By the time I was interested in a relationship, the hours and amount of travel I needed to do for work had become all-consuming. Dating became too difficult."

He stood staring down at her with a blank expression.

Wishing he'd say something, reveal something, she started pacing. "*Now* do you believe I'm a freak?"

"No, I don't." He ran his fingers through his already messed-up hair. "That night we met in the club, we went to my apartment to have sex."

She nodded.

"Shit." He put his other hand on his hip. "I'd thought I'd picked up a random girl who was down to fuck. We would have had fun, but in the end, it would have meant nothing. Why would you want your first time to be like that?"

Chloe rubbed her palms on her legs. "It was my birthday. I'd just told my friends about my *situation* and my plans for the future. They'd encouraged me to let loose, have fun, and hook up with a few guys before I committed to one." She stood up and walked to the window, looking sightlessly at the traffic below. "I would have been fine with a one-night stand, but I didn't like the thought of having sex with a stranger, nor did I want to stay a virgin much longer. When I saw you, I knew what you wanted from me, so my first time would be with an old friend and someone I—" she stopped herself from saying "love" because nothing could happen between them. Love wasn't an option. "Someone I trusted," she amended. "Then you recognized me and, well, we know what happened next." She turned back to look at him. Embarrassment from that night still rippled through her.

"You trusted Owen enough to have your first time with him?" He did the clenching of the jaw thing again, speaking through gritted teeth.

Thinking back on her time with Owen, it was obvious there'd been no chemistry between them. He hadn't made her melt with one glance. Her heart had never raced when he'd said her name, and her body had never hummed with pleasure with a simple touch. And she hadn't trusted him, she'd been burned so many times that she'd needed to reveal her deepest secret to determine if she was willing to trust him with her heart and her virginity. And Owen had failed. Hard. "It wouldn't have happened."

"Why?"

"It just wouldn't." Even before he'd showed his true colors, deep down she'd known she hadn't wanted to marry or have sex with him. She'd tried forcing something that wasn't there. God, was she that desperate to be married that she'd ignore her gut? Obviously she was, because she'd planned on seeing Owen again. Why did she have to be wired the way she was? There wasn't an easy way to forge a deep emotional bond in only a few dates.

"Why?" he repeated.

"Because even before he turned into an arsehole, I just thought he was nice. That's all. Just nice. He didn't make me feel things. There were no fluttery feelings in my stomach. My heart didn't race with a simple touch of his hand. Worse, I wasn't sure I could trust him. He made me nervous," she said. "He made me sneeze. I wasn't comfortable with him. Not like I am with you. He didn't make me feel things like you do." God, she hadn't meant to say the last part out loud, but the words flew from her mouth. Sick of keeping her feelings to herself, she threw caution to the wind and continued, "When I pictured my first time, it was always with you. I wanted you to be my first when I was eighteen, then when we met again at the club, and... now."

Theo grew still. "Chloe—"

"Don't say it." She held up a hand. "Don't say you can't because of Ethan. That's a bullshit excuse. Don't say you can't because you don't want marriage and kids. I know where you stand." Even though it broke her heart. "I'm not asking for a commitment. You admitted it yourself, there's an attraction between us. We should be able to act on it if we want to. If you're going to ignore what's between us and not face it, you're a coward. Are you a coward, Theo? Or are you going to take what we both want?"

They stared at each other, their chests heaving with every breath. Would he take the challenge, or would he walk away?

Please don't walk away. She didn't think she could handle any more rejection.

With two long strides, Theo stood before her. Her heart skidded to a stop at the fierce gaze he pinned her with. He cupped the back of her head, his eyes dropping to her lips right before he claimed her mouth. Opening her lips with his tongue, he slid it inside her mouth. The kiss—so passionate—knocked the air from her lungs. She clutched his hips to stop herself from swaying on her feet.

He didn't walk away!

His hands moved from her head to her shoulders, pulling her closer. Warmth washed over her skin. None of her other kisses could even hold a candle to this one, and she never wanted the kiss to end. Then his lips broke from hers to scrape his teeth along her neck, teasing her. She moaned. She felt him smile against her skin before he licked her racing pulse. Her head tilted back; desire pooled between her legs.

"Are you sure you want to do this?" he murmured against her ear.

"God, yes. I've been ready for years." Wild horses couldn't drag her away from him right now. Nothing would stop her from achieving her goal of losing her virginity. A giddy bubble flittered in her stomach.

This was actually happening!

He chuckled, low and sexy, the sound vibrating through her. "That's what I wanted to hear." He pulled away and glanced around the room. "I don't want your first time to be on a sofa or up against a wall."

The wall idea sounded hot, but he made a fair point—her bed would be more comfortable, and also bigger. She linked her fingers with his and led him to her bedroom. The afternoon sun filtered through her blinds, bathing the room in bright, blinding rays. In a few moments, Theo was going to see her naked in broad daylight. Sure, he'd already seen and done a lot to her, but it had all been at night or in poor light. Suddenly, she felt shy. Not because this was her first time—her body practically hummed with excitement. It was because she was finally sleeping with Theo. Would her lack of experience show? Would he enjoy it as much as she knew she would?

Like he knew something troubled her, he said, "We can take things slow. Experiment. Let you figure out what you want, what you like." He placed a finger under her chin and tilted her face to meet his eyes, and the tender look in them smacked her in the chest. This man was so beautiful, kind, and giving. He was everything she wanted. She had to ignore the way her heart somersaulted in her chest, or she'd lose herself in the fantasy of spending the rest of her days—and nights—with Theo.

She traced his cheek with trembling fingers. "I don't want to take it slow. I want you. We can experiment later." And she hoped to God there would be a later.

He rested his forehead against hers. "It's your first time. It might hurt."

"My first time with a *man,*" *she clarified with an arch smile.* "I have a battery-operated *friend* in my nightstand I've used for years."

Tilting his head back, he squeezed his eyes shut like he might be picturing her using it. "Good to know." He claimed her lips again, even hungrier than before, and began unbuttoning her blouse, groaning with frustration when his fingers fumbled over the little white pearl balls.

"Let me help you." She held his gaze and one by one popped them open.

Theo stood transfixed as she shrugged the blouse off her shoulders. She reached around to the back of her skirt, unzipped the zipper, and let it slither to the floor. If she'd known this would be happening today, she would have worn sexy lace underwear. Instead, she stood before him in pink cotton undies and a white bra. Not sexy at all. But it didn't seem to matter to Theo. He watched her with desire burning from his gaze like she was wearing the most erotic thing ever. It made her feel powerful. He made her feel that.

His words amplified that feeling. "You're gorgeous." He moved closer, placed a hand on the curve of her neck where it met her shoulder, and skimmed it over her collarbone to circle around her breasts. His other hand joined in the exploration, gently caressing down her waist and over her hips.

Chloe bit her lip to stop from moaning.

"Beautiful," he whispered.

She brought his right hand to her lips, kissing the pad of each finger as she unfastened his cuff link. Repeating the process on his left hand, she carefully placed the monogrammed gold links on her nightstand. Now she could truly get to work. Next, she tackled the buttons of his white shirt. One. Two. Three. Each button revealed more and more, like an exquisitely wrapped present.

Pushing the soft fabric down his arms, her hands lingered on his broad shoulders, and then mirrored his earlier movements, trailing her fingers over his chest, around his nipples, and down to his waist. She took it one step further, though, and flicked open the button of his trousers. Her fingers shook as she unzipped the fly and slid her hand inside the waistband of his underwear, caressing over his erection. He hissed at her touch and squeezed his eyes shut. Taking a firmer grip, she stroked from the base to the tip. His cock jerked in her hand, urging her to continue.

As her strokes grew faster, he clutched her wrist, stopping her. She glanced at him, confused.

"I don't want to finish in your hand," he said.

Fair enough. She'd rather he finish in her.

He pressed a kiss to her mouth and said, "Give me a sec." Kicking off his shoes, he stepped out of his trousers. "So you say you want it rough?"

"I want whatever you want."

A mischievous glint entered his eyes. "Okay then." And with that, he shoved her shoulders so she fell onto the bed, bouncing a couple of times.

She dashed up the mattress, waiting for him to join her, but he stood at the edge of the bed, staring at her. His gaze raked the length of her body. Heat spread across her skin as if he'd touched every inch of her.

When he hadn't moved for what seemed like ages, she asked, "You're not changing your mind, are you? Because if you are, I'm gonna be pissed. You can't leave me in this state again." She rolled over and opened the drawer to her bedside table slightly. "I don't want to have to pull out my vibrator to finish what you've started."

He stiffened his shoulders, clearly taken aback at her threat. "You won't need a vibrator," he said with confidence—like her seven-inch, multispeed rabbit couldn't compete with him. And from the size of his erection pressing against his black boxer briefs, she suspected he was right. Thank God she was positively dripping, otherwise she'd be concerned that he wouldn't fit.

She closed the drawer and settled onto her back in what she hoped was a sexy pose. "Then hurry up, get those boxers off, and join me on the bed." She'd waited years for this day to happen. If he made her wait another second, she'd explode with frustration, *not* the mind-blowing orgasm she'd dreamed about.

Hooking his fingers in the elastic of his undies, he slid them off to stand in front of her in all his naked glory. And oh God, it was glorious. She almost swallowed her tongue because she was drooling so much. He was gorgeous. The most beautiful man she'd ever seen. The *only* man she'd seen in the naked flesh. But even the immaculately carved Renaissance statues couldn't hold a candle to him. She'd bet her last dollar no one, alive or dead, could ever compare to him.

He chuckled low and deep, sending shivers of anticipation along her spine. "Are you having a good look?"

Oh, she was looking all right. She wanted every part of him imprinted in her mind forever. "The years have been kind to you." It was the politest, least thirsty thing that came to mind.

His eyes darkened as they flicked over her. "I could say the same about you."

She had wanted him to join her on the bed, but with his erection practically poking her in the eye, she knelt before him and took him in her hand.

He threw his head back and hissed as she stroked him long and slow. "That feels so fucking good."

She felt the same. He was so large and hard in her hand, and she reveled in the feel of him.

Leaning down, Theo cupped her face and kissed her with a deep, bone-melting kiss. When she was just about out of air, he pulled back. "Lie down," he demanded.

He didn't have to tell her twice!

Waiting with anticipation, Chloe watched as Theo got on the bed. But instead of lying on top of her like she expected, he knelt between her thighs, placed his hands on her knees, and pushed her legs open. His palms slowly inched their way up her thighs to cup her sex, massaging it in languid circular motions. Lust slammed into her, and she lifted her hips from the bed. *Oh God, could this get any better?*

It could.

Bending down, he replaced his hands with his mouth. Once again, Chloe's hips bucked off the mattress, and she clutched the sheets in her fists. After a moment, he seemed to become frustrated with the fabric in his way, so he tore off her panties and tossed them to one side to expose her to his gaze. He grinned, pleased. Diving back in to kiss her with an open mouth, he worshiped her with unmistakable relish. She cried out when his tongue licked over her sensitive bud.

"Do you like that?" he mumbled between licks, not giving her time to answer before plunging back in.

She tried to respond anyway. "Oh... Theo... too much... I'm going to..." She couldn't form a sentence; his tongue turned her mind to mush.

"Not yet, love." Her heart hammered at the word "love." While she knew he didn't mean it in the heat of the moment, it didn't stop her from noticing it and hoping.

All thoughts of words and their meaning were excised from her mind when he drew her clit into his mouth. She cried out at the feeling—a wordless cry that did nothing to articulate the emotions roiling inside her. Sensing how close she was to falling over the edge, his lips moved from her hot center, traveled over her stomach, and inched ever higher to her breasts. Sucking on one nipple while twisting the other between his fingers, Theo drove her toward even greater heights. Chloe raked her fingers over the rippling muscles of his back and ass, encouraging him to take the next step.

When he kept paying tribute to her chest, it all became too overwhelming. Chloe grabbed a handful of Theo's hair and tugged it so he faced her, their eyes locking with intensity.

Understanding what she needed, he positioned himself between her legs. He met her eyes, "Are you ready?"

"More than."

Taking her at her word, he entered her hard and fast. She cried out as he filled her; her rabbit hadn't prepared her for the real thing. He was so hot, his length throbbing through her core. Chloe stilled, taking a moment to adjust to the new sensation. *Oh, wow!* This was it. This is what it felt like to have a man inside her. And not just any man, Theodore Campbell. Was this really happening? Was she dreaming? If she was, she never wanted to wake up. She'd never felt so alive in her life.

"Are you okay? Did I hurt you?" Concern flittered over his face.

She shook her head, unable to speak. The emotion of the moment overwhelmed her. She wanted to sear this memory into her skull so she could replay it over and over in her dreams.

Theo simply waited for her to respond.

When she finally found her voice, she said somewhat breathily, "It feels amazing."

He gave her a cocky grin at the compliment and slid back and forth within her for good measure. In the blink of an eye, Theo froze. "Shit, I forgot a condom."

"Don't worry. I'm on the pill." She had been ever since she'd been fifteen and had terrible cramps.

"That's not... I'm..." He paused as if struggling to find the words. He frowned, then said, "I'm clean."

For a second, Chloe wondered if he was going to say something else. What else could it be?

The thought flew out of her mind the second he moved again. It started out slow at first like he was checking if she was okay. When she grabbed his ass and pushed against him with encouragement to prove she was ready for more, he drove into her harder and faster. Wrapping her legs around his waist, she caressed her hands over his broad shoulders and back. Muscles quivered under her touch. Theo kissed Chloe with a crazed enthusiasm as the air around them thickened with desire. She was getting closer. Closer. She arched herself against his mouth and chest. She wanted to be consumed by him.

Breaking away, Theo dropped his head on her chest to catch his breath, taking deep gulps of air before swirling his tongue over her hardened nipples. She bit her lip but couldn't stop the moan from escaping. Theo pumped into her at a fast pace, and she met him stroke for glorious stroke until the pull of an orgasm trembled through her body.

"Come on, love, you're almost there."

The word "love" was her undoing! Her insides clenched around him, and the orgasm spread deep inside her, fanning wildfire over her already-heated skin.

"Oh, yes... Theo!" she cried out and bucked under the weight of his body as it hit hard, knocking the breath from her lungs. He thrust into her once. Twice. Three times before letting out his own groan of pleasure.

Tangled in each other's limbs, they panted into each other's necks. A satisfied grin spread across Chloe's face. She wasn't a thirty-year-old virgin anymore. And even better, Theo Campbell had rid her of it, just like she'd always dreamed of.

When he could finally move, Theo rolled onto his back and flung his forearm over his eyes with a satisfied groan. God, that had been incredible.

"You're not having regrets already, are you?" she asked, and though she tried to hide it under the guise of teasing, he could hear the hint of apprehension in her voice.

"No regrets," he answered. He turned to look at Chloe, her body shimmered with sweat, her lips red from his kisses. God, she was beautiful. He'd thought she was gorgeous when she was eighteen, but maturity had made her stunning. He'd tried convincing himself that being with Chloe was a bad idea, and he had to stay away, but after having his hands all over her body and being buried deep inside her, he couldn't think of a reason why. "What about you? Want to take it all back?"

She shook her head. "No. It was wonderful."

Theo's chest puffed with male pride. He'd been the one to put the satisfied smile on her face, and *he had been* the first man to ever do it. The word "first" deflated the air from his lungs. The first man but not the last. She was on a mission to find a man to marry and father her children.

"Is everything all right? It looks like you're having second thoughts." She reached over and rubbed a finger over his eyebrows.

"I wasn't gentle, are you sure you're okay?" He needed to think about something else, not Chloe living her happily ever after without him.

She ran her finger down the side of his face and tapped it on his lips. "I'm fine. Great. Thank you for making my first time everything I hoped it would be and more."

He reached over and kissed the tip of her nose. "I'm glad I didn't disappoint you."

Before he could pull away, she hooked her arm around his neck and pulled him to her lips, kissing him with the promise of round two. As their lips parted, his cock sprang to attention, ready to go again.

He reluctantly broke away. "This was a one-time thing." Although it wouldn't be if it was up to his dick.

"Why?" She frowned. "I still have so much to learn, and who better than someone I'm comfortable with to teach me?"

He chuckled at her reasoning.

"I'm serious!" she said, and if she'd been standing, he had no doubt she would have stamped her foot. "I have so much lost time to make up for. I've missed a lot. So many positions to try and places to do them in." Her gaze grew sultry, and her hand splayed on his chest, heading south.

He clamped his hand around her wrist. "What positions and what places?" he asked even though he knew he shouldn't. Why torture himself that way? But his curiosity couldn't remain unsated.

"Well, we've done missionary. But there are so many other things we haven't done." She turned to her side, propping her head on her fist, leaving her body totally exposed. He loved how she wasn't shy about lying there nude in the midday sun. She bit her bottom lip while she thought, and damn, it was sexy. "I can be on top. You can take me from behind. There's reverse cowgirl, just to name a few. Oh, and I liked your idea of up against the wall." She tapped him on the nose. "Then we could do it in the shower or bath, at a party, in the bathroom at a club, in a car... Mmmm... I really want to do it in your car—all that leather..."

He jerked his head back. "You want to try all that?"

She nodded and giggled.

Covering his face with his hands, he groaned, "You're gonna kill me."

"At least you'll die a happy man." She smirked.

Theo shook his head. Damn, it would be a hell of a way to go. There was still something he needed to make sure of before they did this again, not only for Chloe's sake, but also to remind himself he couldn't fall in love with her because he couldn't give her what she wanted. He rolled to his side to mirror her position. "This is only sex, right? Things won't change. This is not a relationship. I am not your happily ever after."

She glanced down and lightly plucked at the hairs on his chest. "I know. I haven't forgotten what I want."

Which meant that while she fucked him, she'd still be looking for a husband. A sharp pain stabbed him in the chest. To take his mind off it, he rose from the bed, pulling her along with him. "Time to tick off something from your list."

"So, you'll do all those things with me?" Her eyes sparkled.

He'd be crazy to agree. He was preparing her for another man. How sick was that? But when he looked at her still glowing from their tryst, how could he say no? She was too damn tempting, and he wanted her again. After doing all the positions and places she wanted, hopefully he would have fucked her out of his system even though a tiny part whispered that would never happen. He plastered a smile on and said, "I'm sure I can manage a few. Where's your bathroom? It's time we got wet."

Her face split into a huge grin, and she bounded off the bed. "This way. Are you sure you're up to it so soon?"

Grabbing her wrist, he guided her to his hard-on. "Glowy, you'd better believe I'm ready."

CHAPTER TWENTY-FOUR

The following morning, Chloe awoke early, feeling deliciously refreshed. She stretched languidly, and muscles she'd never even known she had protested in response. *I guess this is what it's like to not be a virgin anymore.*

"Hey, beautiful," Theo's husky voice came from her left side. "How are you feeling?"

"Fabulous." She smiled and shifted closer to him. "Want to check off just-woke-up sex from the list?"

"Sure. Just let me go brush my teeth first."

That was probably a good idea, and she should definitely take care of a few other things before they settled down into round... three? Four? Five? She'd lost track. As she mentally cataloged the things she needed to do, her phone started vibrating and flashing with an incoming video call. She picked it up and frowned. What was Aiden doing, calling her at... four thirty in the morning? Was everyone okay? Had something happened? Picking up Theo's discarded shirt, she hastily shrugged it on and clicked "accept."

Instead of her brother's rugged face, her six-year-old nephew, Noah, filled the screen, a grin spread across his lips. "Hi, Aunt Chloe!"

Chloe pasted a smile on her face and triple-checked that everything important was either covered or out of view. "Hey, Noah. What are you doing with your dad's phone? Isn't it your bedtime?" she asked. Noah was technically Aiden's stepson, but Aiden had adopted him when he'd married Mya.

"He gave it to me," Noah said slowly, a sure sign that he was lying.

"Did he?" Chloe asked. "Did he really?"

Noah looked down, and she'd bet money that he was scuffing his foot on the floor. "No... he left it on the table when he went to the toilet."

That sounded more like her nephew. He had an adorable-yet-annoying habit of absconding with people's phones. "So why are you calling?"

"I miss you, Aunt Chloe!" His little lip trembled. "When are you coming home?"

She was saved from having to answer by her brother's face swimming into view. "What are you doing? Who are you talking—oh, hey, Chloe!" he said when he saw her face. He looked back at his son. "Why were you calling your aunt in America? Don't you know it's..." Aiden looked at her. "What time is it there? I can never keep it straight."

"Four thirty in the morning," she said, then yawned.

Aiden winced. "I'm sorry."

"As you should be."

Aiden ignored the hint and settled down into full catch-up mode. "So how are things going in the Big Apple? Are you meeting lots of new people? Not too many men, I hope."

The door to the bathroom opened, and Chloe frantically motioned for Theo to shush before he said something and gave the whole thing away. Wouldn't that just cause trouble?

Oh my God, what is it with big brothers thinking that they can control my sex life? She rolled her eyes for effect. "I am not going into this with you. You're as bad as Ethan."

Aiden's mouth dropped open in mock affront. "How dare you say that? You take that back."

Chloe shook her head. "Nope. Not gonna. First Ethan asked Theo to spy on me, and now you're telling me the number of men I can and cannot date. Meanwhile, you got to 'be *friends* with'"—she was mindful of Noah listening—"half the women of Sydney until you settled down with Mya, and no one got to say 'boo.'"

Ignoring the last part, Aiden tilted his head. "Ethan asked Theo to spy on you? I know he's overprotective, but that doesn't sound like Ethan."

"Well, he did."

"Hey, I believe you."

By the door, Theo shifted, and the hardwood floor beneath his feet creaked loudly. He froze midshift, staring at the phone with growing horror.

"What was that?" Aiden and Noah asked in unison.

Her eyes darted to Theo for an instant before returning to the screen. "Um... rats. Huge, stinking rats. My super's been setting traps for them. You know how New York is, yup they've got huge, stinking rats, big enough to haul a slice of pizza under the subway." She'd only seen one rat since moving to New York, and it had been in a subway station. There definitely weren't any rats in her apartment. There had better not be any rats in her apartment. She'd be on a one-way flight back to Australia if there were.

"Whoa, wicked!" said Noah.

But Aiden wasn't so easily convinced. His eyes narrowed, and he craned his head as if he was trying to get a better view of what was just out of sight of the screen. "Are we calling at a bad time?" he asked archly.

"Yes. Yes, you are. It is four thirty in the morning on a Saturday. You are absolutely calling at a bad time. Four thirty is never, ever, a good time."

Aiden laughed. "Fair enough. Well, we should say goodbye, Noah, so your aunt can get back to having a good time," he said in her direction, giving her a broad wink.

"Bye, Aunt Chloe!" Noah said as he waved at the screen.

"Goodbye, squirt. Goodbye, Aiden."

"Take care," her brother said, his voice becoming serious. "And remind any good times you might have that you have two overprotective older brothers and they'd better make sure that you are having a good time. Or they'll have to deal with me."

Chloe rolled her eyes. "Goodbye, Aiden." She hung up. Once she made sure the phone was off, she placed it face down on the bedside table. No more interruptions. "Okay, it's safe now," she said to Theo. "Kids. They have no sense of privacy." She paused. "Or time zones."

"So I gathered," he said, coming over and pulling her into his arms.

She placed a finger on his lips. "Hold that thought. I'm going to go take care of a few things, and when I come back, you're going to show me that good time. Because if you don't, I've got at least one brother who will be very disappointed."

By the time Monday rolled around, they'd definitely checked off the majority of her list that they could do in an apartment, and she was having to come up with new items. This predicament had led her to some fairly interesting websites, which she'd hastily scanned while alone in the bathroom.

So when the day dawned bright and the weather report indicated that it was going to be an unseasonably warm day for the beginning of March, she suggested, "We should go on a picnic."

Theo blinked.

She gave him a wink. "I mean a sex picnic."

"Okay…" A slow, sexy smirk slid across his lips. "I'm intrigued. Go on."

"So, I've always"—"always" meaning since last night—"had these fantasies of having sex somewhere where we could get caught. You know, public bathrooms, airplane lavatories, in an alley—"

Theo interjected, "There aren't very many alleys in Manhattan. We'd have to go to Brooklyn."

She waved the correction away. "We'll figure it out. In any case, there's another one: sex outdoors. And since we're so close to Central Park, it'd be criminal not to take advantage!"

That wasn't the real reason she was suggesting it, though. Because if she was being honest with herself, she was beginning to feel a little bit… sore. No, the real reason she wanted to go on a picnic with Theo was because she wanted to steal a moment that might be close to a "real date." Sure, there'd be sex—and she was looking forward to the sex—but a picnic in the park? That was peak romance. And she wanted the romance.

Unaware of her real motives, Theo thought it over and nodded. "Sounds good. Let me make a few calls."

"What for?"

"It's a bit of a hike to Central Park from here." He gave her a sly look. "And I was wondering if having sex in the back of a limo was on your list."

"Well, it is now."

While Theo made his calls, Chloe took a quick shower and got herself ready. By then, the hired limo had arrived, and they drove first to Theo's penthouse—where he picked up some clean clothes and a picnic basket filled with goodies. Theo had winked at her when he'd said that, and she guessed that the goodies in question weren't fried chicken and brownies but something a little more risqué.

By the time they reached Central Park, it was approaching lunchtime, and that's when they discovered that they weren't the only people to have the idea of playing hooky at the park on this lovely day.

"I don't suppose getting arrested for indecent exposure was on your list?" Theo asked, eyeing the crowds.

Two teachers and about six or seven preschool-aged kids holding on to a rope and wearing bright-yellow pinnies strolled by, and Chloe winced. "No, definitely not. Let's avoid jail."

"Good call."

Disappointment flooded through her; she'd so wanted to have this moment with Theo. She wasn't sure what to do.

Theo turned to her and asked, "So, since we can't tick that off your list, how about I treat you to a New York delicacy instead?"

"Delicacy?" she raised an eyebrow. Where were they going to find a delicacy in the middle of a park?

"Yep." He took her hand and led her toward a man standing by a pushcart under a wide umbrella. "Let me introduce you to a staple New York delicacy: chestnuts roasting under an open light bulb."

The street vendor grinned. "Last of the season," he said. "Better get them while they're here!"

"One, please," Theo said, pulling out some cash to pay while Chloe just stood there and tried to wrap her head around the concept of roasting nuts with a light bulb.

They strolled through the park, eating the light bulb-warmed chestnuts, which were surprisingly good. When they finished, Theo pointed to another food cart. "So tell me, have you ever had a real New York hot dog?"

She shook her head. "No? I've had hot dogs, though. They weren't anything special."

"Ah, then you're in for a treat. There's something about a real kosher hot dog in New York." He approached the vendor and ordered two hot dogs. He pointed to an array of condiments. "Now, you can get pretty much anything you want on these within reason, but in my opinion, it's really all about the mustard."

The vendor nodded her head emphatically.

"The classic New York hot dog is steamed onions and mustard, sometimes a hint of sweet pickle relish," Theo continued.

Chloe wrinkled her nose at the mixture of onions and kissing. "Can I just have my hot dog with ketchup?"

Theo looked taken aback. "I suppose you can..."

"One children's dog coming up," the vendor said.

A couple of minutes later, Theo held his mustard-and-onion-slathered hot dog out to her. "Just humor me. Take a bite."

Chloe took the smallest bite she could and then paused as the flavors exploded over her tongue. Theo was right: it was surprisingly good. She could do without the onions, but the mustard... She held her ketchup-covered dog out to the vendor. "Do you think I could get some mustard with this, please?"

"Ah, I see you have graduated to teenager," the vendor said approvingly.

The three laughed, and Chloe and Theo continued through the park, enjoying the pleasant spring day. This was nice. Almost like a date. And Chloe lost herself in the moment.

When they finished their hot dogs, Theo turned to her and said, "So I know this doesn't really check anything off of your list, but is there something else that you want to do?"

"Other than you?" she said with a wink.

He pointed to a cop on horseback nearby. "I don't think that he's really up for voyeurism."

"And I'm not really an exhibitionist. So let's not." She thought about it. "I know that it's super touristy—"

"Please tell me you don't want to go to Times Square," Theo said, interrupting her. "The Elmos are scary, and you can get M&M's anywhere."

She blinked; that seemed random. "What? Uh, no. I wanted to go ice skating at Rockefeller Center." She blushed and mumbled, "I may have read one too many romantic comedy scripts where the couple goes and does that."

He gave her a look, then said, "Let me check on something." He pulled out his phone and typed something. "Supposedly the rink is still running." He glanced around the park. "But considering the temperature, we might want to hurry."

Theo texted the limo driver, and they headed toward the pickup point. As they were leaving the park, Theo's phone rang. Theo pulled it out, looked at it, and frowned. "I told Annabelle not to bother me unless it was an emergency."

Disappointment welled up within her. "Then you should take it."

He nodded once and accepted the call.

She didn't hear much of the conversation, as Theo had walked away, but she was able to make out his frustrated shout of, "What do you mean, he canceled? We've got a contract!" A few seconds later, Theo rejoined her, scrubbing a hand through his hair. "Fucking DJ."

"Do I want to know?"

"Not here," he said, eyeing the crowd. He led her to the waiting limo, and they got inside. "Remember when I told you about that DJ on our practice date?"

"Vaguely."

"So, apparently Julius Seizure—that's the DJ, by the way—has decided that it would be bad luck to play Alto's Saint Patrick's Day event. I don't know why, apparently he said something about the full moon, never mind that Saint Patrick's Day is two days after that."

Chloe patted his arm sympathetically. If anyone could understand the temperamental nature of creatives, it was her. Exhibit A: Ethan Doyle. Exhibit B: Aiden Doyle. Exhibit C: her entire client list.

Theo rested his head in his hands. "I don't know what we're going to do. We've got a deal with MTV to stream the event on their website. It'll be great publicity for the club—and for our company. Julius Seizure was our headliner. Without a big name, MTV could pull out."

What Theo was describing wasn't that unusual in her line of work. She ran into this kind of thing all the time. Contracts in entertainment lived and died based on who was headlining or starring in any given project. Studios were notoriously quick to pull the plug at any sign of trouble. Hell, it had happened to Aiden. As an agent, she'd spent hours going over the cancellation clauses in her clients' contracts to make sure that they weren't screwed over if some network executive got cold feet.

"I know that this really isn't any of my business," she said tentatively, "but what exactly does your pull-out clause with MTV state?"

He stared at her. "Pull-out clause?"

"It's not the technical term, but it's what will cause MTV to cancel. Is Julius Seizure in the contract by name, or is it just 'the headliner'?"

"Let me find out." He called his office, getting Blake on the phone. Unlike the phone call with Annabelle, this time she could hear Blake's side of the conversation. Blake sounded even more panicked than Theo, demanding that Theo come back to the office to deal with this mess. But once Theo calmed his brother down enough to actually read the contract, they discovered that, thankfully, Julius Seizure wasn't named in it.

"Okay, this is good news," Chloe said, her mind landing on a possible solution.

Theo just stared at her. "How? Saint Patrick's Day is less than two weeks away! There's no way I'm going to be able to pull in a big-name DJ within two weeks. Not with every other club competing with me."

"I may have the answer to your prayers."

"I'm all ears."

"Have you heard of Emily Kaminski?"

"Isn't she that actress who starred in that show on Hulu?" Theo asked, confused. "The Mary Mistress Mysteries one."

"Netflix, but yes," Chloe corrected. "Before she got her break on Marrying Miss Mystery, she paid her bills by DJing pop-up raves. She's not a Skrillex, but she is a name. A big one in certain circles."

Theo considered her words. "I've heard of her at least. But do you think she'll do it?"

"Well, I know she's between projects at the moment."

"And how do you know that?" he asked, suspicious.

"She's the client you kicked out of my apartment"—she gave him an arch look—"well, you remember when."

"So you're my potential savior's agent."

"Yep."

"Isn't this a conflict of interest? Insider trading?"

"There's no such thing in the entertainment industry," she countered with a grin. "Do you want me to pick up my phone and save your arse, or not?"

"How much is this going to cost me?" He scrubbed a hand over his face.

"How much is your arse worth?"

He rattled off a number that she knew was way too low. "Please," she said, rolling her eyes. "If that's what you were paying Julius Seizure, no wonder he bailed on you. You're going to rake in eight figures in alcohol sales and cover fees alone." Saint Patrick's Day was big money in New York, with some clubs even staying open for thirty-six hours straight, only pausing the service of alcohol between four a.m. and eight a.m. on those days. "That's not even counting the streaming revenue or the potential residuals."

Theo winced, and then gave out a much more realistic number.

She nodded. "I'll call her and ask."

"I should let you know I don't bargain. When I name a price, that's what I'm willing to pay," he said, narrowing his eyes.

Chloe laughed. "Clearly you have never worked in the entertainment industry. Everything is a bargaining point: clothing, publicity, residuals, up-front pay, even what kind of scene the client is willing to do. We haggle more than a used car salesman."

"I don't haggle." His voice was flat.

She reached out and patted him on the cheek like he was a child, and in her world, he was. "That's why your acts cancel on you. I bet you money that Julius Seizure got a better deal that covered the cost of whatever his cancellation clause was. There's an art to getting the best deal where everybody walks away happy. And it's an art I happen to be an expert at."

"So how much is this going to cost me?"

"Honestly?" she asked.

"Yeah, honestly."

"Without haggling?"

He nodded.

She named a price that was twenty-five percent higher than his second offer.

He blinked, then blinked again. "That's outrageous."

"You've got less than two weeks' notice. Emily's going to have to assemble a playlist, make sure that the music rights have been cleared, along with set aside time that she could be doing other things to do rehearsals and tech runs." She ticked off each obstacle and annoyance on her fingers. "You're not just paying for a DJ for a night. Putting together a show like this can take months of work."

He made a face, and she knew she had him.

"Fine."

She smiled sweetly. "I'll make the call."

An hour later, Theo had his new headliner for Saint Patrick's Day and Chloe had earned a nice commission, considering she was playing hooky. In all, it was a good day.

She smiled at him, the thrill of victory making her feel frisky. "So, I was thinking." She eased closer to him, sliding her hand up his thigh. "We could skip Rockefeller Center."

"Oh? And do what?"

She took his face in her hands and pressed her lips to his. "So we have this limo, and we never actually got around to having sex in it."

His eyes darkened, and his voice became husky. "No, we did not."

"I think that's something we should remedy." She kissed him again, this time more seriously.

When they surfaced for air, he asked, "Another check off your list?"

"Yep."

"I could go for that," he said and gathered her into his arms.

CHAPTER TWENTY-FIVE

As the credits to episode four of Marrying Miss Mystery rolled, Theo had to concede that the sitcom was actually good. But even better than the show was the person he was watching it with. Chloe was nestled against his side, and Theo let himself forget, just for a moment, that this "whatever they had" was temporary.

He could get used to this. This whole making love in unusual places or trying new sex positions. He had to admit that his current favorite was reverse cowgirl with Chloe riding him while he watched her in the mirror hanging from the back of her door. Or was his favorite her going down on him in the back of a limo? Both were pretty spectacular.

Chloe was spectacular. Magnificent. Marvelous.

Despite having her in many different places in many different ways, he couldn't seem to get enough of her. He felt like he was stocking up on memories of their time together, so when this inevitably ended, he'd be able to survive without her.

Hitting pause on the remote, Chloe climbed into his lap, straddling him. "So," she said, "how are you liking the show?"

"It's not bad."

"Which in Theo-speak means 'it's bloody brilliant.'" She bopped him on the nose.

He grinned, grasping her hips and pulling her closer to grind against his erection. "You know me too well, Glowy."

She screwed up her face at the nickname, but he wasn't about to stop using it. Not when it fit her so perfectly. "You should be nicer when talking about the woman who saved your big Saint Patrick's Day extravaganza," she said.

"Are you talking about yourself or Emily?"

"Both."

She wasn't wrong. The Saint Patrick's Day event had gone off better than he'd expected. Who knew that cute actresses who beat-match with the best of them were so popular? MTV had been ecstatic with the results, and Alto had raked in some great reviews.

As she bent to kiss him, the intercom buzzed.

"Are you expecting anyone?" Theo asked.

She shook her head as the intercom buzzed again.

"Impatient, aren't they?" she said rhetorically. She climbed off his lap and went to the intercom, pressed the button, and asked, "Who is it?"

"Chloe, let me up. It's an emergency," a feminine voice came through.

"Blair?"

"Chloe, open up. I need you!" The woman sounded frantic.

She hit the button to release the door and turned to him. "It's one of my best friends. This isn't like her. She normally would text first."

A couple of minutes later, there was a knock at the door, and Chloe opened it to reveal a frazzled-looking woman around his age, carrying an infant of indeterminate gender while holding the hand of what looked like a four-year-old girl.

The woman shoved the infant into Chloe's arms and bent down to whisper to the little girl, "Why don't you go find something to watch on Auntie Chloe's TV while Mommy has a chat with Auntie Chloe?"

The little girl scampered off while Chloe looked at her friend askance. "Not that I don't love seeing you and the kids, but what's going on?"

"Mitch was in a car accident," Blair said, tears filling her voice. "He went out to get bagels, and someone hit him. The cop I talked to said a car hopped the curb, and that's it. I don't even know how he is; they won't tell me anything until I get to the hospital." She started unloading a veritable pile of things from her arms and purse as she half babbled, half cried. "They've taken him to Mount Sinai West, and you were along the way. I tried calling you, but your phone kept going to voice mail, and thank God you're home. I can't bring the kids to the hospital! And Hazel's on vacation, and Daniela's at the Oscars, and Mitch's parents are in Poughkeepsie. I need you to watch the kids until my parents get here from Jersey."

"Of course I'll watch them," Chloe said, shooting an apologetic glance at Theo. "Give your parents my address and my number." Picking up her phone, she switched it off "Do Not Disturb." Then she gently ushered her friend out of the apartment. "Call me if anything changes."

"I will," Blair said. "Thank you again!"

And then she was gone.

As the door slammed closed behind her, Chloe started cataloging what Blair had left behind, gently bouncing the infant. "You don't have to stay. I know you don't like kids."

That wasn't it at all, but he couldn't say that. Part of him wanted to run away as far and fast as possible, but another part of him knew that he would be an absolute asshole if he abandoned Chloe with a toddler and an infant. "I can stay."

"Thanks." She sniffed. "And I think I need to change this little man's diaper." She grabbed the diaper bag from the pile of things.

"Speaking of, what are the kids' names?"

"Oh, right, yes. So this is Carter." She held out Carter's pudgy hand for him to shake. "He's eight months old, and I really hope Blair has some formula in that diaper bag. Because I only have oat milk in the house, and these"—she motioned at her breasts—"are currently only for decoration."

And wasn't that a giant reminder that she one day wanted to have kids of her own? Kids he couldn't provide. His heart twinged. "And the girl?" he asked to cover his emotions.

"That's Sybil. Keep your phone away from her at all points and times. If you thought my nephew Noah was bad, Sybil is worse. The last time she got a hold of my phone, I ended up having to reassure an HBO exec. that I hadn't lost my ability to form coherent sentences. She's three—"

"Three and a half!" Sybil shouted from the sofa.

"Three and a half," Chloe corrected. "And she hears everything."

That was a hint they couldn't sneak off for a quickie while the kids were there, and they had to watch their language. He didn't think that her friend Blair would appreciate getting her daughter back only to discover that she'd developed a penchant for saying ass, fuck, and shit: three of his favorite words.

Just then, Carter screwed up his face and let out a wail.

"I probably should go change his diaper now," she said, pulling her hand away from his bottom. "And get him some clean clothes. Can you and Sybil play nice?"

He glanced at Sybil. Could they? God, he hoped so. As Chloe retreated to the bedroom, he approached the waiting three-and-a-half-year-old.

"Who are you?" the child asked, staring at him with huge brown eyes.

And inwardly, he panicked. Who was he? How was he supposed to answer? "I'm a friend of your Aunt Chloe's," he tried.

She nodded. "So who are you?"

Hadn't he just answered that? "My name is Theo. Your mommy asked Auntie Chloe and me to look after you and your brother."

"Okay!"

He'd expected that to be harder. He looked at the TV screen to see an animated cat or—was it a tiger?—on it, singing a song about counting to four. "Can you tell me what we're watching?" he asked.

"Daniel Tiger! Don't you know Daniel Tiger?" She seemed aghast at his lack of Daniel Tiger knowledge. "He's a cat like I'm a cat! Meow!" She jumped on the couch, getting on all fours.

"You're a cat? I thought you were a little girl."

"No, I'm a cat!"

He knew he wasn't going to win this argument. "Okay. What kind of cat are you?"

"A tiger! Me-rarrrr!" she half meowed, half roared.

He was fairly certain that wasn't how tigers sounded. But considering that the tiger on the screen was now looking for a special pear and could talk, what did he know?

"You can be a cat too." She pointed to herself. "I'm Sybil Cat." She indicated the bedroom. "That's Aunt Chloe Cat and Carter Cat." She moved her finger to point at him. "You can be Mister Theo Cat." Then she meowed again. "That's how kitties say hello."

He might as well just go with the flow. "Well, hello, Sybil-cat. Or should I say meow?" He hoped that was good enough.

It seemed to be, because her little face broke out in a wide grin. "Come on, sit down! Do you wanna watch with me?"

He wasn't terribly interested in children's programming, but not seeing a graceful way out, he nodded. The little girl snuggled up to him, and they watched the show with Sybil providing not-very-relevant commentary about what was going on on the screen. He did his best to try to keep up, and despite himself, he discovered he was enjoying the experience.

He heard a sigh come from behind him, and he turned his head to find Chloe standing there with a freshly diapered and clothed Carter in her arms. "Is everything all right?" he asked.

"Yep," she said in a somewhat-sad voice. "It's just... you'd make a good father."

Theo struggled to control his expression and his emotions. No. He wouldn't. He'd never be a father.

As much as he'd like to be.

Chapter Twenty-Six

Over the next few weeks, Chloe and Theo covered every position and place she could think of to have sex. They did it in her living room, on top of the kitchen counter, in the shower, and on the desk in her office. Multiple times. When they covered every surface of her apartment, they moved to the back of his Mercedes, in the club's bathroom, and every room in Theo's penthouse. And yet they didn't stop. Nor had she been on another date with another man since they started sleeping together.

If she were being honest, she wasn't dating because she hated the thought of going out with anyone else. She wanted Theo. She'd done what she'd promised she wouldn't do...she'd gotten attached. When he looked at her with his piercing blue eyes, the way he touched her, made love to her... how could she not? Sometimes she wondered if he had feelings for her too. Yes, she knew he liked her; they were friends. Kinda. Friends with benefits might be better. But lately, it seemed like more than that. Or maybe it was wishful thinking.

Her phone rang, and her heart did a little jig. Was Theo calling to meet up? She picked up her phone and saw her mother's name on the caller ID. She was just as excited by this call. With the different time zones, it wasn't easy trying to connect.

"Hi, Mum."

"Hi, sweetie. Happy Easter! How are you? I hope I haven't caught you at a bad time."

"No, I'm taking a break." God, she loved hearing her mother's voice. She missed her.

"How are things going? It's been a few months now, have you settled in?"

"Things are great. I'm loving the city. I think I've finally found my go-to Chinese takeout," she said, sliding onto a stool at the counter.

Her mother laughed. "That's wonderful, although I miss you so much. I can't pretend I don't wish you were back home."

"I miss you too." Hearing her mother's voice and thinking about Sydney made her chest ache with homesickness.

"So, tell me, apart from working, what have you been doing? Are you meeting new friends?"

"I've been hanging out with friends from work most of the time." That and banging Theo like a bass drum.

Naturally, her mother followed up with, "How were the dates you've been on?"

Could she call what she was doing with Theo "dating"? No. Not once after they'd started having sex had they gone to dinner, a movie, or a picnic in the park.

Deciding to go with a half-truth, she said, "They didn't work out."

"Oh, that's a shame. Don't worry, there's someone wonderful for you out there." Theo was someone wonderful, just not available. "Have you caught up with Theodore? Ethan tells me he lives in New York," her mother asked, eerily prescient.

Chloe drew circles on the counter with her index finger. "I've seen him a few times. He owns a club I've been to." It was another half-truth. She hated deceiving her mother like this.

"I've always liked Theo. I remember you had the biggest crush on him." Her mother chuckled.

What? Her mother knew that too? Was her love for him so obvious? "No, I didn't," she lied.

Her mother snorted. "You followed him around like a puppy, and when he left Sydney, you didn't come out of your room for a week. Is he still as sweet as I remember?"

Sweet? That's definitely not how Chloe would describe him. There was an edge, a hardness about him sometimes that she didn't understand, especially when he spoke about marriage and kids.

"He's... nice." The only word she could think of to describe him to her mother. Sexy, hot, and mind blowing was what he really was. "Divorced. Single. No kids," she added, knowing the likely line of questioning her mother was going to take.

"You know me too well," her mother said. "You know, this could be your second chance." She could sense her mother smiling through the phone.

"Second chance at what?"

"To rekindle whatever was happening between the two of you before he left."

"Rekindle what? What do you mean?"

Her mother told her.

At sunset, the city lights sparkled into life. Faint traffic noises drifted up to the penthouse suite's balcony where Theo stood shirtless watching the busy city below. A cool breeze rustled through his hair and chilled his bare chest. He should be in the office working, but he wasn't. It was funny how he didn't feel the need to work all the time anymore. No longer were his days filled with reports, statistics, and the day to day running of a billion-dollar business. He'd begun to enjoy life again—at least temporarily. And it was all thanks to one person.

Chloe.

She'd consumed his mind. Every day, he wanted to pick up the phone to see her, and not just for sex even if that was pretty much all they'd done. He was starting to want more. Chloe made him feel relaxed and comfortable. She made him forget about the shit he'd been through and his day-to-day worries. She even had him even thinking that maybe his infertility wouldn't be a problem. But then she'd tell him about something her niece, nephew, and friends' kids had done, and he'd see the longing in her eyes for children of her own. Better to keep their relationship based on sex and friendship.

The bell to his penthouse rang, and he turned to look into the living room.

"Hello?" Chloe said, opening the door. She was dressed in a long black coat with her hair piled high in a messy bun. He'd told her not to dress up because they were going swimming. Even with no makeup and her hair on top of her head, his heart thudded hard in his chest. She was beautiful no matter how much or how little she wore.

"Hello, Theo?" she called again, setting her purse down and looking around the room.

"Out here."

When she walked onto the balcony, she gave him a thorough inspection from head to toe. "I think I'm overdressed." Slowly, she unbuttoned her coat, unwrapped the belt around her waist, and shrugged it off her shoulders. It slid down her arms and pooled at her feet. When she stood in front of him in a tiny yellow bikini, he almost swallowed his tongue. She gave him a sultry grin. "I'm ready to go swimming."

From the gleam in her eyes, she wanted to do more than swim. He couldn't get her to the pool fast enough. "Follow me." He grabbed her hand and pulled her to a door on the side of the balcony where he pressed a code into the pad. It clicked open, revealing a spiral staircase. Leading the way, they headed down the stairs to the "recreational" floor of the penthouse, which contained a billiards table, a small gym, a sauna, and a heated infinity pool with a corner view.

"So, what do you think?" He wrapped his arms around her waist from behind and dropped his chin on her shoulder. He wanted to hold her like this forever. God, he had to stop thinking shit like that. It wasn't possible, but he was going to cherish it while it lasted.

"Oh my God. This is so beautiful." Chloe's mouth hung open as she looked around the floor that held the pool. He rarely came here—he never had the time. But if she liked it so much, he'd take her here more often. "You can see the entire city from up here." She spun around in a slow circle and looked at the pool. "This is all yours?"

"Mostly. My company owns the building, but Logan lives in the suite below this, and we share this space. The pool table is his." He paused. "I would not recommend having sex on it...it's been....uh... well used."

She laughed. "And what about Blake, does he live here?"

"Nope. He crashes in my guest room if he needs to stay in the city. He's got a house on the ocean out on Montauk. He says the surfing is almost as good as at Macca's."

"And here I thought he'd still be living with your parents," she said, teasing.

"To be fair, if I didn't have this place, I'd still be living with Mum and Dad. They have a huge place up in Mamaroneck. It's right on the ocean, but Blake says the surfing isn't as good." He shrugged. "I've always liked swimming more than surfing."

She motioned to the infinity pool. "And now you've got your own swimming pool."

"I own the building, and technically it has two. One on the sixth floor for the rest of the residential tenants, and this one that's just for me—Logan doesn't swim."

Chloe shook her head. "It still amazes me how successful you've become." She threw her arms around his neck and kissed him. "I'm so proud of you."

He wrapped his arms around her waist. "Thank you." It meant a lot coming from Chloe because he knew she meant it. She didn't try to suck up to him and get close to him because of his money and connections.

Wanting to show her how he felt, he bent his head and placed his mouth on hers, opening her lips with his tongue. The heat of their kiss burned, searing him to his very core. His hands moved to her back to pull the string of her bikini loose. He repeated the act with the tie behind her neck. The top fluttered to the floor. With their lips still fused together, his hands slid up her stomach and cupped her breasts. She moaned into his mouth as he massaged them in slow, circular motions. Carefully, he maneuvered her backward to the large lounge chair by the pool until the backs of her knees hit the smooth wooden edges. Her hands looping around his neck, she sat, and he soon followed her. He positioned her on her back and slid between her legs, covering her with his body.

Her hands skimmed his back as he placed wet kisses along her collarbone. He didn't know how many more times he'd have her like this. Every time they were together could be their last. When she found the man she wanted to marry, it would be the end of whatever the hell this was. But he didn't want to think about that now. All he wanted was to have as much time with Chloe as possible.

God, she was amazing.

His heart swelled with every touch of her body, every gasp of breath she took. When her gaze locked with his, he saw something more than two people satisfying their needs—something that went far beyond friendship. The three little words almost spilled from his mouth.

Almost.

But he yanked them back. He couldn't say those words. Not yet. Not ever. She wasn't his to keep. But while he had her, he was going to savor each and every moment.

They moved slowly, taking their time exploring each other's bodies. He untied the strings on the sides of her bikini bottoms and tugged them off, and she dragged down his swimsuit. This was supposed to happen in the pool—another item on her list—but he was too far gone to move now. They'd just have to tick that box later.

His tongue slid down her neck, over her collarbone, and circled around her nipples. Her back arched off the lounge as he pulled one into his mouth. Traveling lower, he took playful bites of her hip. When he reached a certain spot, he outlined it with his tongue. "When I was younger, this birthmark drove me insane." The heart-shaped mark still did. He planted a kiss on the tantalizing mark.

She giggled, "I can't believe you knew about it!"

"How could I not when you pranced around in skimpy bikinis in front of me?" He traced a finger around it.

"I did not."

"Yes, you did. It was so damn sexy. I wanted to lick it." And he did what he'd fantasized doing all those years ago. He twirled his tongue around the birthmark before moving on to other tempting locations. Lapping his tongue along her body, he drew a line from her birthmark to her lips. Their mouths fused together into a heart-stopping kiss.

Not able to wait a moment longer, he drew her knees apart and nestled himself between her thighs. His eyes met hers, waiting for her permission to continue. She gave it, pulling him closer. That was all he needed; he entered her with a slow thrust. He didn't move for a beat, even though every fiber of his being demanded that he pound into her until she cried out her release. But he didn't. His body shook at the intimacy of the moment. This was more than a quick fuck to tick off her boxes. He was falling for this woman, and he wanted to show her just how much she meant to him with his body since he couldn't say the words.

He dropped his head onto her shoulder, pulling in deep breaths. His body tightened as he pistoned in and out of her. Whimpering with growing need, she tilted her hips up to meet him, and he met her hips thrust for thrust.

God, she was amazing. Magical. Wonderful. He wished he could freeze this moment and keep this beautiful woman with him forever, but he knew it was impossible. But his heart refused to listen. How was he supposed to walk away from her? How could he forget how she wriggled in ecstasy within his embrace? How could he possibly say goodbye?

Unaware of the struggles plaguing his mind, Chloe bucked under him, ready for release. Slipping his hand between their bodies, his thumb circled her clit, bringing her to her limit.

"Theo... this... is... perfect." She panted between words as her body trembled. "Never... want...to...stop."

"I know, Glowy. I know." Although he'd bet that, unlike him, she was thinking about the sex, and not their relationship in general.

Pulling her knees up higher, he drove harder into her with punishing thrusts. Like he needed to castigate her for wanting a life he couldn't give her.

Her body spasmed, and she cried out as her orgasm hit. Her sheath fluttered around his length, and he soon followed her into ecstasy.

As he lay by her side, he waited for the trembling to ease. There was no denying how he felt about her. Even though he would never say the words out loud, they'd burrowed deep into his heart. But he wouldn't hurt her like he had Layla—couldn't live with himself if he couldn't give her everything she wanted. So, he wouldn't say the words—wouldn't even think them. He would just have to live with the fact that Chloe would soon be leaving his life for good.

When they caught their breath, he led her to the pool. "You know, I always used to love swimming with you—even if you were scrawny."

She splashed him with the heated water. "I wasn't scrawny."

He quirked an eyebrow. "Pencil thin," he joked, pulling her to him. And she had been scrawny, there was no other word for it. Then she'd gone through puberty, and suddenly there had been nothing *scrawny* about her.

"Speaking of when we were kids, I spoke to Mum yesterday." She rubbed a finger over his collarbone.

He welcomed the shift in conversation, the better to take his mind off things he'd rather not think about. "How is she? She was always so good to me. Even when Ethan and I got into trouble from time to time."

"'Time to time'?" Chloe rolled her eyes. "More like always. Anyway, she's good. She had something interesting to tell me, though." She paused for a moment and bit her bottom lip like she was unsure whether she should continue.

"And?" he urged.

She fiddled with a lock of her hair. "*And*, she said when you lived in Sydney, you had a crush on me."

"She was right." He chuckled. "How'd she know?"

"She said she saw the way you looked at me." She jerked her head back as though she'd finally processed what he'd said. "Wait... you did?"

"Maybe a little." Definitely more than a little. Actually more like a lot.

"What?" She stepped out of his arms. "Why didn't you tell me?"

"Because you were Ethan's little sister, and he would have killed me." He wanted to add a "duh," but he manfully restrained himself.

"Oh, for fuck's sake," she swore, her eyes snapping. "I'm going to *kill* Ethan. If I'd known, then maybe we could—"

He held out a hand. "Nothing would've changed. By the time I realized how I felt, I was moving to New York with my family."

Wrapping her hand around his, she took a step closer. "How did you feel?"

"Mostly horny," he chuckled. The sparks of young love for the first time had squeezed at his heart.

She burst out laughing. "If you'd acted on it, I wouldn't have been a thirty-year-old virgin."

"We're making up for it now." He tugged her to him and wrapped an arm around her waist. This was where he wanted her to be—in his arms. Forever.

"Yes, we are." She slid her hands up his hard torso and around his neck. "Things could've been so different if you'd stayed in Australia."

"Maybe." Or maybe he would have ruined a great friendship.

Either way, he couldn't live in the past. The future was what mattered, and he didn't have a future with Chloe. If Layla didn't want to stay married to him because he couldn't give her a baby, why would Chloe?

CHAPTER TWENTY-SEVEN

Monday morning, Theo met Blake at a café two blocks from their building. Theo only had time for a quick coffee. He'd spent so much time with Chloe lately; his work had piled up to colossal levels. Not that he'd complain. Chloe was a beautiful distraction.

Theo glanced at his watch and then at his brother. "Make it quick. Why couldn't we meet in the office?"

"It's not work I want to talk about," Blake said, taking a sip of his latte. "If we're in the office, you'll tell me you're too busy to talk."

This must be important if Blake needed his undivided attention. "Are you okay? Is there a problem?" Too occupied with spending time with Chloe, he hadn't had the chance to catch up with his brother.

"Yes, there's a problem."

With concern Theo asked, "What is it?"

Blake folded his arms on the table and leaned forward. "You."

"Me?" Theo asked, taken aback.

"And Chloe," Blake amended.

Theo's eyes narrowed. "What the hell is this about?"

"I know you're spending a lot of time together."

There was no point lying to Blake, he'd see straight through it. "Yeah, so?"

"This is Chloe. Your best friend's sister. Someone who you'd never get involved with unless you were serious about them." Blake took another sip of his latte. "You wouldn't risk your relationship with Ethan if you were just fucking her."

"Watch your mouth," Theo said through gritted teeth.

Blake rolled his eyes at Theo's threat. "See, that's what I'm talking about. You're acting strange. And it's not just this overprotective grumpy thing you've got going on—which by the way, I've heard that Owen's put in for a transfer."

Good. "Do you have a fucking point?"

"What I'm trying to say is, I've seen a change in you. You're more relaxed—happy. I've seen you smile and laugh. And you've finally started going out again." He stared at Theo pointedly. "Something you haven't done for over a year. I like it. Chloe's the reason, and I hope you make it work with her."

He wished he could make it work too, but he needed to burst Blake's bubble. "It's not like that. She knows this isn't going anywhere."

"Right, so you *are* just fucking her then?" Blake raised an eyebrow.

Theo's nostrils flared, and he gave his brother a hard stare. Clenching the arms of his chair, he said, "If you say shit like that again, I'm going to put my fist through your face."

Blake leaned back in his seat and held up his hands. "Jeez, calm down. Stop threatening people, don't make me sign you up for mandatory anger management training," he half threatened, half teased. Then he sobered. "But look at yourself—threatening friends and family, skipping work, actually smiling. You must care for her... a lot."

Theo slammed his lips shut. Yes, he cared for her. His life would be so much easier if he didn't.

"Do you love her?" Blake pressed.

No way was he going to answer that question. "This is what you dragged me here to talk about? My love life? It's none of your damn business."

Ignoring Theo's demand to stay out of his business, Blake asked, "Have you told her about your problem?"

Theo rubbed the back of his neck. "No, and she doesn't need to know."

"Damn, you're thick. What if it doesn't matter to her?" That pointed look was back. "If she loves you too, she might want to try treatment or adoption or other options."

Theo's shoulders tensed. "I don't want to put her through that."

"Shouldn't she decide what she wants to do? Just because Layla chose differently doesn't mean Chloe will." His brother had a point, not that he'd admit it.

Theo cupped the mug in his hands. "She deserves to be happy."

"And what about you? Don't you deserve the same?"

There was a time when Layla had made him happy, and he her. They'd been happy right up until the moment the doctor told them their chances of having a baby were extremely low, and it was his fault. He'd failed her, and she hadn't been able to look at him the same way again. He didn't want to see the same disappointed look on Chloe's face. With Chloe, he was happier than he'd ever been, even more so than with Layla. Not being able to give her the one thing she wanted... he couldn't bear to fail her too.

He placed a few more bricks on the wall he'd built around his heart after Layla left. "It doesn't matter what I deserve. Chloe wants kids. End of story."

"Do you love her?" Blake asked again.

God, he'd tried so hard not to, told himself he was only helping her until she could find her life mate. What a load of shit. He stared into his coffee. Yeah, he loved her. He wanted her more than he'd ever wanted anything in his life.

Blake pointed his stirrer in his direction. "I'm taking your silence as a yes. If she loves you too, *really* loves you, it won't matter."

Theo twisted the cup in his hands. Did she love him? The way she looked at him, touched him—something strong pulled them closer. The night beside the pool when they'd made love had been more than just friendship or lust. But was it enough? Would she accept the fact he might never give her a baby? Would she be willing to go through the pain and heartbreak of fertility treatments or adoption?

A knowing expression on his face, his brother said, "Think about it before you let her go."

Before you let her go. The words stabbed his chest like a blunt knife. If things were different, he'd never let her go.

———————— ◆◆◆ ————————

"I'm falling in love." Chloe dropped her head on her raised knees as she sat on a bench under the shade of an oak tree along Wien Walk in Central Park. "And I don't know what to do about it." Chloe had asked Blair and Hazel to join her for lunch—a.k.a. emergency meeting—on one of her rare days in the office. Thankfully, they were able to clear their schedules for her.

"We both knew this would happen. Especially since I saw you with Theo the day Mitch broke his leg." Blair patted her on the shoulder. Then said, "Pay up, Hazel, I win."

Hazel screwed up her face as she dug into her handbag, pulling out a twenty-dollar bill from her purse. "Damn it. Why couldn't you have waited another week before you announced it?"

Chloe stared with shock at her friends. "Wait... you bet on me?"

Blair gave a sheepish smile. "Just a little one."

"Pfft. You're not the one who's had to hand over twenty bucks," Hazel grumbled.

Chloe's gaze flicked between her friends. "You bet on me falling in love with Theo? Was Daniela in on this?"

"Of course she was. She had you down for next month," Hazel answered. "She's going to be soooo pissed."

"Speaking of... Are you mad at us?" Blair's brow wrinkled.

Chloe leaned back on her hands. "I should be."

"But you love us too much to be angry?" Hazel teased.

"Something like that." Chloe rolled her eyes.

"Before we get into the details, we need food. Hazel, as the winner of our bet, I order you to get us hot dogs." Blair motioned imperiously toward a brightly colored umbrella and the food cart underneath.

"Sure, whatever, I guess this is my treat. You want one?" she asked Chloe.

Remembering her outing with Theo when he'd bought her her first hot dog, she nodded. She felt a low blush spread across her cheeks.

"Oh God, she's blushing! I think we're really on to something."

Ten minutes and three hot dogs with extra mustard later, Chloe was finally willing to talk.

"So, you're in love. When did you finally work it out?" Hazel asked, wiping her fingers with a Wet-Nap.

"I think I've always known," she said, shredding her napkin into a neat pile. "My feelings for him have never gone away even after all these years we've been apart. And seeing him again, what was once a teenage crush bounded to the surface, only this time as something stronger."

"That's so romantic." Blair placed a hand over her heart and sighed. "It's like you're in a romance novel. A really good one!" Blair winked suggestively.

Chloe rolled her eyes at Blair. "Except this story won't have a happy ending. We all know Theo doesn't want marriage and kids."

"And that's a deal breaker for you?" Hazel asked gently.

Was it a deal breaker? It was the reason she'd flown across the world. To change her life and get what she wanted: a marriage and a family. "I came to New York to find those things."

"Maybe he's changed his mind?" Blair said.

Chloe stared at the shredded napkin pieces fluttering in her lap. There was a metaphor in that somehow, but she didn't care to think about what it might mean. Her heart was too heavy. "No, he hasn't." Not once had he said otherwise.

Always the sensible one, Hazel asked, "How are you going to find what you're after, if you keep seeing Theo?"

That was the problem. It had been on her mind for days. She loved Theo, couldn't see a future without him, but he didn't want the same things she did. She needed to step away and stop seeing him if she was ever going to get over him and be able to move on. "I know I have to end things soon." She hung her head.

"Are you sure?" Hazel placed a comforting hand on her shoulder. "Is this what you want?"

"No, but what else am I supposed to do? I can't keep making lists for him to tick off, as much fun as it's been." And it had been fun. "I need more. I deserve more." She wanted Theo to change his mind about marriage and kids, but it wasn't fair to ask him to change for her when she wasn't willing to consider changing for him.

"Yes, you do. Don't settle for anything less." Blair said.

"Just remember, you can always change what your happily ever after looks like," Hazel said, picking up their trash including Chloe's now-confetti napkin. "You can decide your fate."

But she'd already decided, hadn't she? She'd already changed her mind. After Isla had died, she'd changed from wanting to be the highest-paid agent in Australia to wanting to be a wife and mother. She couldn't change her dream again so soon, could she? She couldn't. She wouldn't.

So when the time came to end their relationship, would Chloe walk away from him with her heart intact? Not a chance.

CHAPTER TWENTY-EIGHT

L ater that week, Theo had a surprise visitor. It wasn't often Theo's dad came into the office. Since retiring five years ago, he'd left the running of the business to Theo and Blake. Theo smelled a rat.

Said rat met Theo in his office with a grin on his face. Almost too happily, he dropped into a chair and put his feet on the desk, crinkling some papers.

"Do you mind?" Theo frowned and knocked his brother's feet away. They landed with a heavy thump on the floor.

"When's Dad coming?" Blake asked, unfazed by Theo's bad mood.

Theo glanced at his watch. "Should be here any minute."

Right on time, their father came through the door. For a man close to seventy and in a wheelchair, he carried himself well. His full head of hair had gone completely gray, which gave him a more sophisticated look. Blue eyes, the same shade as Theo's, twinkled as he smiled at his sons.

"Dad, great to see you." Theo gave him a hug.

Blake rose from the chair, did the same, and asked, "How was your trip?" Their parents had just got back from a month-long tour of Italy.

"We had a great time. Lots of pizza, pasta, and gelato." He chuckled and tapped his stomach.

"You can tell us all about it over lunch," Theo said.

"Sorry, boys, I've got other plans for lunch. I just dropped by for a quick hello and to tell you your mother's planning a barbecue at the house this weekend. She said to pack an overnight bag. She doesn't want you driving back at night."

Blake grinned. "Mum always worries too much."

Their father shrugged. "She's never going to change. See you on Saturday." Their father started to leave then paused at the door. "Oh, I nearly forgot." He wheeled to face Theo. "Your mother insisted you bring Chloe."

If his dad said to come dressed in full birthday clown regalia, he'd be less surprised. "Chloe? Why would she want me to bring Chloe?"

His father's gaze flicked between Theo and Blake. "Aren't you two seeing each other?"

"Who said we were seeing each other?" he asked even though he had a good idea who had opened their big mouth.

His father answered blandly, "Blake was on the phone with your mother last night and told her all about it."

Theo glared at his brother. Blake gave him a huge smile back. "Oh, he did, did he?"

"You're not seeing Chloe?" His father frowned.

"Not exactly." Why did Blake have to bring their parents into this? How was he supposed to explain his situation with Chloe to his mother? "It's complicated."

"I don't know what that means, but your mother said she's not taking no for an answer. Don't be surprised if she calls Chloe herself with the invite. She's excited to see her after so many years." He waved at Theo and Blake. "See you soon, boys." With that, he left the office.

Theo dug his hands into his pockets. Safer to restrain them because if he didn't, he'd wrap them around Blake's scrawny neck.

"This weekend's gonna be fun." Blake sat in the chair and kicked his feet back onto the desk. The man was looking for a beating.

"Why the fuck did you tell Mom I'm seeing Chloe?"

Blake shrugged. "She asked how you were doing. I told her."

"And you just happened to mention Chloe?"

"Well, no." Blake rolled his eyes like Theo was an idiot. "She was worried about you after your divorce and wanted to know if you were happy." He paused, then added, "I think she was about to set you up with some of her neighbors' kids, but don't quote me on that."

"She could have talked to me," Theo grouched.

"Mum thinks you'd tell her what she wants to hear so she won't worry. When I told her you were happy, you know what she's like, she pried the information from me."

Theo blew out a breath and ran his fingers through his hair. "I bet you tried really hard to keep my personal business private. You two gossip like teenagers."

"You're just jealous I'm her favorite." He gave Theo a smug smile.

Theo pulled a face. "Whatever."

"So, do you think Chloe will go?"

Theo rubbed his hand down his face. "I'm not telling her."

"Mum will be pissed if you don't bring her," Blake warned.

"I can deal with Mum; she'll get over it." He'd rather her be pissed at him than have to bring Chloe along and have his mother look too closely into their relationship.

Blake chuckled, "Good luck."

Theo's cell rang, and he picked it up from the desk. Swiping the screen, he answered, "Hello."

Chloe didn't even bother with returning his greeting, immediately asking, "Can you please explain why your mother just called me inviting me to stay at her house in Westchester for the weekend?"

"What?" Oh shit, his father had been right! His gaze darted to Blake.

"Did you give her my number?" she asked.

"No, I didn't give her your number. But I have a good idea who did." He glared at Blake. The guilty look on his face told him who the culprit was.

"I'm going to go." Blake mouthed, pointed to the door, and hurried out before Theo could protest.

Yeah, you better run, you fucker. Returning to his conversation with Chloe he asked, "What did you tell her?"

"At first I said I had plans, but somehow by the end of the conversation, I heard myself saying I'd love to see her on Saturday."

Theo pinched the bridge of his nose. What was his mother up to? She obviously knew he wouldn't bring Chloe up to Mamaroneck so she went straight to the source.

"Should I call her back and tell her I can't make it?" Chloe asked, confused. "I mean, I'd love to see her, but this is so weird. Why is she inviting me to a family gathering?"

Time to come clean, but at least he could lay the blame squarely at his brother's feet. "Blake opened his big mouth and told her we were seeing each other. This is her way of checking out what's going on between us."

"Oh. Then I should cancel."

"No. She'll just keep inviting us until she decides that the only way to satiate her curiosity is to just 'pop in' for a chat, and she's got the code to the elevator and the keys to my penthouse." He left it unsaid that his mother might just decide to show up at the least opportune time. "It's better that we just get this over with. When she sees we're just friends, she'll leave us alone."

"Okay, if you're sure." He heard the uncertainty in Chloe's voice.

No, he wasn't sure. But there was nothing he could do about it. "I'll pick you up on Saturday."

He hung up, sinking into his desk chair. He had to convince his mother that he and Chloe were just friends. Easy, right? All he needed to do was keep his hands off her for a couple of days. Oh God, this was going to be impossible. Because lately, touching Chloe was the most natural thing in the world.

He was screwed.

CHAPTER TWENTY-NINE

Theo pulled off the road and onto the longest driveway Chloe had ever seen. Manicured hedges lined the driveway leading to Theo's parents' house. At the sight of their home, Chloe's eyes almost bugged out of their sockets. It stretched over the large property with pitched roofs and gray shingled walls with white trimmings. Wide verandas wrapped around the house with wicker baskets of colorful flowers hanging from the eaves.

"This house is amazing," she said, getting out of the car and tilting her head back to take it all in.

Theo smiled. "Mom found the city too busy for her liking, and they moved out here when Dad retired."

Chloe's stomach twisted in knots at the mention of his parents. Could they convince his mother that nothing was happening between them? Technically, they were actually friends so it should be easy, right?

Oh God, how were they going to manage this?

After pulling their overnight bags from the trunk of the car, Theo asked, "Ready?"

"No" is what she wanted to say. Instead, she said, "Yes."

He must have noticed her hesitation. He put the bags down by their feet and ran his hands up and down her arms. "It will be okay."

She wished he had his confidence. She drew in a deep breath and nodded. "Let's go."

If Chloe thought the outside of the Campbell house was amazing, the inside was gorgeous—pure luxury overload. Her boots clicked over pale-gray marble floors. The walls—painted in a crisp white—were decorated with subtle statement pieces from artists whose works she'd only seen in museums, a Gorman here, a Frankenthaler there. They moved past a living area with plush, oversized furniture in subtle blues and light timber, a painting by Winslow Homer hung over the fireplace. A wall of glass filled the room with natural light and displayed a beautiful view of the ocean.

"Mum, Dad?" Theo called.

After a moment, Theo's mother scuttled from a room; his father followed close behind. Felicity beamed at them both with a huge smile. "Oh, Chloe, look at you. You're so grown up and just as beautiful, if not more, than I remember." She pulled her into a hug that almost squeezed the oxygen from her lungs. Theo's mother pulled back and cupped Chloe's face. "I'm so happy you could join us." Chloe hadn't had much choice, but she didn't bring that up.

"It's lovely to see you too. You haven't changed a bit." A few extra laugh lines crinkling at the edges of her sparkling hazel eyes were the only difference. Her hair sat in a neat light-brown bob below her ears.

"Hey, Mum." Theo leaned down and kissed her cheek while his father, Michael, gave Chloe a hug in greeting.

"Let me take your bags to your room," Felicity said.

Alarm bells went off in Theo's head. "We need two rooms, Mum."

Felicity's eyebrow rose. "I thought you'd be staying together."

"No. We're just friends. Blake doesn't know what he's talking about." Damn Blake for making them go through this.

"Oh." Her face dropped. "Okay, I'll set up another room."

"I can help you with that," Chloe offered.

Felicity waved her hand. "Nonsense, you're a guest. Blake's out back, and I invited Rachel, her kids, and her brother, Jordan. Rachel's husband is away for a few days, so I thought it'd be nice to have them come around too." She paused, a thoughtful expression on her face. "Why don't you go join them out in the backyard? Michael will help me with your room."

Chloe must have looked confused because Theo said, "Rachel is my parents' neighbor."

When they made their way outside, once again Chloe was struck by the beauty of the property. The grass looked spray-painted bright green and hand cut with scissors. The gardens bloomed with colorful flowers and an Olympic-sized pool with white lounge chairs surrounded the crystal-blue water. Theo leaned down and whispered in her ear, "They're not as comfortable as mine." He pulled away with a smirk.

Chloe's face grew warm. "Stop it," she whispered back. "I can't be at your family's home and be thinking of what we got up to. We're supposed to be acting like friends!" The night they'd made love by the pool filled her mind.

"Sorry, it won't happen again." He pulled a serious face.

Chloe rolled her eyes. "Come on. Let's get this weekend over with."

They walked around the pool to a covered outdoor area. The backdrop was a picturesque ocean landscape. The scent of salt drifted in the breeze. Blake, and she assumed the neighbors, sat on plush lounges with drinks in hand.

Theo waved and made the introductions.

Chloe noticed two small boys with black curls playing soccer on the grass. "They're mine," Rachel informed her.

"They're gorgeous," Chloe said, watching them wistfully.

"Thank you." Rachel smiled at them with pride.

"Can I get you a drink, Chloe?" The breeze blew a strand of hair onto Chloe's face, and Theo brushed it away. His hand cupped her face a little longer than allowed if they were "just friends." Like he realized he shouldn't be touching her, he snatched his hand away.

Chloe cleared her throat and stepped back. "Yes, please."

Once they had their drinks, they spent the next few minutes chatting with Blake and the neighbors until Felicity and Michael arrived carrying trays of meat and vegetables for the barbecue.

"You boys are in charge of the cooking." Felicity handed over aprons and utensils.

"Yes, ma'am," they said in unison.

"I'll go get the salads," Felicity said.

"I'll help," Chloe offered.

"So will I." Rachel put her glass of water on the table.

She waved off their offers as she hurried into the house. "No need. It won't take me long. Enjoy the beautiful day."

While the men busied themselves with the barbecue, Chloe and Rachel got to know each other. "Felicity mentioned your husband's away," Chloe said.

"He's a journalist and often travels for work. My brother Jordan stays with me when David's away. He doesn't like me in the home alone with just the kids." Rachel rolled her eyes. "Between you and me, I think he does it because he's a lousy cook and is sick of takeout." Chloe laughed, and Rachel continued, "Big brothers can be such a pain in the ass."

"Tell me about it. I have two of them. One's worse than the other." Rachel made a sympathetic noise. "I moved to New York a couple of months ago, and my brother Ethan doesn't think I can take care of myself."

Rachel shook her head. "Brothers." Then she nodded her head toward Theo grilling steaks. Even wearing a pink floral apron, he looked hot. "How does your brother feel about boyfriends? Mine treated David like he was an escaped prisoner from a maximum-security prison when we started dating."

"Theo and I aren't dating. We're friends." The words stung, but she needed to keep up the facade.

Rachel blinked. "Oh, when I saw you together and from the way he looked at you, I just assumed..."

The way he looked at me? He always looked at her like he wanted to peel her clothes off. "No, just friends." To change the subject before Rachel questioned their relationship further, she said, "How old are your boys?"

"Timothy is five, and Alexander is seven and a half. The half is very important according to him." Chloe laughed. "And I have a four-month-old baby girl, Abigail, who's asleep inside."

"You're very lucky." Having three beautiful children was the dream, but Chloe would be ecstatic to have at least one.

"I know. Sometimes I want to pull my hair out and scream, but I wouldn't change it for the world. What about you, do you want kids?" Her eyes grew round. "I'm sorry; that's a bit personal."

"No, that's okay. I'd love to start a family someday. Hopefully soon, if I can find the right guy." Her gaze flicked to Theo.

Rachel pointed to her brother, who had ditched the cooking and was playing soccer with the kids. "Jordan is single, and I can vouch that he'd be an awesome father. He's great with my boys and Abigail has him wrapped around her little finger."

Chloe picked up on Rachel's not-so-subtle hint. Her gaze drifted over to Jordan. She could see the appeal. He was cute in a surfer-dude kind of way with shaggy brown hair and tanned skin. The boys looked like they adored him as they rang rings around him. He had potential.

But he paled in comparison to Theo. Was that going to be her problem from now on? All men wouldn't live up to him? Every time she was on a date, would she think of him and how he made her feel?

Alexander ran over to Rachel with the ball. "Come and play with us, Mommy."

A small, crackled cry came from a monitor sitting on the table. "Maybe later, I have to go inside and feed your sister." She kissed his cheek and made her way to the house. The boy's smile faded as he spun the ball in his hands.

"I'll play with you if you'd like?" Chloe hated seeing the disappointment on his face. Would she be a sucker for a dropped lip when it came to her kids? Probably.

Alexander's mouth screwed up at the side.

"I'm pretty good. I doubt you can beat me," Chloe said.

He nibbled on his bottom lip. "Okay." And he kicked the ball over to Jordan. "We have another player," he yelled to his uncle.

Jordan kicked the ball up and juggled it on his knees. "Great, happy to have you on the team."

"Glad to be here." Chloe giggled.

"Right, the teams are Chloe and me against you two boys. The rules..."—his eyes squinted, he placed his hands on his knees so he was eye level with the kids, and he put on a fierce expression—"there *are* no rules."

Chloe hid a smirk behind her hand.

"But you're big." Timothy scratched the side of his face.

"You think you can't beat us?" Jordan dropped the ball at his feet.

"We can beat you." Alexander puffed out his skinny chest, slapped his hands on his hips, and bolted toward his uncle. Jordan flipped the ball around until Alexander won it. He took off toward the makeshift goals made with two large white rocks taken from the garden.

"Run after him, Chloe," Jordan called.

"I'm trying. He's too fast." Chloe swung her arms like she was running as hard as she could.

Alexander kicked the ball, and it went flying through the stones. "Yes!" He fist-pumped the air.

"Lucky break. Isn't that right, Jordan?" Chloe said, pulling a mock-serious face.

Jordan folded his arms across his chest. "Yep. We're coming for you now." He charged toward Timothy who had possession of the ball. His little legs ran as fast as they could, and Jordan bumped into Chloe as she chased him too. They tumbled onto the spongy grass, letting Timothy score a goal.

"Woo-hoo!" He danced around the ball.

"I wish you watched where you were going. We could have won that one." Jordan winked at Chloe, bounded to his feet, and held out his hand to help her up. His grip was warm and strong, but Chloe didn't feel a spark of interest.

The game continued. Jordan and Chloe ran, tripped, and lost the ball over the next few minutes. Finally, Jordan scored a goal.

"Eat dirt, boys." He jogged over to Chloe and gave her a high five. "Okay, boys. Time-out!" Jordan announced. "I need a break. Go grab a drink. You look hot and sweaty."

They watched the boys scurry to the barbecue area.

"Oh, thank God. I didn't think I could've lasted much longer." Chloe bent over and placed her hands on her knees, drawing in deep breaths. "I need to exercise more often."

Jordan chuckled. "These kids can wear even the fittest person out." It looked like he might say more, but Felicity called them for dinner.

With the table piled high with excellent food, the conversation was light and fun. They chattered about many different topics. Blake and Jordan debated which beach had the best surfing. Jordan waxed poetic about their recent trip to Italy. Chloe dished some innocent behind-the-scenes stories from her job. And Felicity told stories about their time in Australia.

Rachel's boys were disappointed Australians didn't ride kangaroos to school and have pet koalas, but they recovered well. Everyone was enjoying the evening. Everyone, except for Theo. He sat stone faced and almost sullen, hardly speaking a word throughout dinner. Every time she tried engaging him in the conversation, he gave her the cold shoulder.

She frowned, then quickly covered it up. They were supposed to be acting as friends not enemies. What the hell was wrong with him?

<hr />

Later that night, after Rachel, Jordan, and the kids went home, Chloe and Theo's family sat in the kitchen drinking tea. Felicity glanced out the window. "Oh no, the wind's picking up. I forgot to bring the tablecloth inside." She started to get up. "I'd better get it before it blows away."

Theo slid off the stool. "I'll go."

"I'll go with you." Chloe followed him outside.

They strolled in silence toward the barbecue area. The moon cast a silvery glow over the grass, and she breathed in the smell of the sea breeze. As the wind picked up, she shivered and wrapped her arms around her body.

"Here, take this." Theo shrugged out of his jacket and draped it over her shoulders.

Chloe put her arms through the sleeves and was immediately surrounded by the masculine scent of Theo and woodsy cologne. "Thanks."

Once they reached the privacy of the barbecue, Chloe placed a hand on Theo's arm. "You seem tense. What's wrong?"

"Nothing." He picked up and folded the tablecloth. Even in the dim light, she could see his clenched jaw.

"You haven't said two words to me all evening."

"That's not true." He turned to go.

She stood in front of him to stop him from walking back to the house. "Oh, really? Ever since dinner, you've acted like you're mad at me."

He folded his arms over his chest. "Did you have fun with Jordan?"

The way he stressed the other man's name told her exactly what he was upset about. "Do you mean playing soccer with *the boys* and their uncle, Jordan?" She rephrased the question, trying to soothe his ruffled feathers.

It didn't work. A spasm of pain flashed over his face. "You looked good together. It's obvious he's interested in you." He attempted to smooth his features, although she could still make out the tenseness of his jaw. "You should set something up. He could be husband material."

"He did ask me on a date," she admitted. While talking on the lawn after dinner, he'd asked for her phone number so they could arrange something. Conflicted, Chloe hadn't given Jordan an answer, and before he'd been able to press further, Felicity had interrupted them, giving Chloe time to make her escape.

But Theo didn't know that, so his head whipped around to glare at her. "What did you say?" Her suspicions were right; he was jealous.

"Would you care if I agreed to go to dinner with him?" She should tell him the truth, that she would have said no, but she wanted to know Theo's answer first. His answer mattered. They were more than just friends with benefits now. Somewhere along the way, they'd crossed over the line. She loved him. Couldn't see a life with any other man. Surely, he could feel it too.

Theo scoffed and turned his face away. "No."

Her heart sank. Had she been wrong? Was she seeing...feeling things that were only one sided? To be sure, she said, "So you won't care if I date him? You won't care if we hit it off, if things moved forward."

He nodded. Even with the silvery light of the moon shining on him, his face darkened like a midnight sky. "If Jordan is the man you choose to share that life with, he's a lucky guy."

The man you choose. He didn't place himself in that picture. A weight pressed on her shoulders, and tears pricked the backs of her eyes. Maybe all of those dating sites were right, jealousy wasn't a sign of caring. He might be jealous, but he still didn't want a life with her. "So, you really don't care if I see him again?"

"It's none of my business." His hands slid into the pockets of his jeans, and he looked away.

"I don't believe you. You have feelings for me." His actions belied his words.

"Of course I do, we're friends."

Chloe shook her head. "No, it's more than that. I can feel it." She placed a hand over her heart. If she wanted Theo in her life, she had to speak up now, or she'd regret it forever. "I don't believe you can look at me the way you do and touch me with so much passion if you didn't lo—care for me." She wanted to say "love," but she pulled back when she saw his eyes widen. Better to ease him into it. Maybe he wasn't quite there yet.

"Chloe—" He stepped closer but stopped himself.

Don't stop! She wanted to say. *Hold me. Tell me all the things I want to hear.*

Screwing up her courage, she continued, "My feelings for you have changed." She took a deep breath. "And I know yours have too. This is more than 'just friends.'" She took another step toward him. "Look me in the eye and tell me you feel nothing for me." The breeze picked up and whipped her hair in front of her face. With jerky hands she twisted it and slung it over her shoulder.

Theo blew out a breath and dropped his head to stare at his feet. When his head rose, he said, "I can't."

The tension coiling through Chloe's body eased, and her shoulders dropped. She'd been right. "So why are you telling me to go on a date with Jordan when we can be together?"

Theo kicked the leg of the table. "Because no matter how I feel about you, we can't be together. Go and find someone who is good for you."

Chloe's voice shook. "*You* are good for me. I only want you."

Theo took two strides forward and clutched Chloe's face in his hands. "Don't say that. Please, don't say that!"

"Why?" She stared intently into his eyes. "Because you don't want to get married again or have children? Is that it? Did your first marriage mess you up that much?"

He flung his arms away, turning his back to her. "Yes."

Damn that woman! Chloe wanted to find his ex and give her a piece of her mind, but she needed to try to salvage what she had with Theo first. "It doesn't have to be that way again." She put a hand on his back. "I lov—"

Stopping her from admitting her love for him, he spun around, grabbed her shoulders, and crushed his lips against hers. She leaned into his heat even as the cold wind swirled around them.

When he pulled away, he said, "No matter what you say. This is all we can have."

"I want more," her voice cracked.

He sighed with regret. "I can't give you more."

She couldn't accept that. "Why?"

"Because you deserve to be a wife and mother, and I can't give you that. Seeing you with Rachel's kids today confirmed that." He caressed her cheek. "You're going to be a wonderful mother someday. Whoever you choose to marry will be the luckiest man alive. But that man won't be me. I can't be a husband"—he drew a shaky breath—"and I can't be a father." He said it like it was immutable, final. A fact as irrefutable as the sun rising in the east rather than a choice he'd made.

But it was a choice.

She could stand out here all night arguing until she froze to death, but she knew she wouldn't change his mind. The words she desperately wanted to hear—the life she wanted him to tell her they could have together—would never be spoken.

She couldn't bear it any longer. She spun on her heel and raced toward the house.

Her body shook. Was it from the chilly breeze ripping through Theo's borrowed jacket or Theo himself not being in her future? She knew it was the latter.

And her heart shattered at the answer.

CHAPTER THIRTY

"Morning, sweetheart. Just in time for breakfast." His mother bustled around the kitchen placing plates of eggs, bacon, sautéed mushrooms, and tomatoes on the table. A tray of fresh fruit and a basket of thick sliced toast sat on the counter, and Theo carried them to the table.

"This looks and smells amazing." He scanned the kitchen, noting that someone was missing. "Is Chloe still in bed? I can call her down for breakfast." Last night had been one of the hardest nights of his life. Telling Chloe he couldn't give her what she wanted had ripped a hole in his chest. In the long run, she'd probably see it was for the best and thank him. Still, it hurt like fucking hell letting her down.

His mother sat down and patted the chair next to her. She gave him a long, sad stare. "Chloe left early this morning. She seemed upset."

"What!" He'd hurt her that much she couldn't face him? He shouldn't be surprised; he'd been a right fucking asshole to her. But he'd hoped they could walk away from this as friends, and now that didn't seem likely.

Unaware of the turmoil her announcement had caused, his mother continued, "She said something about needing to see a client urgently and caught an Uber to the train station. I suspect there was more to it. By the look on your face, I'd say I'm right. You know something, so spill."

"I don't know what you mean." He plucked a slice of toast from the basket, put it on his plate, and grabbed the butter and a knife.

His mother gave him a look, clearly unimpressed by his pitiful attempt at dodging her question. "What's going on with you and Chloe?" When he opened his mouth, she held up her hand. "And before you say you're just friends, you should remember I know when you're lying."

He blew out a breath and set the knife on the table. No point trying to deny it. Like she said, she'd know. "It's not what you think."

"Then tell me, because I can see more than friendship going on between the two of you." His mother reached for the coffee carafe, poured steaming brew into two mugs, and slid one toward him.

Blowing on his coffee, he said, "We've been spending a lot of time together...as more than simply friends."

"Is it serious?" she asked, able to read between the lines.

Saying no would cheapen his and Chloe's relationship because they shared more than a fling, but he couldn't say yes either. "It's complicated." And wasn't that an understatement. "I'm not able to give her what she needs."

His mother's brow creased. "What does that mean? Does this have anything to do with your divorce? People often find love again after heartbreak."

"No, it's more than that. But something I don't want to get into right now." If he told her about his infertility, she'd worry and then throw herself into trying to find a solution.

She placed a hand on his forearm. "Do you love her?"

His heart squeezed. "It's complicated," he repeated. "Things are going on with me that aren't good for her. She deserves better." When his mother's eyes grew round with concern, he hurried and added, "It's nothing for you to worry about. I'm fine." He wasn't fine, but he also wasn't dying, which was what she was likely worried about.

Her shoulders sagged with relief. "Well, whatever it is, have you told her about it?"

He drew circles with his finger on the crisp, white tablecloth. "No."

"Why not?"

Blake walked into the kitchen and interrupted their conversation. "Don't bother, Mum. I've had this same chat with him. He's too thickheaded to understand that Chloe will probably take him warts and all if he just opens up to her."

His mother nodded, visibly pleased with her other son. "Love doesn't happen often, Theo. Whatever is holding you back, tell her. If she loves you, you can fix anything."

It was a lovely sentiment, but it was also dead wrong. Love wouldn't fix his problem. Thankfully, his father joined them, ending the conversation.

Were his mother and brother right? Although love wouldn't fix his problem, if Chloe knew everything about him would she accept him anyway? Could she give up her dream of motherhood to spend a lifetime with someone like him?

⚫

Theo rarely took the whole weekend off, so after spending a couple of days at his parents' house, he had loads of work to catch up on. But every time he tried getting work done, thoughts of Chloe invaded his thoughts. He'd picked up the same file three times, forgetting its contents as soon as he put it back down.

He missed Chloe. He wanted so desperately to tell her he loved her, hold her in his arms, and promise to never let her go. Without her he could barely breathe. Theo rubbed a hand across his chest like it physically ached.

Could he do what Blake and his mother suggested and tell Chloe about his infertility? If he did, how would she react? He swiveled his chair around to stare out of the window. The sky had grown overcast. A light sprinkle trickled down the glass.

He loved Chloe. He had to tell her everything. She deserved that much. He needed to let her decide if she still wanted him. Right now, he was making this decision for her, and it wasn't fair—it wasn't right. Things could go one of two ways: this could either end badly, or he'd have the woman he loved in his arms for the rest of his life. It was as simple as that. Either she accepted him and loved him warts and all, or Chloe would react just like Layla and break his heart.

Well, he'd recovered from a broken heart before, he could do it again. There was no point waiting. He needed to know now. Pulling his phone from his pocket, he sent her a text:

I'm so sorry for how we ended things on the weekend. I feel like a jerk for upsetting you. We need to talk. I'll see you at your apartment soon. If that works for you.

A moment later a text pinged his phone.

It's okay. I'm sorry for leaving without saying a word. I'll be waiting.

His heart pounded. This was it. Time to get everything off his chest.

The intercom buzzed on his phone. Annoyed at the interruption, he pressed the button. "What is it, Annabelle? I'm on my way out."

"I'm sorry to disturb you, sir, but Layla's in reception wanting to see you. Should I ask her to leave? She says it's urgent."

What the hell was his ex-wife doing here? He hadn't seen her since they'd finalized the divorce. His gut reaction was to tell Annabelle he didn't have time for her. All he wanted to do was get to Chloe, but he was trying to be a better person. He took a deep breath and said, "Send her in."

He took a seat and waited for the door to his office to open. When it did, Layla sauntered in. Perfectly styled auburn waves bounced around her shoulders. Her creamy skin looked flawless, her makeup meticulously applied. Tall and slim and wearing designer clothes, she had once graced the cover of various fashion magazines. Even now at thirty-nine, she still could. He rose to greet her.

"Theo, darling. It's so good to see you." She placed her hands on his shoulders and kissed each cheek.

"Layla, how are you?" He gestured for her to take a seat while he sat on the edge of his desk.

"I'm great. Busy with work. I've signed up a bunch of new models for the agency, and we're booking them for practically everything."

"Good for you." After retiring from modeling, Layla had started a modeling agency and built it into a successful, well-sought-after agency.

"How's the family? Are Blake and Logan still getting up to mischief?"

Surely, she wasn't here to catch up? He glanced at her hands, and they slid up and down the tops of her thighs, betraying her excitement. "Why are you here, Layla?" Better to get straight to the point so he could get to Chloe.

To stop the fidgeting, Layla linked her hands together. "I wanted to tell you how sorry I am for the way things ended between us. I could have handled it better."

Was that it? She was here to apologize? But he didn't want her apology. Theo clutched the edge of the desk. "You didn't look too sorry," he said, anger seeping into his voice. "You looked more like disgusted because I was infertile, and then relieved when I left." They'd been over this before. Why was she bringing it up again? He'd thought he'd healed, and now she was ripping open the wound.

She dipped her head and glanced at her clasped hands. "I did love you. Truly I did," she rushed to say when he lifted a doubtful eyebrow. "You have every right to be angry. I'm sorry I didn't handle the situation very well."

"You didn't love me enough to want to stay," he snapped. When he told Chloe the truth, would she look at him with disappointment and disgust? Or would she love him enough to stay?

She tilted her face up to look at him. "I wanted a baby."

"We had options, but it wasn't good enough for you." There was no point rehashing the past. "I'm on my way out, if that's all—"

"I'm pregnant," she blurted.

He froze, his gaze falling to her stomach.

She rubbed a hand over her still-flat belly. "I'm fourteen weeks along. It's too early to show."

"Congratulations," he said somewhat woodenly. She'd gotten what she wanted.

She gave a small smile. "Thank you."

He crossed his arms over his chest. "You came here just to apologize and tell me you're pregnant?"

"Yes... No." She sprang from the chair. "Two months after we broke up, I met Jeremy. We fell in love, and after our divorce was finalized, we got married." She lifted her hand and wiggled a flashy big diamond on her ring finger. "Without even trying, I became pregnant."

"So now you have the life you always wanted. Great." It stung a little that her future was set while he didn't know what his looked like.

"Yes, I did, and I'm so happy. I never thought I could ever feel so fulfilled." She placed a loving hand on her stomach. "I came here to apologize, and also to thank you for letting me go."

He pushed away from the desk and dug his hands in his trousers. "What else was I supposed to do?" Beg her to stay without the guarantee of having children? No, he didn't beg.

"You could've made it difficult—made the divorce complicated—and maybe I wouldn't have found Jeremy and gotten pregnant when I did. I'm sorry I hurt you so much, I truly am. But thanks to you, I get to be a mother."

She came here to thank me for her fantastic new fucking life? Unbelievable.

He couldn't keep listening to this. "Apology accepted. I'm happy you've gotten everything you wanted. Good luck with the baby." He kissed her on the cheek, putting an end to the conversation.

She smiled. "I wish you all the happiness, too." He watched her walk out, and then sank down onto the chair.

Thanks to you, I get to be a mother.

Her words struck him like a bullet to the chest. Layla had practically glowed with happiness. How could he take that joy away from Chloe? All she talked about was becoming a mother. He wouldn't do that to her. She deserved the same happiness as Layla. She deserved to feel that life growing inside her. He couldn't be selfish.

Instead of going to her and hoping she'd accept him the way he was, it was time to let her go so she could have the life she deserved. He had to put an end to this. He had to... for Chloe's sake.

He placed his elbows on the desk and dropped his head in his hands. Layla had *thanked* him for letting her go. But it had been easy to do.

By the time he'd sought a divorce, they'd barely been speaking to each other—the love had long since faded. This was different, the love was new, potent. Chloe consumed his heart and mind like nothing he'd ever experienced before. So, this time letting go of someone he loved would not be easy. It was going to be the hardest thing he'd ever do.

CHAPTER THIRTY-ONE

With a heavy heart, Theo stared at the button for Chloe's apartment for a few minutes before pressing it.

A few seconds later, her sweet voice crackled through the intercom. "Hello?"

"It's me."

"Come up." The front door clicked when it unlocked. He pushed it open and made his way to the elevator and stepped inside. All too quickly, he was on her floor, knocking at her door.

After a few seconds, she swung the door open. "Hi," she said with a timid smile.

"Hi." His voice was gruff, and he cleared his throat.

Stepping aside, she let him into her apartment. She was dressed in gray leggings and a baggy pink sweatshirt. His heart somersaulted in his chest. He wanted to pull her into his arms and kiss her. It took all his strength to hold back.

"I've ordered pizza, it should be here soon."

The thought of food made his stomach churn. "Sounds good," he lied.

She fiddled with the hem of her sweatshirt. "Can I get you something? Coffee? Water?"

"No, I'm good. Thanks." He took a deep, steadying breath. "Chloe, about last weekend—"

She held up her hand. "It's okay. You don't need to say anything. We want different things. You've always been up front about the way you want to live your life. It's my fault I crossed over the friendship line." She dropped onto the sofa and stared at her feet.

God, he wanted to kick his own ass for causing her so much pain. If he could take it away, he would. Sitting next to her, he clasped her hand. Grateful she didn't snatch it away. "It's not your fault. I crossed that line too. All those things you want in your life... I want to give them to you."

Her head spun toward him. "You do?"

He nodded.

Hope sparked in her eyes. Before he could continue with what he had to say, she threw her arms around his neck. "Oh, Theo. I love you! I always have."

Her words knocked the breath out of his lungs. Before his visit from Layla, they would have been the most amazing words he'd ever heard. Now they cut to the bone because he couldn't say them back. Christ, this was not how this was supposed to go. His chest tightened with dread for having to let her down. "Chloe, I have to—"

Her lips slammed against his before he could say the words. Caught up in the moment, knowing this would be the last time they'd ever be together like this, he lost himself in the kiss. He needed to touch her—taste her—one last time. Bank this time in his memory. It was selfish, and she'd hate him for it. But his hands had a mind of their own, and he cupped her face. His thumb brushed over her jaw. It was a goodbye kiss before he told her the truth and she rightfully kicked his pathetic ass out of her apartment. One kiss turned into two, then three. And as her mouth opened up to him, he poured all the passion and love he felt for her into that kiss. This was wrong. He needed to pull away.

But he couldn't.

Any second now he'd put a stop to things before they went further. But it wasn't so easy when her palms slid along his shoulders, down his torso, and began unbuttoning his shirt.

Now... he'd stop. *Come on, stop.*

With her tongue in his mouth and her hands on his body, he couldn't tear himself away. Tugging his shirt out of the waistband of his trousers, she pushed it off his shoulders, and he shrugged out of it. She placed kisses on his neck as she raised a leg and swung it over his lap, straddling him.

Stop... now!

The words screamed in his head, but his hands landed on her hips encouraging her to rock against his erection. Fuck, he was going to hell if he let this continue. She reached for his cock, but he grabbed her before she could cup it. As much as he needed to be inside her, he couldn't go on. Grasping her wrist, he pulled her hand away.

"Chloe, we have to stop. There's something—"

The buzzer sounded. Chloe looked around the room with a frown. It buzzed again. Someone was downstairs at the foyer door.

"It's the pizza," she groaned and glanced at him with regret at the interruption, then raised herself off him. She walked to the door and pressed the intercom to let them up. "I'll grab the beers. Let them in when they knock."

"Chloe, wait—" But she had already walked into the kitchen.

While he could follow her, Theo stayed seated, his elbows on his legs, his head in his hands, and tried to collect his thoughts—and get his erection under control. Chloe had confessed her love for him, and instead of telling her he had to end their relationship, he'd almost fucked her on the sofa. There was a special place in hell for men like him.

At the knock on the door, Theo got up and opened it. The least he could do was tip the delivery person.

It wasn't the pizza.

Ethan stood in the hallway. His gaze dropped to Theo's bare chest, and his eyes widened. Shit, he'd forgotten to put his shirt back on.

"Fancy meeting you here. In the middle of the day, no less." Ethan said in a surprisingly amused voice.

"Ethan... is that you?" Chloe came to the front door with beer bottles in hand. "What are you doing here?"

"I was in town and wanted to drop by to surprise you by taking you out to lunch." He took in Chloe and Theo's appearances. "I guess I should've called first."

"You think?" both Chloe and Theo said in unison.

"Aw, aren't you two adorable?" Ethan said with a smug grin. "I was right, you two are perfect for each other."

What the fuck? Theo had thought that Ethan didn't want Chloe dating. Now he was saying that he'd set them up? He'd played matchmaker? Again, what the fuck?

Apparently Chloe was thinking the same thing because she said, "What was all of this stuff about not letting me date and asking Theo to watch out for me?"

"It was perfect, right? Two birds, one stone." He pointed at Chloe. "I didn't want you dating strange men." He shifted his finger to Theo. "And you needed to find new love after your divorce. And I knew that both of you have had crushes on each other since we were in high school. It just made sense. Who better for my baby sister than my best friend?"

"Why didn't you just come out and say that?" Chloe demanded.

"Oh, please, as if you'd ever listen to me! I knew if I threw the two of you together, this would happen." He rubbed his hands together. "So, how long have you been seeing each other?"

"Oh, for heaven's sake. We don't need to give you the play-by-play." Chloe crossed her arms over her chest. "Besides, do you really want to know about my sex life?"

Ethan blanched. "On second thought, no."

Theo stared at his best friend. "The entire time I've been with Chloe, I thought I was betraying the bro code. And now I find out this whole time you've been setting us up."

"I know, it's great!" Ethan said, clearly pleased with himself. "You would never betray the bro code unless you were serious about my sister."

Theo froze.

Ethan narrowed his eyes. "Tell me I'm wrong. If you weren't serious about Chloe, you'd stay away, right?"

Theo's gaze flicked to Chloe, and just like on the sofa, she looked at him with a hopeful expression, waiting for his answer.

"You wouldn't sleep with her unless you were taking this all the way, *right*?" Ethan pushed Theo for an answer.

Fuck, this was not how he wanted to tell Chloe. She deserved better than that. But if he didn't do it now, things would get a lot worse. "I care about Chloe," he couldn't tell Ethan how he really felt, "but..." he faced her. "I came here tonight to end things between us."

Like a switch had been flipped, Ethan went from pleased to pissed in one second flat. "What the hell?" he yelled.

"What?" Chloe flinched. With anguish etched on her face, she put a hand to her chest. "I told you I loved you, and we... we..." She pointed to the sofa. "You were going to have sex with me knowing how I felt while you didn't feel the same way. You were ending things! How could you do that to me?"

"Chloe—" He took two steps toward her.

She retreated, putting out her hand like a stop sign. "Don't. You're just like all the bad dates I've been on, only worse. They showed me their true colors right from the start. Even Owen. But you"—she shook her head—"you waited until I fell in love with you before you tore my heart out."

She was right. He was lower than dirt. Lower than pond scum. He deserved every invective she deigned to throw at him. God, this was killing him. Better that she hated him. It would be easier for her to move on in the long run. "I didn't mean to hurt you. I do care—"

A heavy hand landed on his shoulder, cutting him off. Ethan spun him around. "Time to go. I think you've done quite enough damage, old friend." The last two words came out in a sneer.

Theo had to stay and make Chloe understand that this was for the best. He needed to tell her why he couldn't stay with her. Ethan couldn't make him leave. "What? No. I'm not going anywhere."

"Yes, you are."

"No, I'm not."

Chloe stopped them before they descended into a Daffy Duck/Bugs Bunny shouting match. "What are you? Children? You!" She pointed at Ethan. "Get out! And you!" She turned to Theo. "Stay. We're not done."

"I'm not going anywhere." Ethan glared over her head at Theo.

"Oh, yes you are. If you're not gone in three seconds, I will throw you out. You know I can." She'd grown up with two rough-and-tumble older brothers. Theo knew she could take Ethan on.

"Come on, Chloe. Tell that fucker to leave, not me." He jerked a finger in Theo's direction.

"One."

Ethan stared wide eyed at Chloe. "You're going to let him stay?"

"Two."

"I'm only trying to protect you." His shoulders sagged. Theo had watched Ethan protect his family for as long as he could remember. This had to be agonizing for him.

She pulled her shoulders back and held her ground. "You need to stop trying to protect me. I can take care of this myself. Please leave so I can talk to Theo."

Ethan scrubbed a hand in his hair. "It's hard for me to walk away."

Chloe put her hands on Ethan's shoulders, staring intently into his face. "You have to. I've got this. I had a good mentor."

A vein ticced in the side of Ethan's clenched jaw. He gave a curt nod, threw Theo another deadly stare, and blew out of the apartment.

Chloe closed the door behind him and stared at it. "Did what we shared together mean anything to you?" Her voice was so low, he barely heard her.

"Chloe—"

She spun around to face him. Her eyes shimmered with tears. "Or was this all a joke to you?"

"God, no." Theo stepped toward her and placed his hands on her shoulders.

She shook herself free. "Don't. Touch. Me."

His arms dropped to his sides.

Holding a clenched fist to her chest, her face screwed up with pain. "I poured my heart out to you. Told you I loved you. I should have known you didn't love me when you didn't say it back." She threw her head back and gave a mirthless laugh. "This is all my fault. Well, the joke's on me now, isn't it? I didn't give you a chance to say anything because I threw myself at you. You've been honest with me from the start, I've been the one who's pushed for more. Wishing for things from you, you can't give. I should have known you didn't love me."

Not love her? He was stepping away to give her the life she wanted because he loved her more than he ever thought possible. "I'm sorry, I should never have let it go so far."

"Because you don't love me," her voice cracked.

He slumped his shoulders and stared at his feet. *Fuck!* Not telling her the truth was ripping out his heart.

She scoffed. "I guess I have my answer." She made her way to the sofa and went to sit down, but like she remembered what had nearly happened there, chose the armchair instead. "This is all my fault," she repeated as she sank into the chair.

He wanted to go to her, wrap his arms around her, and comfort her, but all he could do was watch the misery etched on her face. "No, it's not."

She twisted her fingers together. "I begged you for help. You were only doing what I asked. I'm the one who pushed and pushed. You warned me you couldn't give me more, and I fell in love with you anyway." She lifted her face. A tear slid down her cheek.

God, his insides turned cold at causing her pain. He deserved to have his heart ripped out of him just like he'd threatened to do to Owen. Theo sat on the sofa opposite her, dropping his hands between his legs. "When I came here tonight, I had something to tell you."

"That you were breaking up with me? Got that memo." She shook her head. "Actually, we were never together."

In his heart, their relationship had been real. He shoved his hair back away from his face. "I had a visit from Layla this afternoon."

She frowned with confusion. "Your ex-wife?"

Theo nodded. "She came to tell me she'd remarried and was pregnant."

"Why would she do that?"

"She wanted to thank me. If I hadn't made our divorce so easy, she wouldn't have met her husband and be having his child. That's all she wanted... to be a mother."

"And you don't want children. Is that why you divorced?" She pulled a cushion from behind her back and hugged it.

He rubbed his hands over his thighs. "We didn't divorce because I didn't want kids. It's because I can't have them."

She arched a brow. "You can't have kids?"

He cleared his throat. "I'm...I'm... infertile." The words hung in the air as they stared at each other.

On an exhale of breath, she said, "Oh. How long have you known?"

"For a while. When Layla and I started trying for a family with no success, we both got tested. I'm the problem." Telling her was both harder and easier than he'd thought it would be.

She threw her hands in the air. "Why didn't you tell me?"

He rubbed his palms together. "I only recently told Blake. It's embarrassing. I didn't want anyone to know. I felt like such a failure."

She plucked at the tassels on the cushion. "There's nothing to be embarrassed about. A lot of men have infertility issues. Was the pressure of treatment too much? Is that why you broke up?"

"We never had treatment." His fist clenched.

Chloe tilted her head to the side. "Why not?"

"After discussing our options with the fertility specialist, they told us the process could be a long road, and we weren't guaranteed a successful pregnancy. Layla wanted a family sooner rather than later—she's almost forty. The possibility of never having a baby was too much for her to handle. So, I ended things to give her what she wanted."

Chloe's shoulders sagged. "Theo, I'm so sorry."

He propelled himself from the sofa. The sympathy in her eyes was why he wanted no one to know. *Look at poor Theo. He can't have kids. Can't give his wife a family. What a failure.*

"And that's why I'm here. I knew things were going further than they should. I needed to stop whatever's going on between us because I can't give you a family. I'm sorry I went too far after you... you—"

"Told you I loved you?" The pissed-off expression was back on her face. He'd much prefer that than her pity.

He nodded. "I'm sorry," he said again. "I hope you find everything you're after. You deserve happiness."

Walking to the door, he opened it. Before stepping out, he paused. Was he hoping she'd call him back? Tell him that not being able to have kids didn't matter. That she loved him anyway. If she said those words, would he change his mind and turn back around?

But she didn't stop him, so he'd never know.

CHAPTER THIRTY-TWO

Four days later, Chloe curled up under a blanket on the sofa watching *Say Yes to the Dress*. The only time she'd gotten up was to take care of her most basic needs. She still wore the same clothes—leggings and an oversized sweatshirt—as when Theo had left her apartment. She hadn't combed her hair, brushed her teeth, or showered. If she Googled the definition for "hot mess," she'd find her photo.

Pizza boxes and Chinese take-out containers littered the coffee table, and she pushed them aside to find the tissue box. She'd cried after every bride found her dream wedding dress and was marrying the love of her life. They were so happy, bursting with excitement for their big day and beginning a new life. How fucking fabulous. She knew she should turn the show off. But for some sick reason, she liked torturing herself. She should binge reruns of Seinfeld to make her laugh, but her face felt like stone. Would she ever be able to crack a smile again? She doubted it.

The buzzer for the foyer door rang. Had she ordered takeout? It was hard to remember. The days were blurring together. The buzzer sounded again, and she pushed the blanket off her lap, got up, and padded barefoot to the intercom. Chocolate wrappers crinkled under her feet. "Yes?" she said into the speaker.

"Chloe, it's us. Open up," Daniela's no-nonsense voice came through the crackly speakers.

Chloe took her finger off the button and groaned. Aw crap. Her friends were downstairs. She'd been avoiding their calls and text messages. She should have known they'd eventually show up.

The buzzer rang again. "I'm busy. Can you come back another day?"

"You are not busy," Daniela said. "We've had a client meeting for today on the books for the last six months."

She glanced at the clock and then at the calendar in her phone. Daniela was right: they had had a meeting planned. "Can we reschedule? I'm sick." And she was, heartsick that is.

Hazel's voice came over the speaker next. "That's what we're here for! I've got some good old-fashioned kosher chicken soup, guaranteed to knock any illness out of you."

"And assuming that's not the real problem," Blair added archly, "I've got five pints of ice cream with your name on them."

Chloe almost laughed. Her friends were like a force of nature; she was lucky to have them. But even her friends couldn't help her now, all she wanted to do was wallow in her grief until she became numb. "Go away."

"No, Blair and I will stand here pressing this button all damn day until you let us in."

Chloe leaned her forehead on the wall and squeezed her eyes shut. She wanted to be left alone. Knowing her friends, they'd do what they threatened until they drew the attention of either the super or a passing cop, and wouldn't that just be a steaming pile of dung on top of an already shit sandwich? "Fine," she sighed and pressed the button to unlock the foyer door.

Giving the living room a quick glance, she contemplated tidying up in the couple of minutes it would take for her friends to arrive. Eh, screw it. She was too spent to even think of picking up a single take-out container.

Rapid knocking hit the door. Chloe swung it open. Blair, Daniela, and Hazel charged inside, stopping short at the mess in the living room. They turned to face her, and their eyes widened with shock as they scanned her disheveled state.

"This is worse than we thought," Hazel whispered in Blair's ear.

"Are those noodles in her hair?" Blair whispered back to Hazel.

"When was the last time you showered?" Daniela wrinkled her nose at Chloe.

"Or even eaten a decent meal. I'm glad I brought the soup." Hazel glanced inside an empty take-out container.

"And the ice cream," Blair added.

"Is there a reason you're here? I'm in the middle of something." She had to get back to watching the brides cry tears of joy while she cried tears of misery.

"We've come to check on you. Make sure you're okay," Hazel said. "You haven't been answering your phone."

"Or your texts," Blair added.

"Or your emails," Daniela finished.

"I'm fine." She tried to smile to reassure them so they could leave, but her mouth wouldn't budge.

"You're not fine." Blair went to wrap her arms around her. Chloe stepped back. If Blair comforted her, she'd fall apart. She'd cried enough; she didn't want to fall apart too.

"You are definitely not fine. Look at this place!" Daniela motioned to Mount Take-out Container on the table.

"Yes, I am. I'm always this messy." She waved her arms to take in the room. "Why would you think otherwise?"

Hazel's head tilted to the side, and her mouth puckered. "Maybe because we've been here before? Sit." Daniela pointed at the sofa. "We need to talk."

"I'll grab a garbage bag and clean up a bit." Hazel's nose screwed up when she glanced at the mess then hurried into the kitchen. A moment later, she came back with bags.

"Tell us what happened," Blair said, piling up pizza boxes and handing them to Hazel.

"Nothing happened." Chloe slumped back on the sofa and crossed her arms over her chest.

Daniela pinned her with a stare that said *you better tell me now or you're in big trouble*. "We're not leaving here until we find out."

"That's right!" Blair said, "We'll even sleep here if necessary." She paused and seemed to be reevaluating her proclamation. "I hope your room is cleaner than this."

The sooner she told them, the sooner they'd leave her alone, and then she could get back to her pity party. She brought her friends up to speed about Ethan's matchmaking attempt and everything to do with Theo, including his infertility. When she was done, she buried her face in her hands and cried, letting Hazel comfort her.

When Chloe got herself back under control and blew her nose, Hazel leaned back on the sofa. "So, he broke up with you because he couldn't promise to give you children, not because he doesn't love you?"

"He said he *cared* for me," Chloe corrected, taking another tissue. "That's not love."

"Did you ever think maybe he didn't tell you how he really feels because he was trying to let you live a life you've always dreamed of—having a family?" Hazel raised an eyebrow.

"I flat out asked him if he loved me, and he didn't say a word."

"Why would he? He was probably too scared," Blair said. "Remember that Margaret Atwood quote, 'Women are afraid of being murdered; men are afraid of rejection.'"

"That's not how it goes," Daniela hissed.

Blair waved it away. "Close enough." She turned back to Chloe. "Look at it from his perspective. His ex-wife didn't want to stick around and try when she found out he was infertile. Maybe he thought you'd do the same. All you've talked about is wanting to start a family as soon as possible. This wouldn't be an easy issue for him to deal with."

Chloe propped her elbow on the armrest of the chair and dropped her head in her hand. "No, it wouldn't be easy, but we could have gotten through it. I would think if he loved me, he would've told me." She blew her nose and dropped the tissue into the already-overflowing bin next to her. "I'm so pathetic. I've finally fallen in love, but it's with the wrong man."

"Why is he the wrong man?" Blair frowned.

Chloe pulled a face at Blair. "Because... because... firstly, he doesn't love me, and secondly, he can't have kids."

"Why does that matter? There's adoption, surrogacy, artificial insemination. Hell, I bet his brother would be willing to provide sperm if you're that keen on Theo's genetics," Daniela said, ticking off the options on her fingers.

"Besides, the doctors have said he had a small chance, not that it *couldn't* happen," Hazel reminded her.

"Yes, well, it might take years to conceive or maybe not at all."

"So, what you're saying is, your love for Theo has conditions." Blair rubbed her chin.

Chloe shook her head. "What? No, I want—"

"Want kids, blah, blah, blah. We've heard it a thousand times," Blair waved a hand around in the air.

"If you want kids so badly, why haven't you considered any options other than the 'insert penis in vagina and ejaculate' one?" Hazel asked, a hurt expression on her face. "Because for some of us here it wasn't an option."

"All of us," Blair added. "I had to have IVF because of PCOS. So get off of your high horse and do something about it."

Chloe crossed her arms over her chest. "Well, I'm so sorry I've bored you with my desire to have a family. We're not all as lucky as you are with your perfect lives and kids." Her friends were supposed to be here comforting her, not taking Theo's side.

Blair scoffed. "We are hardly perfect, but yes, I am lucky because I love my husband *unconditionally*. We're not married because of our kids; we're married because we love each other. The kids were a bonus. Mitch didn't leave me just because we had trouble conceiving. And I wouldn't have left him if he'd had a similar issue. We got lucky with IVF, but if we hadn't, I'd still be with him. We'd be two happy DINKS"—Daniela mouthed "dual-income, no kids" at Chloe's confused expression—"instead of two stressed—but ultimately happy—parents. I'll always love him no matter what life throws at us. That's what 'for better or worse' means."

Hazel blinked back tears and sniffed. "She's right. I feel the same about Joyce. If you love someone, you accept them for everything they are. Flaws and all."

Chloe's heart sank. They were right. All she'd been able to focus on was finding a husband and having a baby; she'd forgotten to let herself just love someone.

"Ask yourself this, if you were with Theo—not knowing of his condition and after months or years of trying to conceive with no luck, would he be enough? Would you still love him?" Daniela gave her an intense stare.

Without hesitation Chloe answered, "Yes, Theo is the love of my life." Chloe covered her face, trying to stop the tears of shame prickling the backs of her eyes. Oh, God, she'd really screwed things up. She'd watched Theo walk out the door letting him believe he wasn't enough. She should have told him she loved him no matter what.

Chloe lifted her tearstained face, and her insides shook with dread. "What if it's true that he only *cares* about me?"

"There's only one way to find out," Blair said.

Chloe shot from the sofa. "I have to see him—now. He needs to know how I feel about everything." Her heart hammered. She raced to the door.

"Wait," Daniela called and waved a hand up and down Chloe's body. "You can't go like that. You look like you've rolled out of a dumpster."

Chloe glanced down at her body and laughed. "Gee, thanks."

"Get in the shower. We'll finish cleaning up this pigsty," Daniela said, pulling out her phone—probably to call her housekeeper.

"That's right. We got this! Now, go get your man," Hazel said.

Her *man*. She loved the sound of that.

CHAPTER THIRTY-THREE

The intercom on Theo's desk buzzed. "Excuse me, Mr. Campbell, I have a Chloe Doyle here to see you," Annabelle announced.

Theo's pen paused over the document he was about to sign. "Send her in."

What was Chloe doing here? The last time he'd seen her she'd looked so wounded; he thought she'd never want to see him again. His heart filled with happiness at seeing her. Just as quickly, disappointment deflated him because nothing had changed.

After a moment, the door to his office swung open, and she stepped inside. God, the sight of her slammed into his chest. He hadn't seen her in four days, and each day that passed made it harder and harder to stay away. So many times he'd picked up the phone to call just so he could hear her voice only to stop himself. Rising from the chair, he walked around the front of his desk and slid his hands into his pockets, stopping himself from touching her. "Chloe?"

She took two steps closer. "I hope I'm not disturbing you." She gave a nervous glance around the room. "Do you have time to talk?"

He should tell her he was on his way out to an important meeting. Staying in the same room without pulling her into his arms was torture. "Sure," he answered and gestured for her to take a seat.

She stayed standing. "I want to talk to you about the other night."

Of course, she did. That night was the worst night of his life. Walking away from her was the hardest thing he'd ever had to do. And now, he was about to relive it all over again.

"I feel like I left some things unsaid. You opened up about your infertility and how it affected your marriage. Thank you for that." She took a deep breath. "I'm sorry I didn't respond then. I should have. When you told me, I was shocked. Confused. I didn't know what to say, and I let you leave." She crossed her arms in front of her, cupping her elbows. "What I should have said was: whether or not we have children, I'm willing to try even if it takes months or years. We can try IVF or even ask Blake for a sample, if you both are okay with it. We can try adoption. Or fostering. We've got options." She met his eyes. "And if it doesn't happen, that's okay. You're all I need. But maybe if our paths don't lead to parenthood, we could get a dog." She smiled warily. "I like dogs. I'm allergic to cats, but I like dogs."

Hope for their future shimmered in her eyes, and seeing it killed him. "Chloe, don't—"

"Let me finish. What matters more to me is you. With or without kids. I want you in my life because I love you, and I always will. Love shouldn't have conditions, and I placed them on you." She reached out for him, but when he didn't take her hand, she dropped it. "I'm sorry."

Theo dropped his head and stared at his feet. "You'll change your mind about the way you feel when you've done a dozen rounds of IVF treatments, and you're not holding a baby in your arms."

She shook her head. "No, I won't."

"You don't know that." He couldn't continue a relationship with Chloe with the threat of her leaving him when it all got too much. This time, he wouldn't recover.

Her eyes shimmered. "Yes, I do. Because I'll have you."

He couldn't believe that. "For months it's all you've talked about."

"I know. I got a little too single goal focused. I tend to do that," she said with a self-deprecating laugh. "Now I know how I truly feel, and I know what's important in my life. It's you." She stepped closer. "With or without children."

Theo moved away, putting his desk between them. It took all his control to stop himself from touching her. Even though he wanted to believe her, he couldn't take that chance. "I'm not prepared to put you through treatments. You'll hate me in the end."

She threw her hands in the air. "You're not *listening*. I'm happy to live the rest of my life with only the two of us. Wait... unless..." She covered her cheeks with her hands. "I've been going on and on about how much I love you, and you still haven't said it back. While we were hanging out and sleeping together, I was falling in love. You were just helping me out. Having a fling."

"It was more than that." Emotion clogged his throat.

"Was it? Do you love me?" Her voice cracked.

The sound tore his chest open, ripping out his heart. She'd asked him the same question in her apartment, and he hadn't been able to give her an answer then either.

Yes, he loved her. The thought of not having her in his life crushed him. He loved her so much, and it was why he needed to do this for her. One day when she had the family she'd always dreamed of, she'd thank him just like Layla had.

"Do you love me? Yes or no." Chloe's voice rose as she asked the question again.

He drew in a deep, shuddery breath and hoped the words he was about to speak sounded convincing. "I wish I could tell you what you want to hear. We're friends, I care for you, but it's not love," he lied. He lied through his teeth.

Her lips rolled inward, and she nodded. "Okay, sorry to have wasted your time."

"Chloe, I'm sorry." He reached out to her, but she stepped away. His arm dropped to his side.

"Goodbye, Theo." Her voice wobbled, and tears welled in her eyes. She spun away and raced out of the office. The door closed after her with an audible click, signaling the end of this time in his life.

"Fuck!" Theo swiped his arm over the desk, scattering paperwork over the floor. He linked his fingers together, cupped the back of his head, and took several deep breaths. What was he supposed to do now?

Blake walked into the room. "Was that Chloe running into the elevator? She looked upset."

He didn't answer. Looking up from his ruined desk, Theo said, "Get out of my office, and tell Annabelle to cancel all my appointments. I'm in no mood for anyone's shit."

His brother refused to leave. "What the hell did you do to her?"

"I said, get the fuck out!" he growled.

Blake slapped the folder he was carrying on the desk. "What are you doing? You're letting a great woman get away. Why don't you tell her the truth? If she loves you, she'll understand?"

"She knows."

Blake's eyebrows rose. "Is that why she ran out of here like her ass was on fire? She couldn't accept it? If that's the case, you're better off without her."

He couldn't stand to have anyone bad-mouth Chloe, especially when she was entirely blameless. "She doesn't care about my infertility.

Doesn't care if it takes years of IVF to conceive. She's even willing to adopt or ask you to be the genetic donor." Blake's eyes widened at that. "She even said it would be okay if we never have kids; she's happy for it to be the two of us."

Blake threw his arms up. "Then what's the problem?"

"Me," he said succinctly. "I won't put her through it. She might think she'll be happy without a baby, but she'll change her mind."

"Oh, so you know this for sure, do you?" his brother said, arching a brow. "Come on, Theo, this is bullshit. You love her, and she loves you. You can get through anything. If she says she's happy to try even if there may not be a baby, then believe her."

"It's for the best." Theo held on to the back of the chair and dropped his head.

"I don't know why you're punishing yourself," Blake said. "So what, you're infertile. A lot of people have bigger problems. Get over yourself."

Through clenched teeth, Theo said, "This is *my* problem, and I'll deal with it the way I want to."

Blake shook his head. "Well, if you're prepared to let her go, you deserve your miserable life without her. One day, you'll realize you've made a huge mistake, and it will be too late." With that, his brother walked out of the office.

Scrubbing his hands over his face, Theo blew out a long breath. Was Blake right? Would he wake up one day and realize he'd made a mistake?

No. He'd made the right call. He couldn't picture Chloe childless. She deserved to have the family she'd always wanted. Although Blake was right about one thing: he would have a miserable life without her.

CHAPTER THIRTY-FOUR

With a heavy heart, Chloe stared at the boxes filling her living room. It had been a week since that disastrous day in Theo's office. A week since she'd called her mother and started making plans to move back home. It seemed like yesterday she'd unpacked the boxes with excitement, dreaming of what her new life in New York would hold. Thankfully, she hadn't signed a long-term lease. Or worse, bought an apartment outright. Moving to the city had been a big mistake. No, that wasn't true. She could never regret moving here. After all, if she hadn't, she wouldn't have met Theo again. And despite everything, meeting Theo again after so many years hadn't been a mistake. She'd fallen in love for the first time, and she'd hold on to that for the rest of her life.

There would never be another man who could ever make her feel the way he did—a man who she wanted to spend the rest of her life with. From now on, she didn't want to think about other men because they'd never compare to Theo. Maybe, when she was ready, she'd go to a clinic and get artificially inseminated like Daniela and Hazel had done. There was no reason why she couldn't be a single mother—if

Mya could do it, she could too. While she'd like to raise her child with a father, she couldn't imagine wanting to spend her life with anyone other than Theo.

She tossed the remaining clothes hanging in the wardrobe into the luggage she'd take on the plane. Hazel was organizing to have the packing boxes shipped to Sydney. God, it was hard saying goodbye to her friends. They'd tried convincing her to stay, but she reminded them she'd be making frequent trips to New York for work so they wouldn't have time to miss each other. But there was no point living in New York anymore. She'd moved here to find love, and she had. Theo just didn't feel the same way. So, she'd go home to Sydney and go about her life like normal—before Theo. Hopefully, if she threw herself into work, she wouldn't have time to think about him.

She'd made all the necessary phone calls to her clients telling them she'd be in touch in a few days. There was one person she should be talking to, and she'd been putting it off. After the way Ethan had manipulated her and Theo, she'd been avoiding his calls. She was too mad to speak to him. But Ethan had a right to know she was leaving the country. She dialed his number.

"Chloe, finally. I've been trying to call you," he said.

"I know." She didn't bother with an excuse as to why she hadn't answered them. "Ethan, have you got a minute to talk?"

"Sure, are you okay?" She could hear the concern in his voice.

"I'm calling to tell you I'm leaving New York."

"Where are you going?"

"Home to Sydney."

There was a long pause. "When will you be back?"

She scuffed her toe along the join of the floorboards. "I'm not. Well, only when I have to for work. I'm moving back to Australia to live."

"But you just got there."

"Yes, and it didn't work out like I'd planned."

"If this has to do with Theo, I'm sorry. I never expected my best friend would turn out to be such an arsehole. If I'd known, I would have never tried to push you two together." There was another long pause, then he said. "I'm sorry he hurt you."

Chloe dropped onto the sofa. "He didn't mean to hurt me. He warned me he couldn't give me more, but I fell in love with him anyway." She brushed a tear from her cheek. She'd been crying a lot lately.

"Just because things haven't worked out with Theo, doesn't mean you need to leave. I'm done with the reshoots for that movie, I can be there in a couple of hours. Look, I'll stay with you for a few weeks and we'll play tourist. We'll go to the Met, ride the roller coaster on Coney Island. It'll be fun!"

She picked lint off her pants. "I want to go home. There's nothing for me here."

She heard him sigh. "Are you sure?"

"Yes." The sooner she got out of the city the better.

"When do you leave? The least I can do is come down and see you off."

"Don't bother. My flight from JFK leaves at six thirty-five, tonight. My taxi's picking me up in an hour."

"Okay, travel safe," he said, giving up. "I'll talk to you later."

"Bye, Ethan." She hung up the phone, fell back onto the sofa, and stared at the ceiling. It was time to get her old life back. But she doubted it would ever be the same again.

Theo, Blake, and Andrew Vandersluis sat in a meeting in the board-room of Andrew's office. Discussions about purchasing Andrew's building near the Javits were getting heated. Andrew was still convinced that the property was worth twice as much as what they were offering and had made one last appeal to increase their offer. While Theo and Blake had already agreed between them that even though they'd originally told Andrew that they would not offer more, they were willing to pay an extra two and a half percent.

Tired of listening to the negotiations, Theo unfolded from his chair. "We are withdrawing our offer." He started to gather his papers.

"Wh...what?" Andrew spluttered.

Blake gave him a wide-eyed "what the fuck are you doing?" stare.

"You need to sell. We wanted to buy. You're fucking us around with the price. I'm not in the mood to play games." Theo plucked his jacket from the back of his chair and shrugged into it. "Good luck in selling it. You're going to need it."

With that, Theo left the office. Ignoring Andrew's plea to stay and work things out—he needed their money to get himself out of shit, and both Campbell brothers knew it. He kept shouting progressively lower and lower offers, but Theo kept walking, knowing that Blake would follow his lead despite hating when Theo pulled this kind of thing. He didn't need to look at Blake to know he'd be pissed. He didn't have the energy for this bullshit anymore.

Once back in his penthouse, he poured bourbon in a glass and made his way onto the balcony. The last time he was out here, Chloe had stripped her coat off and blown his mind in a tiny yellow bikini. Everywhere he looked reminded him of her, and it tortured his heart.

Placing the glass on the ledge, he leaned his forearms on the balcony and stared at the city below. Where was Chloe? What was she doing? Was she feeling as shitty as him? He'd left work early. His mind hadn't been able to concentrate since letting Chloe walk away. He'd only been able to remember her. The way she smiled. The way she made him laugh. The way he felt complete with her in his arms. Without her, the building he lived in could crumble with him in it, and he wouldn't care.

Someone knocked on the front door, then let themselves in. He didn't bother turning around. It would be Blake coming over to chew his ass off for losing the building they wanted.

"Theo," someone called. It wasn't his brother.

He glanced over his shoulder and turned back to stare at the lights. "Ethan."

"I wanna talk to you." Ethan came onto the balcony toward him.

"You could've called." He picked up his glass and swirled it around.

"I fucking chartered a helicopter to get here to talk to you in person." Ethan put his hand on Theo's shoulder and spun him around.

Alcohol sloshed over his hand from his still unconsumed drink. "I'm not in the talking mood. Sorry you wasted your time and money." He shook the liquid from his fingers.

"Too bad. I'm going to talk; you're going to listen."

"Say what you need to say, then get out." He loosened his tie, lifted it over his head, and tossed it on the floor.

"What the hell happened to you? Where did my best friend go? Because this guy?" Ethan motioned to Theo. "I don't know him."

Ethan wasn't saying anything that Theo didn't agree with. He couldn't blame Ethan for not wanting to be his friend anymore; after what he'd done to Chloe, he didn't like himself much either.

"Chloe's going back to live in Sydney," Ethan said suddenly.

That startled Theo out of his pity party. "What?"

"She's moving back to Sydney. She's heartbroken and can't bear to be in the same city—no, country, no, hemisphere as you. That's the kind of arsehole you were. That's how much you hurt her." Each word was pointed like a dagger. But Ethan wasn't finished. "Surely, you could see she was falling for you. Yeah, I was pushing you together, but you should've stopped it before it went too far. Instead, you treated her like a tissue to wipe your arse. Did she mean nothing to you?"

Chloe mustn't have told Ethan how their relationship had started, and Theo wasn't going to tell him about his sister's sexual history—or lack thereof—before she'd met Theo. "Yes, she meant something to me. I fucking lo—" He cut himself off, pushed away from the balcony, and marched into the apartment.

Ethan followed him inside. "What were you going to say?"

"Nothing." He knocked back the remnants of his drink.

"Were you going to say you love her?" Ethan stared at him.

Theo gave a curt nod. No point denying it; it was probably written all over his face.

Ethan lifted his palms up. "Why the hell haven't you told her?"

"Because I'm no good for her."

Ethan shook his head with a frown. "What does that mean? You used to be one of the most decent guys I know. I wouldn't have tried to hook you up with my sister otherwise."

He might as well tell Ethan about his problem. Hell, he should just put up a billboard in Times Square.

Ethan frowned when Theo finished bringing him up to speed. "If Chloe knows and understands, what's the problem?"

"I can't give her everything she wants." Was everyone around him dense? Why couldn't they see that this was a major problem?

"My sister knows her own mind. For some reason, you're who she wants." Ethan shook his head. "If she says she wants you with or without kids—believe her. You love her. She loves you. Don't be a fucking idiot and let your pride get in the way."

Theo froze and stared at Ethan. *Don't be a fucking idiot and let your pride get in the way.* The words smacked him over the head with the force of a sledgehammer. He'd let Chloe walk out of his life because of his *pride*.

His pride had had him keeping the secret from his family. His pride had him believe that no one would want him for who he was. His pride had made him believe he wasn't good enough for Chloe. God, he really was a *fucking idiot*. He'd ruined everything. Chloe was the greatest thing to happen in his life, and he'd let her slip through his fingers. Now he needed to fix his mess. He prayed Chloe would forgive him. He wasn't too proud to beg if he had to. "I have to go." Theo set his glass on the coffee table and raced out the door.

"Where are you going?" Ethan called after him.

"To see Chloe," he said over his shoulder.

CHAPTER THIRTY-FIVE

After arriving at the Sydney airport, Chloe's sister-in-law Mya drove her to her mother's house.

"Are you sure you don't want to stay with Aiden and me?" Mya asked, regarding her over her glasses.

"No." Chloe leaned against the window. "I just want to go home."

But even there she couldn't. While she'd had the foresight not to sell her terrace house immediately upon moving to New York, she'd rented it out to a couple for several months. Now she had to wait until their lease was up before she could cocoon herself in her house where she could be safe.

Mya gave her a look. "Well, the offer's open if you need it." Then to Chloe's relief, she turned on the radio so the rest of the drive was blissfully conversation-free.

When she got to her mother's house, Mya brought in her things while her mother fussed over her. "Oh, sweetie, come inside and I'll make you a pot of tea. You must be exhausted after that long flight."

"Thanks, Mum."

Mya finished with the bags. "Do you mind if I impose on you for a bit? I haven't chatted with you in ages."

"Of course, I always have time to catch up with family."

Chloe's heart twinged guiltily. She'd been so laser focused on finding a husband and having a baby that she'd forgotten she already had the most wonderful family—a family who from half a world away would drop everything to help her. God, she'd been self-centered. Just like she had been with Theo, she'd assumed he'd want the same things she did if she pushed enough. But what right did she have to force someone to change their mind? This broken heart was as good of a lesson as any, she supposed.

Vowing to try to do better, she listened as Mya chatted with her mother about her sister-in-law's next book before slipping into a lighthearted recap of her mother's latest film. The conversation was delightfully mundane and mercifully free of discussion of children or relationships. It was like both women were deliberately avoiding those topics so as not to upset her.

Eventually the travel and the emotional upheaval got the better of her. She yawned. "I'm going to take a shower and get some sleep." Suddenly, exhaustion weighed her down. It was an effort dragging her butt off the sofa.

"There are clean towels in the bathroom. There're fresh sheets on the bed in the guest room," her mother said, patting the back of her hand. "Have a good sleep."

Chloe trudged up the hallway and into the guest bedroom. Stripping out of her clothes, she dropped them on the floor as she walked into the en suite and took a long, hot shower. When she reentered the room, she found that someone had picked up her dirty clothes and laid out pajamas on the bed. Chloe smiled for the first time in days. She'd made the right decision coming home. She needed the love and comfort only her family could give her. Getting dressed, she slid between the sheets and pulled the quilt up to her chin. Her eyelids fluttered closed, and she fell into a restless sleep.

———◆———

Chloe slowly blinked her eyes open, and for a second, she didn't know where she was. Then the past couple of days came flooding back and with it the gut-wrenching pain. She rolled to her side and tucked her knees to her chest, hoping it was a nightmare. But the pain burning through her chest was too real for it to have been a dream.

With heavy curtains covering the windows, she didn't know the time. She'd left her phone in her purse in the living room, and there wasn't a clock in the guest room. Her stomach rumbled; she'd eaten nothing since leaving New York. She should probably do that. Reluctantly, she got out of bed and found her mother in the kitchen.

"Morning," Chloe stretched and yawned.

"It's more like, good evening." Her mother filled a kettle with water and switched it on.

"What's the time?"

"It's ten at night. You slept over twelve hours." Her mother pulled two cups from the top cupboard and dropped tea bags in them.

"I can't believe I slept so long." Chloe slid onto a stool at the breakfast counter.

"I can. You were exhausted." Her mother poured water in the cups and passed one to Chloe. "Are you feeling better?"

No. Would she ever feel normal again? "A little," she lied; she didn't want to worry her mother.

Her mother gave her a look telling her that her lie had been noted but was being ignored, for now. Instead her mother suggested, "Let's go out. We'll walk around the harbor to get some fresh air."

"Maybe tomorrow, I'm still tired. Jet lag's a bitch." Chloe didn't want to go anywhere. She wanted to curl up in bed and bury her head under the covers.

"Whenever you're ready." Her mother squeezed her hand.

The doorbell rang.

"Are you expecting anyone?" Chloe asked.

Her mother shook her head and wiped her hands on a dishcloth. "No, I'll see who it is. Be right back."

Chloe drank her tea and grabbed a biscuit from the jar on the counter, waiting for her mother to return. When she didn't, Chloe left the kitchen to make sure she was okay. At the living room entrance, her steps faltered, and her breath caught in her lungs.

Theo was here. In her mother's living room. But how?

She drank in his features like a woman lost in the desert. His hair was mussed, there were dark circles under his eyes, and the shirt and trousers he wore were creased. Even disheveled, he was still the most beautiful man she'd ever seen. A pang of longing clutched at her chest.

"What are you doing here?" The words came out in a whisper.

He whipped around to face her.

Her mother glanced at her watch. "Oh, look at the time. I have a thing at the place. I should run; I don't want to be late! I won't be back for hours. See you later!"

Chloe watched her mother rush out the door. There was no appointment. Her mother was giving them privacy. Although if she knew her mother, she was actually going to go sit in her car to make a swift reappearance if needed. Chloe just kept staring at the door because if she looked at Theo, she might crumble to the floor.

"Chloe." The sound of his voice warmed her insides. God, she'd missed him. "Please, look at me."

Locking her knees before her legs gave out, she slowly turned her head toward him. "What are you doing here?" she asked again. "How did you find me?"

"Ethan told me. I tried to catch you before you boarded your plane, but I didn't make it." Then his gaze traveled over her, and he gave a small smile. "Cute pajamas."

Chloe blushed; she'd forgotten she was still wearing her favorite Winnie the Pooh pj's. "Thanks."

"Chloe," he stepped forward, then hesitated like he wasn't sure she'd want him near her before taking another step closer. "I'm such an ass for letting you walk away from me. I'm sorry. It was the biggest mistake of my life. I fucked up. I let my insecurities—my *pride*—get in the way, and I lost the best thing to have ever happened to me."

Chloe's heartbeat accelerated, slamming against her chest. Her breath caught in her throat, and she was left unable to speak.

His eyes boring into hers, Theo continued, "I've been miserable without you. You're all I can think about. All I've ever wanted." He inched closer. "You're the only person I see myself waking up to every morning for the rest of my life. The only one I want to come home to. The only one I want to grow old with." He took a deep breath, then said, "I love you, Chloe. I've always loved you. I loved you when we were kids. I loved you when you stumbled back into my life, and I love you even more now."

Chloe wrapped her arms around her stomach. Was this really happening? His words were too much to hope for. "But when I asked you how you felt about me, you said—"

"I lied." He hung his head for a beat before returning his gaze to her. "I'm sorry. I hated telling you I didn't love you. I'll never forgive myself for the pain I caused you. I thought I was doing the right thing for you." He sighed. "But I don't get to make that decision for you."

"Theo..."

He held up a hand. "I still believe you're better off without me. But I'm selfish; I love you too much. I don't want to live the rest of my life without you."

Breathless, she held shaking fingers to her lips as tears filled her eyes. "You love me?"

"So much." He reached out to clasp her trembling hands. Or were they his hands that shook? "I want us to be together. I want to do all that I can to make you happy." His eyes shimmered, and love poured from them.

Chloe's smile grew wide, and her heart pounded so hard like it wanted to burst from her chest with happiness. "Theo—"

"Wait. Before you say anything, I want to give you something." Pulling away, he picked up a yellow box from the coffee table and handed her the package.

"What's this?" She glanced from the box to Theo.

Theo shuffled his feet. Was he nervous about something? Why did he want her to open a box when all she wanted to do was throw herself into his arms and kiss him like there was no tomorrow?

He nodded toward the present. "Open it and find out."

Taking the box from him, she sat in a chair and lifted the lid. It was filled with pale blue and pink tissue paper. On top of the paper sat a round, clear tube of plastic with some cloudy liquid in it. She plucked it out, put the box back on the coffee table, and slid the tube through her fingers.

"It's a glow stick from the disco. The one you crashed with Isla way back when." Her eyes flicked up to Theo. "You were wearing so many you didn't notice when you dropped one. I picked it up and put it in my pocket. I was going to give it back to you, but instead, I kept it. To remind me of you, Glowy." He smiled.

Her fingers trembled as she ran her fingers along it, the color long ago faded. "I can't believe you kept it all these years."

"Even when you were a scrawny kid"—his lips quirked at her frown—"I knew you were someone special and wanted to have something to remember you by. Now, open the rest." He pointed to the box.

Bending over, she parted the paper and pulled out a white baby's onesie and an envelope with a sheaf of papers. She swung her head toward Theo. An eyebrow raised in question.

He drew in a deep breath. "If you still want to try and have babies with me, I'll do everything I can to make it happen. The outfit should speak for itself, but the papers are the forms we'll need to fill out to adopt." He gave her a wry grin. "I should warn you, some of the agencies only give children to married couples." He pulled out a small light-blue box and slid it toward her.

"Is that what I think it is?"

"Open it."

She did. Inside, lay an emerald and diamond ring. She looked at the ring, and then back at him. "Where... How..."

He seemed to know what she was asking. "Would you believe that there's a Tiffany & Co. in the Singapore Airport?" He shook his head. "I picked it up on my layover."

"Oh, Theo." She sniffed, clambered to her feet, and went to go to him. She was so desperate to hold him.

"There's more." He nodded to the first box.

What more could she want? Theo was everything she needed. She looked inside the box and pulled out a photo of a black-and-white ball of Staffordshire terrier mix. "A dog?" She stared at him. "When did you have time to do all this?"

"It was a long plane ride from New York, and the plane had complimentary Wi-Fi in business class," he explained before motioning to the photo in her hand. "So, Daisy is waiting to be adopted if you want to start our family with her." He seemed to think of something. "Or we can pick out our dog together, but I liked Daisy's story, and Annabelle and Blake insist that she's the sweetest dog ever." He laughed. "I think Blake will adopt her if we don't. But if you're okay with it, I'll ship her to Sydney and move here too, if you'll have us... me. I love you so much, Chloe."

Slipping the ring on her finger, Chloe dropped the photo, the papers, and the onesie to launch herself at Theo, throwing her arms around his neck. Her love for this man and the happiness at being back in his arms brought her to tears. This time, though, they were happy ones. "Yes. Oh, God, yes! I'll have you." She sniffed. "You're all I ever wanted. I love you, too. I want the dog, the adoption, and everything. Most of all... I want you."

Theo wrapped his arms around her waist and hugged her tight. Dropping his forehead to rest against Chloe's, he said, "I'm going to do everything I can to make you happy."

She cupped his face in her hands. "You already make me happy. So, so happy!"

He lowered his head and kissed her with so much passion, she felt it down to her toes. Chloe couldn't remember a time she'd ever been happier. Even if they never had children, Chloe's life was complete. She felt like the luckiest woman in the world.

She had everything she needed standing right in front of her.

EPILOGUE

Three years later.

"You're nearly there, Chloe. Just a couple more pushes," Dr. Rebecca Morgenstern, her obstetrician, encouraged.

Chloe dropped her head back on the bed. "I can't do this anymore. Make it stop!" she cried.

"Glowy." Theo kissed her sweaty brow. "Yes, you can. You're doing great."

Chloe squeezed her eyes shut and tossed her head from side to side. "No, I can't. I've changed my mind. I want all the drugs—now," she wailed on the last word as another contraction gripped her body.

"It's too late for drugs. You need to push." Dr. Morgenstern looked up from her place between Chloe's legs. "Now!"

Chloe clutched her knees, leaned forward, gritted her teeth, and groaned. The sound echoing through the room.

She clutched his hand through the contraction. If Theo could take his wife's pain away, he would. Why the hell did women put themselves through such torture? Adoption had been so much easier. After adopting their two oldest children Matthew and Makayla—a brother and sister aged two and six—Chloe had gone through multiple rounds of IVF to go through what looked like a hell of a lot of pain. She needed a medal. Fuck that, he'd buy her the goddamn moon.

"That's it. Good job. The baby's almost here. I can see the head," the doctor said.

Theo was stunned by what he was witnessing. Never had he seen anything so amazing. Thanks to Chloe, he had the family he'd always dreamed of, and now their third child was being born. He watched as the doctor maneuvered the baby into position. Chloe gave another guttural scream as Dr. Morgenstern pulled the baby out.

Chloe slumped back on the bed with a groan of exhaustion. "Is the baby okay?"

"She is! Congratulations, it's a girl!" the doctor announced.

"A girl." Chloe beamed with pride. The smile replacing the pain etched on her face only moments ago.

The doctor handed Theo a pair of surgical scissors. With some minor trepidation, he cut through the umbilical cord and the nurse placed the baby on Chloe's chest.

"Oh my God. Theo, we did it. She's so beautiful." Tears spilled from her eyes as she kissed the top of their daughter's head.

She was. They both were. He wanted to savor this moment, sear it into his memory so that he'd never forget.

Pride emanating from every pore, he kissed Chloe on the lips, then their baby's cheek. "She's perfect. You're perfect," his voice cracked with emotion. "I love you."

"I love you, too." Chloe reached out and clasped his hand. "We're so lucky and blessed."

He cleared the tight knot of emotion in his throat. "Yes, we are."

Damn, his life was good.

ACKNOWLEDGMENTS

Firstly, I want to thank my loving family, Tom, Jaime, Ryan and Leah. They're always so encouraging and supportive and my number one fans! A huge thanks to TL Swan and her Facebook groups, Cygnet Inkers and S S Cygnets. The ladies in those groups are amazing. Without them, I wouldn't be doing this. To my wonderful better readers, Becky, Michelle and Kirstie. Thank you for taking the time to read this book and for your feedback. A massive thank you to BJ Alpha for being my personal cheer squad. You have taken the time to answer many of my questions and supported my books! Thank you. A special thanks to LM Fox for reaching out to me when I was ready to give up. Thanks for helping to keep going!

Finally to my amazing readers. I can't tell you how much I appreciate you reading my books. It makes my day! Thank you, thank you, thank you.

ABOUT SONIA STANIZZO

Sonia Stanizzo is a contemporary romance author living in the beautiful south coast of New South Wales, Australia with her husband and three children. When she's not dreaming up stories about couples and their road to finding love, sometimes bumpy but always a lot of fun, she can be found taking pole dancing lessons, reading and writing.

Thank you so much for reading Matchmaker. I hope you enjoyed meeting Theo and Chloe and loved them as much as I do.

SAY HELLO!

Want to follow me on social media? Follow me here:

Facebook: facebook.com/soniastanizzowriter

Instagram: instagram.com/soniastanizzowriter

Ticktock: ticktok.com/@soniastanizzowriter

Sonia's Website: soniastanizzo

Sonia's email: soniastanizzo@gmail.com

Join my newsletter for free books, new releases and giveaways:

Newsletter

MORE TITLES BY SONIA STANIZZO

www.ingramcontent.com/pod-product-compliance
Lightning Source LLC
Chambersburg PA
CBHW031546240626
47153CB00002B/401